OUTBACK

STEPHEN WILLIAM CHESHIRE

COPYRIGHT

ISBN eBook: 978-1-990080-07-4

ISBN paperback: 978-1-990080-08-1

Editors: Dianna Chan, Rhonda Chieduch

Publisher: On the Way Publishers

Box 944, 4755 47 Street, Onoway, AB TOE 1VO Canada

ACKNOWLEDGEMENTS

Many, many thanks for purchasing my first-ever zombie novel. I started writing this just before I went off to University, something I have always wanted to do write a zombie horror. So got some happy memories of writing this in the student halls with a cup of tea. And many thanks to On The Way Editing & Publishing for taking this from being self-published to traditional.

S W Cheshire

stephencheshire@rocketmail.com

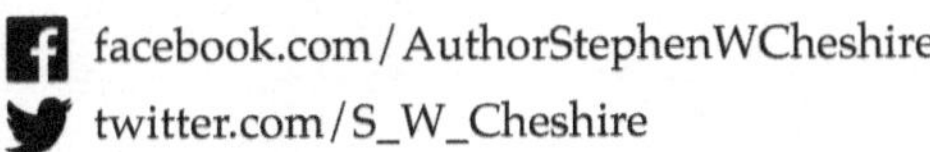

facebook.com/AuthorStephenWCheshire
twitter.com/S_W_Cheshire

CHAPTER ONE

It was thirty-seven degrees. Inmates of the prison wandered about their day, with hands in their pockets, looking down at the dusty burning ground, feeling the sun scorch their necks. The prison was located in Texas about ten miles from the nearest town and held some of the United States' most dangerous convicts and criminal masterminds. Guards, scattered about the prison, were armed with loaded shotguns. Their eyes, behind regulation sunglasses, were locked onto the inmates.

Ticiano sat in the far corner of the sports court. He had a skinhead and tattoos up his arm. A blade, which he had carved out of some plastic he found was hidden in his back pocket, and he had a small stick in his mouth. He was inside for the murder of a rival gang member who had been killed in a drive-by shooting that took place last year. He was serving a life sentence. At the tender age of twenty, he knew he would never see the world outside of the prison walls again.

Ticiano looked down at the ground. He felt the sun burning his neck and sweat running down his forehead. He looked to see that one of the opposing gang members from the prison was looking over at him.

"Are you sure you want to go through with this, homey?" Joshua McAllen asked.

"Got to, bro," Ticiano replied.

"He'll kill you, bro," Joshua replied.

"No, he won't," Ticiano replied "I can take him."

"Bro," Joshua pleaded.

Ticiano looked up and over at Sotero.

"Yo!" Sotero called. "Ready when you are, bitch."

Ticiano quickly got up, looking over at the prison guards to make sure they weren't paying him any attention. He turned away from the court. Now was the time to begin the fight and to take over the prison. Ticiano got up, making sure the plastic blade was still firmly secured in his black shorts. He spat the piece of stick out of his mouth while looking into the eyes of Sotero. The two prisoners locked eyes as the rest of the prison inmates began to surround them. The guards were not looking. The fight was going to begin. Ticiano advanced, his arms by his side and his fists clenched. He raised his fists ready to fight. Sotero did the same thing, but then Ticiano felt a sudden jolt through his chest. His heart began to race extremely fast. He put his hand on his chest.

"Damn, man!" Ticiano gasped.

"What is it, bro?" Joshua asked.

Ticiano fell onto his knees with his hand on his chest. "I…" Ticiano panted, "think I'm having a heart attack."

"Don't be stupid, bro," Joshua said. "You're, like, twenty-something man."

"My chest," Ticiano panted again

Ticiano fell onto his back. The heat he felt from the sun, was burning his head, but that was the last of his worries.

"Hey!" Joshua called. "Guard!"

One of the guards ran over to the side of the fence, looking down, he reached for his radio.

"Ticiano!" Joshua yelled. "Hey, man, stick with me. Think of your mom, bro!"

Ticiano coughed, gritting his teeth in pain.

The guards entered the yard staring at the two men that just moments before were going to fight. "Everybody back. Now," one of them ordered. The guards looked at Ticiano as he laid on his back.

"Knife!" The guard yelled.

Joshua looked at Ticiano. The onlookers just watched as Ticiano closed his eyes. "Hey," Joshua called. "Bro, think of your ma. She loves you very much, man."

Ticiano closed his eyes. The prisoners and the guards could only stare down at him.

"He's dead" A subtle voice said.

* * *

SYDNEY, AUSTRALIA

It was 8:30 a.m. People were beginning their day. The roads were jammed with commuters as Officer Lewis Jackson, a Sydney-based police officer, climbed into the New South Wales patrol vehicle. He listened to the crackling packet in his hands as he sat down in the left-hand seat of the patrol vehicle.

"What you got today?" asked Bob Hudson.

"Bacon roll—the usual." Lewis opened the paper bag taking a bite into the soft white bread roll.

Bob watched as the food ran down the front of Lewis' clean, clear sky-blue uniform. "You like them, don't you?" He asked with a smile.

"Oh, yes." Lewis stated wiping his mouth as he turned his head to see Bob pull out something from under the seat.

"What's that you got there?" Lewis asked when he saw Bob had brought a small portable radio with him on duty.

Lewis continued to eat the sandwich he had just bought at the bakery.

"What, this? This is my little friend," Bob replied.

Lewis looked at Bob who was holding onto the small portable radio. "Your friend?"

"Oh, yes," Bob replied. "This has kept me more than amused some days on duty here in Sydney."

"Amused?" Lewis asked.

Bob turned the radio on. "Let's see what's going on in Oz today; Juliana Reeves will be on in a minute, just for you."

Lewis watched as Bob tuned the radio. "Oh please," Lewis pleaded, "not that woman, please"

"Agggh, here we are." Bob smiled at Lewis as he finished tuning the radio.

Lewis watched as the tiny bit of roll fell onto his uniform.

"Good morning Australia," Juliana Reeves said. "This is Juliana Reeves with you on this fine summer's day"

"Morning," Bob replied. "Your fan Lewis is here listening to you."

Lewis smiled as Bob rested the radio against the window of the car.

"It's 8:30 a.m., and it's another beautiful day here in Sydney. After this small break, we're going to look at your favourite Australian holiday hotspots as the holidays are nearing. Stay tuned. I'm Juliana Reeves."

Lewis listened to the radio.

"I know what I meant to ask you," Bob said. "How's Gemma?"

"She's very well, thank you," Lewis stated. "Still tolerates me."

Lewis finished the sandwich, looking out the front window as the everyday Australians wandered around doing their day's business or leisure activities. Children played in the adjacent park.

"Oh yeah," Lewis said, "I've got something to tell you."

"What?" Bob replied, still listening to the radio.

Lewis felt the sun heating the side of his head through the window. "You know I and Gemma were trying…" Lewis said.

"What? Oh, yes, I remember you saying," Bob said. There was a small pause. "She isn't?"

Lewis smiled at Bob, looking him in the eye.

"Oh, my boy," Bob replied. "Give me a hug." Bob hugged his partner after being told the news that Lewis's fiancée, Gemma, was pregnant. "Oh, I'm so pleased for you two," Bob said with a laugh before sinking back down into the seat of the car.

"Not long now for you," Lewis said.

"'Til what?" Bob asked. "Margaret isn't pregnant—not that I am aware of."

"Your big day," Lewis replied.

Bob had to think for a few seconds as Lewis looked at him. "Oh, my retirement," Bob replied. "Yes, not too long."

"What are your plans?" Lewis asked.

"Vacationing," Bob replied. "Maybe move to the Gold Coast, away from all this city noise and life. You can always bring Gemma as for the weekend—and the little one when he or she arrives."

"I may do that," Lewis replied. "I think Gemma will need a break after all she will have been through."

Bob turned, looking at Lewis. "You mean *you'll* need a break. What do you think about the new station?"

"I love it," Lewis replied. "A lot bigger than the other; everything is run from there, is it?"

"Yep," Bob replied. "Everything, even my pay-cheques, and soon retirement cheques."

Bob and Lewis heard some static on their radios. "All units in the vicinity of Highbury Street," the operator said, "please attend. Reports of a disrupted person"

"That's us," Bob said. "Let's roll."

Lewis clipped the seat belt in as Bob pulled onto the main road.

"Let's see what Sydney has to throw at us today," Bob said.

* * *

The onlookers on the Sydney street looked at the middle-aged man as he stood in the middle of the street. He had his head bowed, and his eyes were closed. He was not making a sound. Bob swung the car around the corner of the dead street, turning off the siren. There were only a few people on the sidewalk looking at the dazed individual. He was smartly dressed, an every-day man with his laptop bag strapped over his shoulder, just looking down at the sidewalk, oblivious to his surroundings. Bob slammed the door with force, trying to capture the attention of the dazed man as he continued to stand on the side of the street, edging into the road and oncoming traffic.

"Well, he's not asleep," Bob said, stating the obvious. "Come on, let's go and see if he needs our help."

People sitting in the café chairs watched as Lewis and Bob slowly walked over to the man just standing by the side of the street, looking down, unaware of his surroundings.

"How long has he been like this?" Lewis asked an onlooker.

"I don't know," she replied. "I just arrived. I wonder what is wrong with him."

A waitress for the café walked over to Lewis and spoke to him. "I believe he works in the offices over there," she said. "He buys coffee here every morning but look—he dropped it."

Lewis looked at the burst coffee cup on the ground as Bob approached the man.

"Sir," Bob said, "Can you hear me? Are you alright?"

The man didn't reply, but he continued to breathe as if he was choking.

"Come on, sir," Bob said again, gently shaking the body of the man. "Let me help you."

Bob watched as the middle-aged man slowly started to lift his head after the gentle shake on his arm. The top of his shirt creased as he slowly started to open his eyes. His eyelids slowly opened, revealing a gruesome pure yellow where the once-black pupil was. Some of his skin had started to wrinkle as though it was dying. Bob looked into his eyes as the man just stood there.

"Shit," he gasped. "Okay, sir, come here and sit down." Bob tried to guide the man back onto the pavement. "Lewis, radio for an ambulance. It's urgent," Bob demanded.

"Got it," Lewis replied. Lewis pulled out his black bulky radio as Bob tried to pull the man away from the street and onto the sidewalk.

"Sir, we'll find you help, I promise," Bob said. "Please, come away from the edge of the street. It's too dangerous. Look. There are cars coming." Before Bob had time to blink the man's mouth shot open. Bob jumped as the man fell onto him, piercing his teeth into his neck.

"Aggghhhh!" Bob bellowed. "Lew— Lewis!"

Lewis, hearing the horrific bellow, looked at Bob as drops of blood dropped onto the ground from his neck.

"Get him off!" Bob pleaded. "Lewis!"

Lewis ran over, grabbing the man and trying to rip him away from Bob's neck. The man's upper-body strength seemed to have increased. Lewis grabbed onto the side of the man's head, managing to pull him off Bob's neck. Pieces of Bob's skin ripped away and were stuck in the man's teeth. Lewis fought to get to Bob, pushing the man away. People stood along the side with fear widening in their eyes as the blood ran out of Bob's neck and down onto his clothes. Bob fell to the ground, choking as the blood gushed from his throat.

"Hey!" Lewis yelled. "You still hear me, Bob!? BOB!"

Lewis focused his attention on the wound on Bob's neck

as Bob struggled to breathe. "Where is that ambulance?" Lewis demanded into the radio.

"ETA: two minutes," the controller called back.

Lewis looked over at the café and saw the scared onlookers as he struggled to stop the blood spurting from Bob's neck.

"Get me some tissue!" Lewis screamed. "Come on!"

The waitress ran over with a tissue as Bob continued struggling to breathe and the blood continued gushing from his neck wound.

"Come on, man!" Lewis yelped. "Please don't do this! Come on, Bob!"

Something caught Lewis's eye. He looked over his shoulder and saw the smartly dressed man starting to get up off the dirty street. His eyes were still a yellow, pasty colour. He started scraping his foot along the ground moving towards Lewis. Lewis got up. His first priority was ensuring the safety of others around him. He ripped the black handgun from his pouch.

"Get back!" Lewis screamed. "Now!"

The onlookers watched as Lewis grasped his handgun. The middle-aged man was still slowly creeping towards him, his eyes still gleaming yellow.

"I said stay back!" Lewis screamed to the man. Lewis continued looking through the sight of the handgun, pointing it at the man's heart. "I will shoot!" he screamed at the top of his voice. Lewis watched as the man continued creeping towards him, desperate to get back to Bob as the blood broke through the pure white tissue.

"Son of a bitch," Lewis mumbled squeezing the trigger. The golden bullet launched from the canister slamming into the chest of the man. The man stopped in his tracks. Blood penetrated his blue shirt. He continued standing there with his head down, facing the ground, with blood running out of the bullet wound.

"What the. . .?" Lewis grumbled. Lewis re-focused his

attention as the man started walking forward towards him again, blood dripping now from his teeth. Lewis squeezed the trigger again, launching another round into him. The man fell back a few inches, still looking at Bob. He snarled and ran towards Lewis. Lewis didn't hesitate; he squeezed the trigger again. The bullet flew through the air, slamming into the head of the man. The body froze, falling back onto the street. Lewis dove to the ground as the sounds of police and ambulance sirens got louder by the second.

"Bob!" Lewis screamed. "Stay with me, old boy."

Bob didn't respond. Lewis felt a slight pulse on Bob; almost all the blood had left his system. The ambulance skidded around the corner onto the road and pulled up to the street.

"Come on!" Lewis bellowed to the paramedics. "He still has a pulse!"

The medics sprinted over, looking down at Bob, seeing the blood all over the ground. "Oh my God," the medic said.

"Come on," Lewis said. "Is he going to be okay?"

The ambulance was reversed over. Bob's body was placed on the stretcher. The back doors were slammed closed as the engine revved.

"Jesus Christ," Lewis said as he looked up to see Ben Crayfellow, a colleague in the New South Wales police—one he joined with.

"Lewis, what happened?"

Lewis took a few seconds to think. "He, he. . . Fuck," Lewis said. "He just bit into Bob's neck."

"Bit?" Crayfellow asked, gasping.

"Yes," Lewis replied. "Just pierced his neck. Blood was everywhere, and Bob was screaming for help. There was nothing I could do."

Crayfellow looked into Lewis' eyes. "Come on," he said. "Back to the station."

Lewis and Ben walked to the waiting police car. Lewis

stopped as the other officers pulled out the man's wallet to see his driver's license.

"Bradley Briggs," the officer said.

Lewis didn't reply as he stepped into the police cruiser, slamming the door shut.

CHAPTER TWO

Lucas, an American, on his first trip to Australia, looked out the window of the 747 jet as they descended towards Sydney.

"Flight attendants," the captain said, "please be seated for landing."

Lucas looked out over the left wing as Kingsford Smith came into view, the full flaps of the airplane ready for the heavy landing. He grabbed the armrest next to him as the craft touched down with a bump onto the runway. After a ten-hour flight from Honolulu, the jet pulled up to the stand as the seat belt sign was switched off.

"Damn," Lucas said to himself. He got up, looking at the Australian couple as they stood next to him.

"Tired?" the Australian asked Lucas.

"A bit," Lucas replied, stretching.

"Holiday?"

"Yes," Lucas replied. "I've always wanted to come here for a vacation."

"Well, you are here now. I've lived here all my life," the man replied.

"We loved Honolulu," the wife said. "The beaches were lovely, as were the people and the culture. We must go again."

The passengers started to disembark. Lucas grasped his

bag, staring out of the window onto the airport, heading towards passport control. This side of the airport was quiet. Not many people were there. Lucas waited in the queue for his turn. The queue seemed to be moving very slowly.

"G'day," the border agent said.

"Hey," Lucas replied.

"How long you here, and what brings you to Australia?" he asked Lucas.

"Vacation," Lucas replied.

"Holiday?" the border agent said stamping the passport.

"Yep," Lucas replied. "Quite happy I am finally here."

"Have a great stay," the border agent said.

Lucas walked through into the arrival's hall. He looked up at a Sky Australia desk in the corner. A young female sat on the chair, waiting to help somebody. He power-walked over.

"Hello, sir," she said. "How can I help you?"

"Howdy," he said with a smile. "I was looking the other day for flights to Ayers Rock, but the flights seem to have sold out. Do you know of any that are free?"

"One moment, please," she replied.

Lucas leaned on the counter as the Sky Australia employee typed something into the computer.

"I'm sorry, sir," she said. "There are no seats on any flights this week; shall I have a look for next week?"

"No, it's okay," Lucas replied. "I'll drive."

"If you want to leave me your number, I will call you if we get any cancellations."

Lucas wrote down his number and handed it over to the girl. "You'll call me straight away if a seat turns up?"

"Yes, I will do. Have a nice stay."

Lucas walked over towards the exit, seeing one of the taxi stands. An elderly driver was sitting on the bonnet waiting for a trip. "G'day mate," the elderly gentleman said. "Need a ride?"

"Yeah, please," Lucas replied.

"Where to?" he asked.

Lucas unfolded a sheet of paper. "The Grand Opera House View."

"One of the best in Sydney."

Lucas climbed into the back of the cab. The taxi pulled out, heading away from the airport and crossing over the newly built overpass.

"So, where you from?" the driver asked.

"Honolulu."

"Honolulu?" The driver smiled. "Lovely group of islands, great people… You here for holiday?"

"Yeah," Lucas said. "Vacation season is on for me"

"What do you do for a living?"

"I'm a security guard at a mall in Honolulu."

"Sounds fun," the driver replied.

"You got family?" Lucas asked.

"Yep," the driver replied. "Wife, daughter, and a granddaughter."The taxi pulled into the city. "There it is. The Grand Opera House View." The driver pulled into the bay outside the hotel. "There we are. That will be forty-five dollars."

Lucas handed over a fifty. "Keep the change—a present from me."

The porter walked over. "Good morning, sir. Checking in today?"

"Yes," Lucas said. "I have a reservation."

The floors gleamed, as if they had just been cleaned. Tall plastic plants stood in all corners of the lobby.

"Good morning, sir," the check-in girl said to him.

"Hi," Lucas said. "I have a reservation for a week."

"Can I have some identification, please, sir?" Lucas handed his passport over, smiling at the young female. "First time to Australia?"

"Oh, yes," Lucas replied. "Feeling the jet lag now." Lucas leaned on the counter.

"Go and have a lay-down after I check you in," she advised. "It will do you good."

Lucas stood up feeling a burst of energy as he stood straight. "How long would it take to get to Ayers Rock from here?"

The check-in girl took a few seconds to think. "It's right in the middle of Australia. Have you tried the airlines?"

"Tried them. How about driving?"

"Oh, God," the female replied. "Day and a half to Alice Springs nonstop, and another half-day to Uluru… Two, three days at least."

"I'd better get driving then," Lucas replied.

"Is it a place you have always wanted to visit?" the check-in girl asked.

"I live for the place; it's the only place in the world I have wanted to visit."

"Can I have your signature here for me, please?" Lucas signed the A4 piece of paper. "There we are, sir," she said. You are in room 626; it's on the top floor, overlooking the harbour, just as you requested."

Lucas took his electronic key from the counter. He smiled at the young girl as he started walking over to the elevator. The golden doors slowly slid open Lucas got in and the lobby disappeared.

Lucas slid the key card through the reader, opening the door to his room. He sat down on the bed looking out of the window onto Sydney Harbor. His energy was very low after the ten-hour flight from Honolulu. He lay back onto the bed, looking at the widescreen TV. He reached down to pick up the remote. The news of Officer Bob Hudson came to view straight away. He suddenly felt his mobile phone vibrate. He reached down, picked it up, and looked at an unidentified number on the screen. He pressed the 'answer' button and put the phone to his ear.

"Hello," he said in a subtle voice.

"Is that Lucas?" a female voice said.

"Who is this?" Lucas replied.

"We met at the Sky Australia desk about forty-five

minutes ago," she said. "We have just had a cancellation on a return flight to Ayers Rock; the flight is later today. Do you want to take it?"

Lucas smiled as he reached for his wallet. "Yes, please. You are amazing; you have saved my life." Lucas held the phone to his ear, looking at the news as it continued showing images of Bob and his family on the screen.

"Okay, sir, I just need your credit card details and your full name."

Lucas gave her his details. "When's the flight please?" he enquired

"It's at fifteen-hundred hours."

"Thanks, babe."

"Have a safe flight," she said. "If I don't see you."

Lucas put the phone down. He set the alarm on his phone, realizing that he had only four hours until he had to be back at the airport.

CHAPTER THREE

Lewis and Bob pulled up in front of the old estate. The houses were old; some were very run-down. Lewis saw a young man standing on the pavement with his hands in his pockets.

"Is this the one?" Bob asked Lewis.

Lewis looked at the individual who slowly turned his face to look away from the patrol vehicle.

"I believe so," he replied.

Lewis and Bob stepped out of the New South Wales patrol car. They slowly started walking over to the young adult, who was around eighteen years old.

"Arron Philips?" Lewis demanded.

"What?" Arron snapped.

Bob looked at Arron. He knew he was hiding something.

"We had reports of a burglary in the area, and a suspect fleeing the scene matches your description," Bob stated to him.

Arron shrugged his shoulders. "No idea," he replied. "Can I go now?"

"Can you stand here for me, please?" Lewis pulled Arron over to the patrol car—no handcuffs, nothing. "Okay. Where were you ten minutes ago?"

Bob looked around as people looked out of their windows

watching the two officers. He watched as Arron slowly started to put his hand into his pocket. He could tell that Arron was grasping onto something, just as he suspected.

"So, where were you twenty minutes ago?" Lewis asked again.

"I was at home," Arron replied. "I'm out, I told you."

Lewis watched as Arron started to frown. "You're lying."

"I'm not," Arron snapped. "Stupid twat."

Bob continued to observe Arron as he slowly started to reach further into the back pocket of his trousers.

"Hey," Bob warned.

Arron pulled a handgun from the back of his trousers, pointing it at the head of Lewis. Bob pushed Lewis out of the way as Arron pulled the trigger. The bullet slammed into the lamppost behind him. Bob pulled his extending baton out, slamming it into Arron's legs.

"Agggh!" Arron yelled. "Fuck you, asshole."

Lewis got up, looking down at the weapon lying down on the ground.

"Nice try, sunshine," Bob whispered to Arron. "Brace yourself for a long stay inside."

Lewis slowly stood up, gasping for breath, as Bob pushed Arron into the back of the patrol car.

"Hey, fuck you, man," Arron replied. "Fuck you, and fuck you, too."

"Fuck you, too," Bob replied. "Arsehole."

Bob looked over at Lewis. "Lewis."

Lewis looked up at Bob and watched as Bob slammed the door to the patrol vehicle closed. Looking into Arron's eyes he saw the fear starting to show.

"Come on," Bob said, "let's get you back," he ordered. "You're in no fit state for duty."

* * *

Lewis snapped himself out of the daydream. He shook his head and stepped out of the shower cubicle, feeling the hot water running down the side of his face. His blood-stained shirt was hanging on the peg.

"Jesus Christ," he moaned to himself

He could still hear Bob screaming in his head. Plus, in the clear vision of the day, he remembered the day he was nearly shot by a youth in the suburbs of Sydney. He shook his head, slowly walking out of the locker room.

"Jackson," a voice called.

Lewis turned to see Rolf Hepburn, the New South Wales chief of police.

"My office," Rolf ordered.

Lewis followed Rolf to his office, noticing the other officers watching as he was escorted in.

"Come in," Rolf asked Lewis. "Take a seat." He closed the door to his office. "Sit down, Lewis," Rolf asked as he sat at his desk, twiddling his thumbs. "I'm sorry," Rolf began. "Bob didn't make it. He...he died en-route to hospital." Lewis looked down onto the floor. "He lost too much blood from the attack and couldn't be resuscitated by medics."

"Who's going to tell. . .?" Lewis remorsefully asked.

Rolf let his breath out. "She already knows. She'll be here before I announce his death to the media"

Lewis looked down again. "He saved my life."

"After the news conference, you can go home," Rolf ordered.

Rolf looked down onto the form he had to fill out when an officer died. He looked at the pen on the edge of the desk waiting to be used to fill the long form out. Lewis got up. He opened the door and saw Ben Crayfellow.

"Lewis" Ben said as Lewis looked up at him. "Margaret is downstairs."

Lewis let his breath out.

Ben watched as Lewis started to walk off. "You need anything?"

"No, I'm good," Lewis replied.

Lewis walked along the corridor, looking through the glass window of the family room, seeing Margaret—Bob's wife—sitting there on the seat, wiping tears away from her face. She looked up as he walked into the room. Not a squeak or noise was heard from the door hinges.

"Hey, Margaret," Lewis whispered sympathetically.

Margaret sniffled, wiping some tears away from her face. Lewis slowly walked forward closing the door behind him.

"Oh Lewis, what am I going to do?" she wept. Lewis reached out hugging Margaret. "He was just two weeks away from retiring," she added amidst her tears. "We had it all planned, we were going to move to the Gold Coast, and then a few months later, we would travel across Europe. . . London the first stop to see family, Iceland for the northern lights, and —and. . ."

A knock on the door came. "Ma'am," the officer said to Margaret, "you're on in a few minutes."

Lewis and Margaret got up and left the room. Lewis followed Margaret and the officers through to the press room. He stood at the back of the room as the TV cameras were lined up, pointed at Hepburn. Lewis sat down and watched as Chief Hepburn stood up and straightened out his black jacket. He looked into the camera that was pointed at him.

"Today, at 8:10 a.m.," Chief Hepburn began, "Officers Bob Hudson and Lewis Jackson of the New South Wales Police were called to attend a disrupted individual. When Officer Hudson approached the individual, he was bitten by him in the neck. Officer Hudson died en-route to hospital."

The cameras started to flash as Rolf announced the death of Bob. Lewis leaned against the wall, feeling sick. He looked up towards the entrance, seeing the reporter Juliana Reeves walking into the room.

"New South Wales News. Who is the killer of Officer Bob Hudson?" She demanded

Rolf looked over the top of his glasses. "I cannot disclose that information as of yet," Hepburn said.

"But the people of the city have the right to know of the murderer who committed this act of crime."

Lewis clenched his fist; he slammed it into the wall behind him. Hepburn looked up to see Lewis storm out of the media room.

Lewis turned to the left, storming towards the stairs that led down to the car park. He burst through the swinging doors, pulled his car keys out of his pocket, and unlocked the car. He sat down in the driver's seat, pressing the small button on the dashboard. He pushed the accelerator down pulling out of the police station's new underground car park.

CHAPTER FOUR

Ben Crayfellow and Officer Jeremy Sandtown pulled up outside the house of Bradley Briggs. It was a nice house with nicely cut grass; all the flower beds were clean and well-kept.

"Nice house," Crayfellow said.

Sandtown didn't reply as he stepped out of the police cruiser. Crayfellow slowly walked onto the pathway as a young female looked out of the kitchen window, seeing the two officers as they walked up to the front door.

She walked up to the door after Crayfellow rang the bell, still drying her hands from the washing up she'd been doing. "Yes, can I help you?"

"Ms. Briggs," Crayfellow said.

"No," she said. "Well, *Mrs.* Emily Briggs, soon." Ben watched as Emily waved the engagement ring in his face.

"Can we come in, please?" Crayfellow asked.

Ben and Jeremy walked into the house. A young child was playing on the playmat in the front lounge.

"What's happened?" Emily asked.

Crayfellow let his breath out. "It's not good news. Bradley works in the offices in the city center, doesn't he?"

Emily looked at the two officers. "Yes, he does. Why? What's happened?"

"This is going to be hard for you to take in," Sandtown warned.

"What has happened?" Emily demanded.

Crayfellow struggled to get his words out as he looked at Emily, who was trembling from the anticipation.

"This morning," Crayfellow said, "Bradley attacked and killed a police officer of the Sydney Police Division."

Emily started to shake.

Sandtown stepped forward.

"No, please. That's not Bradley. He has never been in trouble in his life. He's a good person. I promise you. He applied to join the New South Wales Police earlier this year but didn't get in. He was so upset but was desperate to try again," she cried.

"Has Bradley been okay these last few days? Did anything seem different about him recently?" Crayfellow asked.

Emily started to weep. "No, we've been okay. We have had Lexi turn up. We had a bit of a hiccup with the bank, but that was sorted."

Crayfellow stood up.

"Where's Bradley?" Emily yelled.

"I'm sorry. Bradley is dead," Sandtown replied.

"Nooooo!" Cried Emily

A white New South Wales police van pulled up outside the house.

"I'm sorry, miss," Crayfellow said. "We have to search this house."

The officers entered her house to search upstairs and downstairs.

"Upstairs," an officer demanded.

Emily trembled while sitting on the settee watching the officers run up and down the stairs of her house.

* * *

Gemma sat at the hospital reception desk. She had been looking at the same A4 document for the last couple of minutes. A small tear began to run down her face.

"Hey," her colleague and friend Jasmine called.

Gemma shook her head, not wiping the tear and trying not to attract any attention.

"Listen," Jasmine said. "Do you want to take five?"

Gemma looked down at the floor beneath her feet.

"I know you and Lewis were close to Bob."

Gemma started to cry again.

"Look," Jasmine said. "Why don't you go and take five? I can cover for you."

"No," Gemma said, sitting up, "I'm good."

The elevator doors opened. It suddenly woke Gemma out of the daydream she had slipped into. There, walking out of the elevator, was Lewis.

"Oh my God," she gasped. "Are you okay?" He fell into her arms hugging her. "What happened?" she wanted to know. Lewis didn't reply as he felt her soft warm body against him. "Come to the family room," she ordered. She escorted him into the adjacent sitting room.

Lewis sat down, looking at her. "We were called to a street," Lewis said in a remorseful voice. "A man was just standing there, looking down at his feet." Gemma looked into his eyes as he continued. "And, as Bob went to help him, he just opened his eyes and bit him."

"Oh my God," Gemma quietly said.

"I had to shoot him," Lewis stated. She stared at him in disbelief. Lewis lowered his head in sorrow.

"Listen," Gemma said. "Go get some rest."

Lewis stood up. He nodded his head walking towards the seating area door. The door creaked open.

"Now, go home," Gemma demanded.

There was a sudden crash from behind. Gemma and Lewis looked up to see one of the medical trolleys wheeled through the doors.

"Serious traffic collision," the medic said.

Lewis and Gemma watched as the medical bed was wheeled past them.

"I've got to go," Gemma said. "Got to go and deal with this."

"Yes, me too." Lewis said. "I'll be back at home if you need me."

Lewis walked over to the elevator. The doors opened. Gemma watched as the elevator doors closed in front of him.

"Love you," she mumbled to him just before the doors closed. Lewis disappeared. Gemma walked over to the man lying on the bed. "What happened?" she asked.

The driver pulled the mask off his face. He was middle-aged. He had a slight beard on his face and had a British accent. "This," he said. "This idiot just ran out in front of me."

"Then what?" Jasmine asked.

"I hit him," he said. "I think he was chasing after someone."

"Chasing?" asked Gemma.

"Yes," the man replied. "His eyes were horrible."

Gemma frowned, looking at the man as he started to cough.

"Here," she said. Gemma put the mask back on the man as she looked at Jasmine.

CHAPTER FIVE

Nineteen-year-old Arron Phillips looked around the running track of the prison grounds. Guards stood on the overlooking balconies, looking down onto the prison yards.

"Times up," the guard yelled. "In. Now."

Phillips walked towards the silver gate. He looked at the guards as they stood there, observing every single inmate. Philips walked into the seating area of the prison. He looked at the secured tables in the block. He sat down and looked up onto the TV screen. He saw the New South Wales news come onto the screen.

"Oh, my God," Philips said as he saw Officer Bob Hudson.

"What?" Arnold asked. Arnold turned around, looked at the screen, and saw the picture of Bob. "Another one dead," he said. "Good. One more of them fuckers off the street."

"You know how I told you about how I tried to shoot that cop??" Philips said.

"Yes."

"He was the one that stopped me and got me put away in here." He said as he nodded at the screen.

"You should have had better aim." Arnold replied.

Philips continued to sit at the table, looking up at the news report showing Bob on the screen. Oscar Beuzeville, the head guard for the prison, was slowly strolling over to Arron. His hands were crossed behind his back. Arron tilted his head, looking forward as Oscar approached, stopped and just stood there, looking down at him.

"Well, well, well," Beuzeville said to Arron, "Officer Bob Hudson, dead. What must you be thinking right now, at this very minute?"

Arron slowly turned his head back at Oscar Beuzeville as he stared down onto him from above, his hands still locked behind his back. His gleaming keychain reflected the light.

"What are you trying to say?" Arron asked calmly for once in his life.

"Oh, nothing," Beuzeville replied. "Just trying to think what you are thinking. You have time to speak for however long you got left in here… Two years, maybe a whole lifetime if I could help it."

"Get out of here, man," Arron snapped.

Beuzeville didn't reply as he slowly walked away from Arron. The squeak of his leather shoes could be heard on the concrete floor as he walked away.

"God, I hate that guy," Arron mumbled. "Can't wait to get out of here."

"What you going to do when you get out?" Aidan asked.

"Find a job," Arron said. "Maybe a woman… Settle down, have a kid, maybe two. I've done my time in here."

"Do you regret what you did?" Aidan questioned.

"Nope," Arron replied looking over his shoulder at the new inmate as he sat down on the plastic chair. "We will have to watch him."

"Oh, yes," Aidan replied. "Trust me. We will."

* * *

It was still early in the morning—two hours behind Sydney. The Porter family was preparing for the day ahead of them. Being isolated in the middle of the outback, around thirteen hundred kilometres from Perth, there wasn't much to do.

Diane Porter walked into the dining area of their house as the sun beamed in through the window. It was scorching hot for that time of day. "Where's your tutor?" Diane asked Jake as Dale, her husband, walked into the front room. "He is on time normally."

"Morning. I'd better get ready for work. It's gonna be a long day today." Dale said.

"You work so hard to support us. Come have some tea. You don't have to leave just yet," Diane pleaded.

"Yeah, well," Dale said. "That's what I do." Dale looked at Diane as he sat down on the wooden chair. Then he said, "Oh, I could use a cup of tea. It won't be long now."

"Till what?" Diane asked.

"We move to Perth," Dale said. "I'll be closer to home and won't have to travel as far. Jake can go to school and finish his education."

Jake looked out and saw the black car with his tutor in it. He watched as it sped towards the house.

Diane walked over to the window, seeing the dust blow up from under the tires "What the…?" She gasped as she watched the car slam through the gate, swerve to the left and slam into the tree.

"Oh my God," Diane gasped. "Dale! Quickly!"

Dale ran over to the crashed car. "Shit," he gasped. Smoke hissed out from the car's hood.

"Hey," Dale said to the tutor. "Can you hear me?" The tutor didn't seem to be moving. "Hey," Dale yelled. The tutor's head slowly started to rise. Dale reached in to undo the seatbelt to allow him to get out. "Hang on," he said. Dale looked at the tutor as he started to turn his head to the left. The tutor's eyes slowly started to open.

Diane turned around to Jake. "Go dial triple-zero and tell them what's happened," Diane said. "You know our location and what to do—like we practiced." Diane walked over to the car.

"Look at his eyes," Dale said.

Diane frowned at the gleaming yellow eyes of the tutor. "Oh my God," Diane gasped

The tutor turned his head to the right, looking at Dale's arm. He opened his mouth, slamming his teeth into the side of the other man's arm. It happened so quick that Dale was not able to get out of the way. Diane screamed as the tutor sunk his teeth even further into Dale's arm.

"Get him off!" Dale screamed. "Please!" Blood ran down from his arm. The tutor wasn't letting go.

Jake watched from behind the curtain as the emergency operator came onto the telephone. "Zero, zero, zero; what's the nature of your emergency?" The operator asked.

Jake, who was now in shock did not here the operator, he continued to stare in horror as the tutor bit into his dad's arm refusing to let go.

"Hello," the emergency operator asked. "What's your emergency?" Jake watched the tutor fall from the car.

Hisses and snarling killed the silence of the outback house. Dale summoned up the energy to pull his arm from the tutor's mouth leaving bits of his own skin dangling from the other man's teeth.

"Jesus!" Dale yelled as the tutor fell back against the car. Dale looked down at the wound in his arm. He tried to stop the blood, but it continued to gush out. "It won't stop!" He panicked.

Diane helped Dale up from the ground. She turned and looked over at the window of the house. "Jake!" She called. "Are they sending help?"

Jake just looked out of the window. He slowly started to lift his hand. He pointed at her.

"What?" She asked.

Diane swung around. Before she had time to blink, she caught sight of Dale and the tutor. They were both just standing there, static, staring at her. The blood on the tutor's mouth was drying from the intense heat. Dale's mouth opened. He sunk his teeth into Diane's neck. Jake stood in shock.

The tutor looked at Jake as he stood by the window, his eyes locked onto him. The tutor sprinted towards the house. Diane lay on the ground choking. Jake stormed through the house, running towards the stairs. Hearing them crash through the door he froze. He stared at the ground at the bottom of the stairs until he saw two dark shadows appear on the wooden flooring. That got him moving. Jake ran up the stairs, diving into his bedroom. He slammed the door shut. Jake frantically looked around the big bedroom for a place to hide. He heard the charging footsteps running up the stairs straight towards his room. It was as if they could smell where he was. Jake spun around and dived into the wardrobe. He slid the wooden door shut just as his dad and the tutor barged their way into the bedroom through the wooden door. Looking at the gleaming eyes of his dad as he sniffed around the room made Jake tremble with fear. He tried to stay still and quiet as the tutor looked through the tiny holes in the wardrobe Jake was hiding in. Watching in horror, Jake managed a small sigh of relief as his dad and the tutor stormed out of the room. The creaks in the floorboards slowly faded as the two zombified people left Jakes bedroom and continued to search for him.

Jake trembled as he listened to the heavy footsteps disperse into nothing. Peeking out from the wardrobe he saw that drops of blood had slowly soaked into the formerly clean carpet. Jake slowly turned his back to the wall of his wardrobe and slowly pulled his knees to his chest.

CHAPTER SIX

Claire Harrison, twenty years old and a student at the University of Sydney, was in her second year of her philosophy degree. She was born and raised in Brisbane; she was the only child in her family. She walked out through the glass door into the university campus socializing area, feeling the weight of the laptop bag she was carrying on her shoulder after the morning's lecture. She looked over at Tom and Ryan, who were congregating, along with a few other students, around one of the wooden benches. Obviously, they had skipped their lectures. She tried slowly walking away so as to not attract their attention.

Noticing her Tom called out. "Claire!"

Claire closed her eyes as she turned around. She strolled to the park bench looking down at the two boys. "Hey," she said. "How you been?"

"I'm good, babe." He said

Claire watched as Tom slurped a tiny bit of alcohol from the can hidden beneath his jacket.

"Oh, that feels good," he mumbled

"Do you know what would happen if you were caught?"

"No. Listen, babe, when we going out?"

Claire looked down at him trying to hesitate. "Listen," she said.

"He's a nice guy," Ryan intervened, squinting in the intense sunlight as he looked up at Claire, trying to persuade her to date Tom.

"Listen," she said again. "I want to finish my studies first."

"Damn, girl," Tom slurred. "When you going to let loose and enjoy life, babe?" "Look," Tom squinted in the sun, "come to my room tonight. All the boys will be there."

Claire felt her phone start to vibrate in her pocket. She ripped it out quickly. "Hang on," she said to the boys as she spun around and answered her phone. "Hello?"

"Hi, Claire." It was Audrey, the café manager where Claire worked. "Do you want some overtime?" she asked. "Emily is very sick."

"Oh," Claire said. "Okay."

"Oh, you little angel, thank you so much," she replied. "See you soon."

"No, thank *you*," Claire replied. Claire turned around to Tom and watched as he sipped another bit of alcohol. "Sorry, I can't make the party," she said. "I have got to work."

"Okay," he said. "Another time, bab— babe." Tom and Ryan both laughed at his intoxication.

"I'll see you around," Claire said, looking down at the two boys. She turned around and walked away, rolling her eyes as she did.

* * *

Lewis pulled up outside the city morgue after the drive from the hospital where Gemma worked. He pulled the handbrake up, got out of his car, and walked towards the entrance. He pushed the brown doors open, staring at the reception in front of him.

"Mr. Jackson?" the receptionist asked.

"Yes, that's me," Lewis replied. "Is Gerald around? I want to talk to him."

"Yes, sir. Do you want to go through and see him?"

Lewis didn't have the time and energy to thank her. He just walked through to the morgue, slamming through the plastic swing doors. He stormed in, looking for Gerald the pathologist, and noticed he was just in the middle of examining Bob's corpse.

"Lewis," Gerald said. "Nice to see you. I'm sorry about Bob."

Feeling deep pain, Lewis looked down at the corpse.

"Cause of death," Gerald added. "Loss of blood and oxygen. But," Gerald invited his attention, "take a look at this."

Lewis and Gerald walked over to the other trolley. Lewis pulled the pure white cloth back, looking down onto Bradley Briggs.

"What about him?"

"Take a look at his eyes," Gerald told Lewis.

Gerald pulled back the eyelid of the corpse. Lewis looked down at the pure black eyes. "Hang on, they were not like that before I shot him."

"What colour were they?"

Lewis took a deep breath before adding, "Gleaming yellow. He was just standing there when Bob approached him."

"Yellow?"

"Yes," Lewis replied. "A pure, glowing yellow, like nothing I have ever seen before."

"I'm going to get some blood samples from this , who has been identified as Bradley Briggs, and run some tests to see what we are dealing with here."

"Has he been to any foreign countries recently?"

"No," Gerald said. "That is the first thing I checked with the New South Wales Police Database and the Foreign and

Commonwealth Office. He hasn't left Australia for over two years."

Lewis looked at Gerald. "I'm going to let you get back to work. I've been dismissed for the day."

"Go home," Gerald said. "Get some rest."

Lewis nodded. He gave Gerald a smile, turned around, pushed the brown door open, and headed towards the main entrance. Lewis stormed passed the reception, walking into the burning light as it beamed in through the door.

Gerald walked over to the body of Bradley Brigg and syphoned a small sample of blood from his arm before it coagulated within the body. He quickly glanced down at the body before going into his lab to examine the blood. Gerald looked down at the blood through the microscope. Words couldn't describe what he saw.

"No," He gasped. "What the hell is that?"

Gerald stood up. He looked over at the two metal cabinets each holding a dead corpse in them. He knew he had to report his findings to the centre for disease control but wasn't quite ready. He walked over to his office, looked at his coat on the peg and the files scattered about the office and desk. He reached down and picked up his tatty leather briefcase. It was old and a few stickers had started to fall off. His heart was pounding fast as he was still in shock from what he had just discovered in Bradley's blood. Gerald threw his coat on intending to leave; but glancing through the glass window he noticed he had left a few documents on the table in the other room.

Gerald slipped his glasses on and walked over to retrieve the documents from the table. As he walked over, he heard some gentle tapping. He lifted his head, listening carefully, and looked towards where he thought the sound was coming from. He could swear it was coming from the metal container that had Officer Bob Hudson in it. As he walked towards it the tapping started to get louder, and faster. Placing his briefcase down on the concrete floor of the morgue Gerald reached out, grabbed the door of the container and pulled the small flap down. He reached in, holding onto the metal rim of the metal bed. His hands grasped the cold metal as he pulled the bed out. The white material covering the body was twitching. Gerald slowly put his hands onto the front of the material and pulled the cloth back, looking down he saw that Officer Hudson's entire body was twitching. Bob's eyes shot open. Gerald gasped, looking down and seeing the gleaming yellow eyes. Suddenly, Bob shot up from the medical table and grabbed Gerald before he was able to understand what was happening.

* * *

SYDNEY ZOO

School children on trips and mothers with their infants gathered round the zoo enclosures looking at the many different species of animals. A young mother of two slowly walked over to the Rhino enclosure. She held onto her son's hand, feeling the beaming sun burn her arms.

"What's he doing?" A voice was heard asking.

Something was wrong. The onlookers stared into the enclosure at the white rhino whose eyes had turned noticeably yellow.

"What's the matter with his eyes?" an American tourist asked.

Claudia Furnell was one of the keepers on duty. She was born in Sydney and had studied in Perth. The sun beamed on her head as she looked at all the people who were gathered around the Rhino enclosure. She walked towards them. "Excuse me," Claudia asked as she barged through the group of people and looked at the rhino as it walked around dazed. It seemed to be snarling.

"Look at his eyes," somebody said again. "What is wrong with him?"

Claudia reached for her radio. The rhino looked up, snarling again, scraping his front right hoof along the ground. He charged towards the other rhino in the enclosure. People watched in horror as he jumped onto the female, slamming his teeth into her neck. Blood rushed out of the female rhino's neck as she yelped with pain.

"What the hell?" Claudia gasped. "They don't do that!"

People, with fear in their eyes, stared as blood rushed down from the neck of the female rhino onto the ground, staining it red. Claudia ran away from the crowd as other staff members congregated around the enclosure. The female rhino fell to the ground. The male slammed his teeth into her again, ripping the skin away.

"He's eating her!" someone yelled.

The people looked down at the female rhino as her eyes reopened. They were now gleaming yellow. The male rhino backed away as the female stood up, blood still running out of her neck.

"Get to the Gorilla enclosure; something has happened there," Claudia heard her colleague say over the radio.

She arrived at the Gorilla enclosure and watched as the gorilla started charging at the concrete pillars, trying to break out. The onlookers looked on in terror as the wall slowly started to crumble as the gorilla continued to slam into the concrete bollards, making chunks of concrete fall to the ground. Claudia turned her head and saw a member of the staff running over with a tranquillizer gun in his hand.

"Do it!" Claudia demanded. "Now!"

The keeper watched as the dart was fired through the air. It shot into the back of the infected gorilla, but the gorilla continued slamming into the wall.

"Do another," she demanded.

The dart was fired and hit the gorilla, but it still had no

effect. The onlookers continued to watch as bits of concrete continued falling to the ground.

"Everybody away," Claudia demanded.

The tourists started fleeing from the enclosure.

"Get the rifle," Claudia demanded. "Now."

"What?" the warden gasped, looking into her wide-open eyes.

"Don't argue," Claudia replied. "If that thing gets out, it will cause havoc, and someone could be killed." Claudia continued to watch the gorilla as it slammed into the metal bars, trying to break free from the enclosure. "Where is that rifle?" She demanded.

The gorilla slammed into the metal bar again, weakening the structure. Claudia watched as he clasped both his arms around the metal bars and started pulling them apart. "Where is that rifle?" she screamed again.

"It's here," the warden said. The gorilla continued ripping the metal bars apart.

"Shoot it," Claudia demanded in a panic.

Claudia stepped back, looking at the warden as he loaded the weapon and looked through the scope of the rifle. As the gorilla was about to break free from the enclosure he squeezed the trigger. The people screamed as the bullets were fired into the chest of the gorilla. He continued to try and break through the metal bars surrounding his enclosure.

"Do one in his head," Claudia ordered.

The warden looked through the scope just as the gorilla finished breaking through its enclosure. He squeezed the trigger once again, launching the round into the head. The people watched as its body froze. Children and even adults were crying aloud as they fled from the scene. The gorilla let go of the metal bars, slowly falling with a thud to the dusty ground. People watched as dust puffed up from under the dead body.

The keeper walked over to the broken cage, looking at the lumps of concrete lying on the ground. "Jesus!" she said.

"What shall we do?" the warden asked.

Claudia didn't have to reply. She turned her head to the right and saw the other gorilla that had been attacked. It was now standing there, with eyes gleaming yellow—just standing there, looking over the broken fence into the compound.

"No," the keeper said. "It can't be."

The warden raised the rifle, aiming it at the infected gorilla as it ran towards the broken fence. The warden looked through the scope once again; he had only one round left to fire. He squeezed the trigger, launching the last round out. The bullet shot through the air, hitting the gorilla's head.

"Close the zoo," Claudia ordered. "Now."

The warden ran off as Claudia stood there, staring at the two dead gorillas as they lay on the dry ground of the enclosure with blood running out of the wounds onto the dry ground. The bodies of the gorillas were still twitching.

"What the hell just happened?" she mumbled to herself.

* * *

Lewis walked into his apartment. The sun gleamed in through the clean windows. A gentle breeze blew the curtains around. They were clean. Not a stain on them. Dinner plates were still left on the table from the meal the night before. The food had dried onto them. He stopped suddenly, feeling his phone vibrate in his pocket. It was Gemma again.

"Hey," he said. "No need to worry now. I'm back at the apartment."

"I just wanted to make sure that you got home okay," Gemma asked.

"Yes, all okay here," Lewis replied. "I will be fine; how's it going down there?"

Gemma stalled for a few seconds before replying. "Oh, you'll never guess what happened."

Lewis interrupted her, "Gemma, I need you here."

"I am sorry," Gemma said. "I love you so much. See you tonight when I finish." Gemma put the phone down quickly.

Lewis was shocked. He put the phone down on the table next to the settee and walked into the bedroom. He lay down on the bed without getting undressed. He looked at the curtains as they blew in a gentle breeze. He lay back into the bed closing his eyes, still hearing the sound of Bob's scream for help in his head.

Gemma stormed into the emergency room of the hospital. "What have we got?" she demanded of her colleagues.

"Serious road collision," the doctor replied.

Gemma looked at the driver as he lay on the bed with his head in a collar.

"What happened?" Gemma asked.

The driver slowly pulled the oxygen mask off his face. "This..." he gasped. "This guy just ran out in front of me. I swerved and..."

"Okay," the doctor said. "Put this back on. Take it easy. You have the best staff here to help you." The doctor slid the mask back on as the plastic doors to the ward slammed open again.

"It's another one of these people," the medic said. Gemma looked down onto the infected individual lying on the bed. Both of his legs were broken so that he could not move. "I mean, look at his eyes. These attacks are popping up all over the city. I have never seen anything like it before." Gemma watched as the two medics walked off.

"Wait," the doctor said. "Where are you two going?"

"Got another call," the medic replied. "Same kind of attack."

"Another bite?" the doctor asked.

"I think so," the medic replied. "We'll let you know as soon as we know."

Gemma looked at the doctor and saw him shrugging his

shoulders as the two medics left the ward. Gemma turned her attention to the injured man. He kept snarling, trying to lift his hands to grab her.

"Sir, can you hear me?" she asked.

"I wouldn't bother," a voice said.

Gemma turned and saw the security guard of the hospital.

"Why?" Gemma asked him.

"I have seen a few of these cases today," the guard replied. "They don't seem to respond to anyone when they are like that."

"What?" the doctor gasped.

"I've heard they just randomly attack people when they are nearby," the guard replied.

The doctor didn't reply as the guard started to walk off, glancing over his shoulder at the bewildered face of the injured man who was showing no signs of civilized life.

Gemma watched as the cable tie holding the man's arms to the metal pole broke. "What the!?" the doctor yelped.

Gemma fell back through the blue curtains to the ward as the man jumped off the bed and looked up at the security guard. The guard continued to slowly walk forward up to the corridors of the emergency ward. He slowly turned his head back, only to see the figure running towards him. The guard looked at the running man. He swiped his handgun from the pouch. He squeezed the trigger. The zombie dropped to the ground. He looked at Gemma, who was starting to get up. People were looking at the guard as he slipped the gun back into the pouch. Gemma watched as he slowly walked away, leaving the twitching body on the ground.

CHAPTER SEVEN

Prime Minister Tony Brown stared out of the black jeep's window as they pulled up outside Parliament House in Canberra. In just his second year as Prime Minister, he had already achieved a lot as he had continued to grow the Australian economy and kept unemployment down. Canberra police were everywhere, with a few members of the Australian Army dotted about the grounds to the house. Brown stared at the soldiers, knowing they had been mobilized by his generals.

"Why has the army been mobilized to the grounds?" He demanded.

"We'll explain once inside, sir," Chief of Staff Thomas Legg said.

Two guards were spotted guarding the entrance as two huge gates opened. Escorted by police motorbikes, the jeep pulled up to the entrance to the parliament. The door was opened for the prime minister. He looked out to the horizon of the capital city. He frowned at the extra police and service vehicles that were present in the city surroundings. He heard a gunshot in the distance, which made him frown.

"This way please, sir."

Brown walked up the steps into the building.

"This way, sir," Legg asked again.

Brown followed Thomas Legg through into the briefing room on the top floor. The chief of the Canberra police was there with some of Australia's service personnel. They were dead silent.

"Bring me up to speed," Brown demanded.

The room went quiet for a few seconds.

"I think I had better start," Police Chief Stanley Rimmer said. "Mr. Prime Minister, throughout the country, we have seen an increase in civil disturbance."

"Civil disturbance?" Brown queried.

"Let me show you something," Doctor Hoskins intervened quickly. Hoskins spun around on his chair and turned on a DVD player in the corner of the room. The picture showed a room in the Center for Disease Control in Canberra,

"This is one of our quarantine centres, sir," Hoskins said.

Brown looked at the individual. He stared at the gleaming yellow eyes of the infected person.

"The hell?" Brown gasped. The snarling echoed around the dead room.

"This is the infection we are dealing with, sir," General Kingsley said. Brown looked at the snarling person. "As you can see, sir, I think we are dealing with an epidemic, the first of its kind in Australian history."

Brown rubbed his face. "What does the ACDC have to say about this?" he asked as he watched Hoskins open his leather bag.

Hoskins pulled out an A4 pad, looked down at the virus that they were dealing with. "This is the virus," he said. "As you can see, it's like any other virus; it has the ability to invade the human body and reproduce in human cells."

"Go on," Brown said, eager for more information.

"But it is a virus that has never been seen among mankind —at least it's not in any records," he replied.

"What?" Brown gasped.

"Yes, sir," Doctor Hoskins stated. "We have run numerous tests at our locations throughout the country and the results all turned up negative."

Brown looked out of the window into Canberra as police cars whizzed back and forward. "How do we go about prevention measures?"

General Kingsley placed a file onto the middle of the table. "Here is the contingency plan for a viral epidemic, such as that which is upon us. They were drawn up after 9/11 in case of the event of a bio-terror attack by a terrorist cell operating here in Australia. According to this, all public transport and public gatherings must close down as soon as possible to prevent further infection, but as we are dealing with a highly contagious infection, I also advise a curfew to take effect."

"How is it passed on to different individuals, this virus?" Brown demanded.

"After the uninfected person has been bitten by an infected individual," Hoskins finally let out, "they return to life in two to fifteen minutes, sometimes longer, as an infected individual and attack anyone who is not carrying the infection."

Brown sat back. "What's the current rate of infection?"

Doctor Hoskins flicked a switch on the remote control in front of him. Brown saw a map of Australia come up on the screen on the main wall. "The red dots you see are the cities and towns that have reported this infection so far."

Brown squinted his eyes as he looked at the map of Australia, noticing that some of the major cities across the eastern seaboard had red dots on them.

"If we calculate the rate of infection including people from other nations that are here in Australia, we are looking at a total infection of almost ninety percent of the country within twenty-four hours if curfew measures are not put into place."

"Have any other nations reported infection?" Brown asked.

"No, sir. No other countries have reported infection so far," General Kingsley said.

"It's only us?" Brown asked. "Just to confirm, we are the only country reporting this disease so far."

"Yes, sir."

Brown looked down onto the desk. "Okay," he said. "I want all public transport within Australia suspended." He went on, "All flights to and from this country are to be grounded."

"What are you going to tell the nation?" Hoskins wanted to know.

"The truth," Brown said.

"I'll get a speech drawn up for you right away, sir." Legg stated.

"Do that," Brown demanded.

"Are you evacuating the major cities?" Kingsley asked.

"It will cause too much panic. If we are to ever stand a chance of evacuating people, it would need to be to somewhere isolated, away from the mainland." Brown turned his head, looking at the map of Australia. He focused his eye on Tasmania, the medium-sized island that is about a one-and-a-half-hour flight from Sydney.

"Have there been any reports of infection in Tasmania?" he demanded. "Answer me."

General Kingsley looked down at the map and said, "No, sir. No reports of disturbance there at all."

"Then that's our safe zone," Brown insisted.

"What?" General Kingsley gasped.

"That is our safe zone," Brown replied again. "It's perfect, it's isolated from the mainland, and it's big enough to hold hundreds of thousands of people. How long would it take to get fifteen-thousand troops down there to begin sweeping the island and securing Hobart?"

"I have an aircraft fully-loaded with troops on standby, about an hour away," General Kingsley replied.

Brown stood up, putting his jacket back on. "Then do it,"

he ordered. "I want fifteen-thousand troops at Hobart and Tasmania."

"Sir?" General Kingsley stammered.

"Get to it," Brown demanded.

"When do you want to start evacuating New South Wales?" General Kingsley asked.

"As soon as we have enough troops and air transport to begin the evacuation," Brown answered. "Get me Mayor West."

HOBART

Mayor Peter West sat in his office chair in Hobart, Tasmania, staring up at the widescreen TV on the wall. The telephone in front of him started to ring. The red light on the plastic casing beamed out, drawing his attention away from the TV.

"Yello," he said into the speaker.

"Sir," The receptionist said, "Tony Brown is on line one for you."

"Tony Brown?" West asked. "Put him through." West picked up the telephone on his desk. "Mr. Brown," West said, "how may I assist you?"

"I need you to listen to me very carefully," Brown said in a monotonic voice.

West knew something was wrong with from the tone of the other man's voice. "Yes, I am listening."

After a short pause, he heard the Prime Minister's clear his voice. "You know the civil disturbances that the country is experiencing?"

"Yes," West replied.

"We are currently going through an epidemic."

West shook his head with disbelief. "Epidemic?" West gasped.

"Are you reporting any disturbances in Hobart or Tasmania?"

"Well," West said, "only the occasional hiccup by some youngsters."

"I mean, bites."

"No," West said. "Nothing like that here."

"A virus unknown to mankind has made it into Australia, and this is what is causing all of the unrest within the country."

West couldn't believe what he was hearing from the Prime Minister.

"What do you want me to do?"

"I want the Devenport shuttle ferry suspended until the military arrive there. All shopping malls and public gathering locations are to be sealed."

"What about the panic and chaos that could happen to us?" West waited for the reply.

"I am sending troops, fifteen-thousand strong, to Tasmania," Brown replied.

"My chief of police is coming to brief me on the crisis on the mainland," West replied.

"Got it" Brown snapped.

Brown and West put the phone down as the chief of the Hobart police arrived. Chief Charles Hazelton walked into the Mayor's office, fully dressed in his uniform.

"You needed to see me, sir?" Charles Hazelton asked as soon as he came in.

"Sit down," West demanded. Hazelton sat down on the chair. "I need to cut straight to the point," West said. "We are not going through a phase of civil disturbance. We are going through an epidemic."

"Epidemic?" Charles Hazelton snapped.

"Yes," West replied. "Now, I have orders from the PM. I need all of your off-duty officers on duty—all over the island."

"But that will cause panic," Charles Hazelton said, expressing his distrust.

"You must remember that Hobart and Tasmania are the

only places in Australian territory that haven't had any infections. We are under quarantine until further notice."

"What virus are we dealing with?" Charles Hazelton asked.

"The end of mankind," West said. Hazelton looked at the Mayor. "Seal off the Devenport ferry," West instructed. "Brown is also sending thousands of troops here to assist the Hobart and Tasmanian police until the infection has cleared."

"Understood," Chief Hazelton said in a weak voice.

* * *

The commander of the C-17 galaxy set the altitude hold switch on the jet as it continued descending to five-thousand feet. He looked out the front window as the city of Hobart slowly came into view.

"Drop time," he said, "T-minus one minute."

The back door of the C-17 opened, as the other C-17 that was following turned to the right, heading off to drop troops into the outback towns of the island. Screaming winds entered the rear of the aircraft. Soldiers of both genders and all ages sat nervous, with their backs to the wall of the jet. Not even a flick of turbulence was felt on that summer's day. The back-jump door of the C-17 finished opening. Only the blue Pacific Ocean could be seen in the distance.

"Enjoy the view, boy and girls," the sergeant yelled. "May be the last thing you'll ever see."

The soldiers stood quietly, looking at the red light beaming into their eyes. It switched to yellow. A slight adrenaline rush hit them as it changed to green.

"Jump, jump, jump!"

The soldiers ran out from the back of the craft. The shoots opened, one after the other. The people on the ground looked up as the C-17 flew overhead, the parachutes opening one after the other. The ground got bigger and bigger. One after another, the soldiers slammed into the ground, rolling.

"Let's move," one soldier yelled. "Go, go, go!'

Carl Farrington, a twenty-seven-year-old, walked into the Mayor's office.

"Mayor West?" He demanded.

West looked at the solider as he barged into the office without permission. "Yes," Mayor West replied. "Yes, that's me."

"Carl Farrington," Farrington said. "I've been ordered to undergo the operation of securing Tasmania and Hobart for the potential site of the mainland evacuation."

"Tony Brown and I had a conversation a little while back."

"Okay," Carl Farrington said. "First, I need you to get a message out to your people here on Hobart about a curfew that is to take effect on my word."

"Curfew?" West asked.

Farrington looked up at West as he unfolded a map onto the table. "Yes, sir." he replied.

"Why a curfew?" West asked.

Farrington looked up into the eyes of the Mayor. "Because we are going to need as much room as possible. There is a very strong possibility that some of New South Wales and other cities in Australia will have to be evacuated to this island."

"How's the mainland?" Charles Hazelton asked.

Carl Farrington didn't reply for a few seconds. "Not good," Farrington said. "Now, let's move."

"I need a car to take me to Radio Tasmania. From there, I can brief the island," West demanded.

"Understood," Carl Farrington replied.

Mayor West stood up, putting his jacket on and catching a glimpse of the view outside the window.

CHAPTER EIGHT

Lucas stormed into the terminal at Kingsford Smith International Airport. He looked over at the Sky Australia check-in desk. Seeing that he only had a few minutes before it closed for the flight over to Ayers Rock he ran over.

"Hey," he said to the check-in agent. "Ayers Rock. I have a booking with you."

Lucas put his passport down onto the desk.

"I'm sorry, sir," The check-in agent said.

Lucas looked into the eyes of the agent.

"Don't you have a booking for me?" Lucas asked. "I was phoned earlier on, and I was booked in for a flight."

"All the flights in Australia have been cancelled."

"Why?" Lucas gasped.

The check-in guy smiled with sarcasm. "Due to the civil disturbances in progress, all flights to and from Sydney have been cancelled."

"Shit," Lucas said. "I'll have to drive there."

"Good luck," the check-in agent said.

Lucas looked up at the flight information board which showed all flights had been cancelled.

"If you go online, sir, you can apply for a refund," the check-in agent said.

"Thanks," Lucas replied. He picked up his bag, but as he left the Sky Australia check-in desk, something caught his attention. He saw a car rental company. He looked at the girl as she smiled at him.

"Hey, sir," she said. "Need a ride?"

"Yes, I do," Lucas said. "Quickly."

Lucas pulled out his wallet, feeling the weight of his bag. He could see more and more people leaving the airport as they found out their flights were cancelled.

"I need you to just sign here," she said. Lucas signed on the line as the small black key was handed over to him. "Take the shuttle bus outside to parking zone two," she said, "and you will see your car."

"Thanks." He snatched the key and ran to the exit. He watched as the mini shuttlebus started to pull away from the parking stand.

"Woah!" he yelled out. "Hey, hey, hey!"

The bus came to a sudden stop. The electric door on the side slowly opened up allowing him to enter the vehicle.

The driver was an African man. "You okay, sir?" he asked.

"Fine," Lucas replied. "Thanks for stopping."

"Not a problem, boss," he replied. "You American?"

"How did you guess?"

The African man smiled as he sped along the streets towards the parking bay where the rental cars were.

"Why are all the flights cancelled?" The African man asked Lucas.

Lucas stopped for a second. He stared out the front window as the bus continued along the street. "Due to these civil disturbances taking place."

The African man laughed, "Makes me laugh, it does."

"Me too." Lucas watched as the bus pulled into the parking bay. The driver pulled up into the stop.

"There you go, boss," the man said.

Lucas stepped down off the bus, holding onto his bag. "You drive safe, okay?" Lucas said.

Lucas walked through the car park, looking for his car. He identified it and pulled the door open. He climbed in and switched on the air conditioning system. He slammed his bag onto the back seat and switched on the engine. He felt the cold air blow onto his face. He looked at the Ayers Rock picture stuck on the rubbish bag that was stuck inside the dashboard.

"Come on," he said to himself. "You can do this." Lucas pushed the accelerator down as he drove away from the airport. He looked up to see the sign that led to the highway. "Come on," he yelled, "need to roll." Lucas sped along the street looking at the highway entrance.

The entrance was blocked by two police cars. "Oh, now what?" Lucas pulled up next to the highway entrance winding down the window. He looked down the ramp and saw two cars piled into each other.

"How long is this road going to be closed?" he asked the officer.

"Don't know. Sorry," the officer said.

"Shit," Lucas mumbled. "Okay, thanks." Lucas sped off wondering how he could get onto the highway that led over to Ayers Rock.

Lucas drove into the city center. People were everywhere. The infection was spreading very quickly. Lucas drove along the road, seeing the other vehicles shooting straight through the red lights.

"Fuck it," Lucas said in irritation. He slammed the accelerator down, dodging the cars as they sped past him. He continued along the main road, keeping his foot near the brake pedal.

He swerved to the right to get out of the way of a car headed straight at him, but he didn't have time to swerve back onto the road before slamming into a lamppost. The front of the new car was buckled up. Steam hissed out of the front of the engine. Stunned from the crash Lucas slowly opened his eyes. He looked out of the window and saw a female police officer banging on the window.

"Hey?" she said. "You okay, sir?"

Lucas opened the door, reaching for his bag. "I'm fine, thanks," he replied. He put the strap of the huge bag over his shoulder still looking at the female police officer.

"Leave the car," she said. "Get home or back to your hotel; the streets aren't safe."

"What's going on?" Lucas asked.

There was a short pause. "I don't know," she said. "Now go, please."

Lucas started walking up the pavement. Hearing a sudden scream he swung around to see the female police officer being slammed into the ground by two zombies. He saw her blood running down into the drain as she slowly started to sit up. Lucas watched in fear as the dead female police officer's eyes opened revealing the gruesome gleaming yellow. She jumped up of the ground, blood still running out of the bite wound.

"Fuck this," he uttered

The female officer sprinted off towards people standing in a group, her arms by her side, her eyes locked onto the closest person.

* * *

The train operator, Eric Stanford, walked into the front of the express train, ready to take it down to Melbourne, unaware of the public transport suspension that was in effect. Born in Sydney, and aged thirty-eight, he lived by himself. He looked around the station. It seemed to be a lot busier than usual. He put his small bag down onto the floor next to him, looking out the front window onto the track ahead of him. He heard a sudden knock on his window which pulled him out of his daydream. It was a vicious knock. Eric swung his head, looking to his supervisor. He pulled the glass window back, looking at the station manager and hearing intense speaking and noises from passengers.

"Siding," the manager demanded.

"What?" Eric asked. "I'm due out in a while."

"Siding," the supervisor snapped. "All trains are cancelled."

"Why?" Eric asked.

There is a short pause. "Due to this disorder," the operator replied. "Now, Siding."

Eric looked onto the platform and saw two New South Wales police officers. They had caught eye on a train station cleaner. He was sitting down on the bench, looking down at the ground and not moving. The officers looked at one another as they put their hands onto their sidearms; they slowly walked over to the individual. The man's yellow jacket was gleaming as it reflected the sunlight.

"Sir," the officer quietly said. The individual didn't respond. "Sir," the officer said again. There was still no movement from the man. "Sir," The officer said louder. The man lifted his head. The officer drew his handgun and pointed it at the man.

"Jesus," the station worker yelped. "I only nodded off for a second."

The officer looked relieved as he holstered his sidearm. "Sorry, sir," he said.

"Not a problem," the worker replied

The officer looked down at the man apologetically as his eyes had opened wide with fear. Hearing a noise the officer swung his head to the left finding himself looking directly into the glowing eyes of a zombie as they stood there, looking at him. Without any warning, one of the zombies lunged forward towards the officer with its teeth slamming into his throat. Blood ran out of his neck onto the floor.

"Oh my God!" a female voice screamed. The onlookers watched as the paralyzed officer was pushed to the ground.

"Everybody out now!" the other officer yelled. The officer

looked down in horror seeing his once close colleague had transformed into a zombie. His eyes were a gleaming yellow.

Eric looked in horror through the front of the train's window onto the platform as the officer stood up, blood slowly running out of his neck, snarling and hissing.

"Holy!" Eric screamed as he picked up his small bag. He opened the door and stepped down onto the platform, seeing people trying to run from the zombies. Eric ran towards the stairs where he saw a clear route to the main station. Blood stained the stairs from the bitten and infected individuals. Eric came to the top of the stairs, looking into the main ticket area of the station. "Shit," he shouted, as he ran towards the main entrance. He looked at the people being attacked by the zombies, one after the other. He looked at the glass doors only to find the doors, usually closed for security reasons, were wide open. Handprints of blood smeared the glass. "Shit" he mumbled

Claire looked out across Sydney Harbor from inside the small café where she worked. She picked up the china cups as she walked into the shop, looking at the TV on the wall. She looked up and saw that the news channel was on. It was broadcasting information about the civil disturbance across the country. She turned her head to see Audrey walk out from the kitchen.

"It's getting worse," a customer said to her.

"Is it?" she asked.

"Yes," the customer replied to Claire. "I thought it was a hoax."

Claire was looking up at the screen when a shot was heard from outside. The people in the café jumped up, seeing police cars rushing back and forth through the streets.

"I'm out of here," a customer said. "Sorry. Here is the money; keep the change."

Claire watched as some of the customers got up and left the café in a hurry. Audrey looked out of the store window. She stormed over to the door and shut it closed.

"Claire," she said, "go home. I mean home—not back to university. It's too dangerous here. This isn't right, what's going on." Claire didn't reply. "Claire," she said again. "Just go back to your accommodation, get packed, and get back to your family. There will still be a job for you when you get back."

"Okay," she replied. "What about you?"

"I'll be fine," Audrey replied. "Now, go on."

Claire put the cups down onto the side as Audrey bolted the lock into place. She watched as the shutters slowly rolled down.

A figure ran past the window. It stopped around half-way up the pavement. Audrey felt her heart pounding faster as the figure stopped, turned back slowly, and mad its way to the café. Audrey stared at the gleaming yellow eyes of the zombie as it looked through the gap in the shutters at her. It was a man, who appeared to be in his late thirties. He was casually dressed and had dried teeth marks on his neck.

"Oh my God!" she gasped.

The infected individual slowly turned its head, looking down at the pavement. Audrey staggered to the right. She knocked one of the small white china cups off the table. The zombie snarled, looking back at her.

Claire walked out the back door of the kitchen. She pushed the door shut, hearing it click. Then, she looked at her car in the small backstreet car park. She reached into her bag and pulled out her keys. Hearing a sudden crash behind her she swung her head to the back door.

"No, no, no!" Audrey was heard screaming.

Claire quickly ran off and got into her car. She placed the keys into the ignition, wiping a tear away from her eye. The car started, but the crash behind her made her jump. She pulled out of the parking bay through the rear fire exit to the café. When Claire looked back, she saw Audrey with a horrendous bite on her neck. She was still alive.

"Claire," she pleaded. "Claire. . ."

Claire stopped as a figure ran out from the back of the kitchen.

"Claire, please," Audrey pleaded.

Claire looked into the rear-view mirror with horror as she saw one of the zombies plunging his teeth again into Audrey's neck.

"Help me!" Audrey screamed.

Claire watched as Audrey was pushed to the ground. Huge lumps of skin were being ripped from her neck. Claire pushed the accelerator all the way down as she left the car park.

SYDNEY ZOO

The group of officers looked at each other as they stood by the main entrance to the zoo.

"Is that the last of the staff out?" Officer Justin Hawes asked.

"Yes, that's it," Officer Marcus Giles replied. "Now, let's get out of here before any of those zombie things come here."

The officers started to walk towards the barriers to return to the patrol cars outside, but the ground beneath them started to rumble.

"What the. . . ?" Max Kirkshop swore in alarm.

The sound seemed to be getting louder by the second. The five officers looked up to see a glowing eye. Before they could blink, the horn of a rhino came into view. The Rhino slowly strolled through the zoo. It stopped, turned its head, and looked at the officers.

"What do we do?" Officer Hawes asked.

"I know what I am going to do," Jack McKinley said, swiping his handgun.

The group of officers swiped their handguns, looking into the gleaming yellow eyes of the rhino as it stopped and looked at them, steam leaving its nostrils as it scuffed its hoofs along the floor, kicking up muck and dust. The officers opened fire on the rhino.

"Why isn't it dying?!" Kirkshop screamed.

The rhino started to charge towards the officers.

"Move! Get back to the cars now!" Hawes shouted orders.

The officers ran through to the main entrance. They heard the barriers click as they stormed through them, one after the other. Kirkshop looked down to his left and saw a toy on the ground—a grey elephant, probably purchased from a gift store within the zoo. It was covered in blood. Only the trunk was grey. The beady eyes from the toy just stared up at him, like they were trying to say something to him. He saw visions of a young mother pulling her child along with her, the toddler reaching out for the toy as she entered the car park, wiping tears from her face, eager to know if her partner was alive and at home.

The sound of a crash woke him from the daydream. He skidded to a stop and looked back. The rhino was now crawling through the tiny walkway that led from the zoo's main grounds. It didn't seem to be giving up.

"Come on," he screamed at the top of his voice.

He spun around, staring down at the sight. The rhino forced its body through the metal work, screaming as it forced its body through the barriers into the car park. The rhino lifted its head up, looking into the sky. It had a sense of freedom. It just stood in the car park, static, breathing heavily. Kirkshop watched as it slowly lowered its head and twisted its body to face the onlooking officers as they stood by the gleaming patrol cars.

"It's just standing there," one of them said.

Kirkshop stood looking at the Rhino. Their eyes were locked. The skin above the rhino's eyes wrinkled and the sound of its huffing got louder as it started to scruff its hoof along the ground.

"Run," Kirkshop muttered. The officers scarpered into the patrol cars. "Come on, come on, come on," Kirkshop mumbled

Officer McKinley jumped into the driver's seat. He trembled as he tried to put the key into the ignition. When he clicked the key into the ignition, he turned the key to the right. Nothing was heard.

McKinley gasped. "Shit, the fucking thing won't start." He eagerly turned the key back and forth, trying to start the engine. He was lucky, the revometer screamed to life. "Got it," McKinley said slamming the accelerator down to the floor . The car slowly rolled, but there wasn't enough time. The rhino slammed into the vehicle, rolling the police cruiser onto its roof.

"Holy shit," Kirkshop yelled, slamming the brakes on.

"What are you doing?" the other officer asked.

Officer Hawes looked at the rhino as it circled around to the driver's side. "Saving my friend," he replied. He got out of his car and ran towards the other vehicle. McKinley looked to the left and saw that the window was smashed. He reached for his seatbelt and unclipped it falling onto the roof. He held onto his neck and squinted in pain. He looked to the right and saw Hawes.

"Hey," he called "Come on, man."

Hawes was dead. McKinley crawled out from the car. He looked ahead seeing the other cruiser.

"Come on," Kirkshop yelled running up to him.

The Rhino looked over the car and saw McKinley staggering from it, his hand on his neck. The Rhino scuffed his hoof and ran towards him. McKinley felt the ground beneath his feet vibrate as the pain from the crash screamed down his neck. He staggered along, overcome by the burning whiplash.

"Come on" Kirkshop screamed again.

McKinley looked back as he fell

Kirkshop skidded to a stop closing his eyes as he did so. He heard a crunch coming from McKinley's location. He slowly opened his eyes and saw the headless body of his colleague. The rush of blood slammed into the ground as the body fell flat onto the tarmac. The rhino slowly lifted his head, locking eyes with Kirkshop.

Kirkshop looked at the rhino. It didn't scoff; it just sprinted towards him. "Oh, shit" He gasped

"Come on," the officer bellowed from inside one of the police cars.

Kirkshop jumped into the cruiser. "Let's go!" he screamed

* * *

George Mahoney, the thirty-eight-year-old bus driver from Adelaide, looked out from the front of his bus as people ran across the streets. There was a sudden knock on the door. It pulled him from his daydream. He swung his head to the right to see a small group of boys.

"Closed," he said. "Sorry."

"Come on, man, please," one student pleaded to George.

"It's closed," he yelled again.

The student reached into his pocket, pulling out some dollar bills. "Thirty dollars," he pleaded. "That's all I've got."

The rest of the people got out their money, showing it to the driver. George could see the look of fear in their eyes as they looked through the glass doors. George let his breath out and opened the front doors.

"Thank you," the student said. "Thank you."

"Put your money away; you may need it later on if we survive this."

"Thank you," the student said again. "Thank you very much."

"It's okay," George told him. "I can take you as far as the depot; then you're on your own."

"That's fine," the student replied. "Thank you again."

George pushed the accelerator down pulling out of the stop.

"So, where you boys going?"

"We don't know," the student replied. "How about you?"

"Any place but this," George replied to the question. "I will get out of this bus, get in my car, go home, pack my bags, and get out of Sydney with my family—and I suggest you do the same thing."

"Where to?"

"As far away as possible until this is over," George replied. "I suggest you boys do the same as well. Find a campsite in the middle of the outback and wait till it is safe to return."

"Yes," the student replied. "Thanks so much again."

"I'd sit down if I were you," George replied. "The streets are in chaos; look at them."

The student went and sat down next to his friend, staring out of the window at the shops and stores being looted out by the mob.

The rhino was still in pursuit of the police car.

"We are not losing him," the officer muttered.

"Leave him to me," Kirkshop yelled. He slipped his last handgun magazine into his weapon. He crawled into the back seat so that he could shoot through the back window. He looked through the sight of the handgun, taking aim at the charging rhino.

George looked out the front right window and saw the police cruiser and the charging rhino behind the vehicle, with its eyes gleaming yellow.

"The hell?" he said.

The onlookers looked at the rhino. George saw a vehicle in front of him skidding to a stop. He slammed the brakes on. The rhino slammed into the police cruiser, flipping it into the air. The car slammed down on its roof. The rhino slowly walked to the window of the cruiser. Kirkshop slowly started to come around after the accident. George watched as the rhino reached in grabbing Kirkshop.

"No, no, no!" He screamed. "Please help!"

Kirkshop was slammed into the ground. Blood gushed up into the air as if from a burst fire hydrant. George and the students looked in fear at the rhino as it chomped onto the dead officer. There was a sudden crash on the window. The student swung his head, looking to see one of the infected people. Bloody handprints ran down the window as it tried to smash its way in. He looked at its gleaming eyes and at the blood dripping out of its mouth.

"Let's go," the student screamed.

George hit the accelerator. He looked into the side mirror and saw the Rhino charging after the bus as they sped through the streets of Sydney. The students and other passengers looked out the side of the bus as the rhino came up the side of the vehicle., looking in with its gleaming eyes.

"Can't this thing go any faster?" the student yelled over to George.

"I'm trying," George yelled back trying to keep his eyes on the road.

George kept the accelerator down to the full as the rhino came up along the side of the bus. George closed his eyes as the rhino slammed into the side of it.

"Come on," a passenger screamed.

George continued to drive forward into the busy Australian streets. The rhino huffed and slammed into the back of the bus again. "Shit!" George screamed

"Come on!" a student yelled

"It won't go any faster!" he screamed back

The rhino slammed into the side of the bus again. The windows started to crack, one after the other.

"Come on!" the student screamed louder.

The rhino slammed into the bus one last time. George lost control of the bus, and it spun onto its side, skimming along the asphalt. George shook his head as he looked ahead down the street. People were not stopping to help; they were just running in all directions.

"Is everyone okay?" he yelled back

"All good," the student said. "Agh, no!"

"What?" George asked

"My arm!"

Georgie shook his head. He looked over his shoulder at the student, who was panting in pain. The student stopped his heavy breathing and looked up. "What?" George asked. George looked forward out of the front window. There, staring directly at him, was the Rhino's gleaming eyes. George opened his eyes wide with fear. The rhino started to move his head away from the front of the bus. George was relieved; he sat back against the seat., but a crash was heard. He looked to see the side of the rhino. It was slamming into the window screen. The crack travelled through the window. "Shit!" He said

The rhino continued slamming into the front of the bus. It suddenly stopped, looking at George. Its head tilted, and its horn penetrated the front window in the blink of an eye.

George froze, looking at the tip of it as he sat back into the seat. The Rhino ripped the front glass window away, launching it into the air. George struggled to crawl over the broken shards of glass, feeling them bite into his palms. Intense pain shot down his back. "Ouch!" he groaned.

George suddenly felt some warm air run down his neck. Ignoring the pain from the tiny bits of broken glass that have dug into his hands, he looked up at the rhino.

"No," he said softly.

The rhino slammed its horn into George and picked him up. Blood ran down the horn as George struggled to keep his eyes open. He looked down at the ground, watching his blood crash down onto it. People in the distance watched in horror.

"Please help!" He struggled to say

The rhino stepped up onto its two back legs. George stared down at the ground. He squinted his eyes closed. The people on the bus watched as George was slammed into the ground. The student turned his head to the left after opening his eyes, seeing one of the zombies looking through the broken window at him. There was nowhere for him to run.

He looked at the young girl next to him. Her eyes were just gleaming at him.

"Please, no!" He pleaded

She reached in, slamming her teeth into his neck. The student screamed as he fell back into the seat.

* * *

Tom and Ryan lay on their beach towels on Bondi Beach as the hot sun beamed down on them. They were unaware of what was going on in the city.

"This is the life," Tom said to Ryan.

"Beach, booze, and women," Ryan suggested.

"I couldn't agree more, man," Tom replied.

Tom reached under his blanket, taking a swig from the can of alcohol he had smuggled onto the beach.

"You do know this is the alcohol-free zone?" Ryan asked.

"What?" Tom replied hiding the can underneath his beach towel.

The lifeguard in the hut to their right saw the can being hidden underneath the towel. He took a deep breath and trekked over the sand towards the boys. He looked down at them as they took in the ultraviolet rays from the burning hot sun. "G'day boys," he said.

Tom and Ryan opened their eyes, looking up at the lifeguard as he looked down. "Is there a problem, officer?" Tom asked.

Ryan closed his eyes, knowing that Tom had just given away that he had been drinking.

"Yes, boys," the lifeguard said. "Have you been drinking?"

"No," Tom replied. "This is an alcohol-free zone."

"Here's the deal: Hand over the can underneath your towel, and I'll say no more."

"Dude," Tom replied.

"It's a two-hundred-dollar fine,"

Tom pulled the can out from under the blanket, handing it over to him. The lifeguard emptied the can onto the beach, staining the golden sand. "Thank you," he said. "If I see you drinking again, it's two-hundred dollars. If you want to drink, go to the alcohol zone. You got me?"

"Yes, babe" Ryan replied

The lifeguard looked back as one of the beach buggies came onto the sand.

"Attention, everyone," another guard was heard saying into a megaphone. "Due to the civil disturbance in progress, this beach is to be closed straight away. This is for your own personal safety. Please make sure that you have all of your personal belongings with you."

Ryan and Tom looked up at the lifeguard as he looked down at them. "Come on, boys," the lifeguard said. "You heard the man." The lifeguard looked over his shoulder after the beach buggy had rolled off onto the beach, but something captured his attention. There was a female in her early twenties. She was just standing in the middle of the beach looking down at the ground. Tom stared at her as she stood there with her blonde hair streaking down her back.

"Remember, boys, no drinking," the lifeguard ordered.

Tom and Ryan watched as the lifeguard walked over to the young female, who was still standing in the middle of the beach, looking down at the sand.

"Woah, dude," Tom said. "Check that arse out. Wouldn't you wanna. . . ?"

"Damn right," Ryan replied. "What's she doing just standing there? Can't she come and stand over here, right over my face?"

The lifeguard looked over at the young female. "Hey," the lifeguard said. "Ma'am, are you okay?"

Tom and Ryan looked up at the lifeguard as he placed his hand on the female's arm as if he were trying to wake her. Her head slowly started to lift. The lifeguard looked at her head as it swung to the right, looking at him, her eyes gleaming yellow.

"What the. . . ?" the lifeguard gasped.

The female leapt forward, slamming her teeth into the lifeguard's neck.

"Dude," Ryan said. "Check it out."

Tom and Ryan watched as the female pushed the lifeguard to the ground, ripping the skin of his neck.

"Hey," the other lifeguards shouted. "What are you doing?"

The onlookers watched in fear as fellow lifeguards ran to assist their colleague. The female looked up at the lifeguards who came near and looked down in horror at their choking friend. The female just stared at the two lifeguards as her eyes continued to gleam a bright yellow.

"What's the matter with her eyes?" one of the lifeguards asked.

The female sprinted towards them all of a sudden. When they realized what was happening, the two lifeguards tried to flee from her, but the soft sand slowed them down. By the time the lifeguard on the ground had gotten up, with blood running down the side of his neck, his eyes were gleaming yellow.

"What the. . . ?" one of the other lifeguards said. "Look at his eyes."

The lifeguards sprinted across the sand towards their fellow lifeguards. Tom and Ryan watched in horror as the now-transformed guard sliced his teeth into one of the other lifeguards' necks. People were screaming in disbelief and terror as Tom and Ryan got up and ran across the back of the beach towards the car park. People were fleeing. Tom and Ryan saw more of the zombies attacking people. Tom jumped into the pickup truck as Ryan hit the accelerator down to full. "Come on!" he yelled. He looked out the back of the truck as the zombies chased after them.

"Dude," Ryan gasped. "What the fuck is going on?"

Tom kept quiet as Ryan continued speeding into the city center. "Hey, look at the mall," Tom yelled. "Awesome, man!"

Ryan pulled into the mall Shopping Centre car park. People were looting the stores. "Do you want to?" he said.

"Hell, yeah," Ryan replied. "I need a new laptop." Ryan locked the pickup truck up and ran up the stairs into the store. People rushed past each other in a frenzy. Ryan and Tom entered the shopping mall. All the shops were filled with looters snatching anything they could lay their hands on.

"Did you see that woman on the beach?" Ryan asked. "Just totally bit into that lifeguard's neck."

"I did, man," Tom replied. "Scary shit, man. What the fuck is going on, bro?"

"Then, he got up and did the same thing," Ryan mused. "Did you see his eyes? It was as if he had metamorphosized.

Tom and Ryan walked further into the mall, looking for a TV store. They both looked through the window at the news which was showing the widespread killings. The highlighted words along the bottom of the screen read, 'Virus Alert Australia.'

"Shit," Ryan said.

Tom and Ryan looked into the store at the dirty wooden floor which people had trampled all over.

"Grab that," Ryan said.

Tom picked up a gas canister. "Why are we grabbing these?" Tom asked.

"Because the cities are going to be overrun with them things soon," Ryan replied. "We might as well stock up and camp in the outback until the city is safe to return to."

"Good idea," Tom replied. Tom and Ryan grabbed the camping gear before they headed back to the pickup truck.

"Get in," Ryan said.

"Now where?" Tom asked.

"Back to uni, and then into the outback," Ryan said. He reversed out of the parking bay and headed in the direction of the university campus.

CHAPTER TEN

Gemma entered the ward of the hospital. She looked at Jasmine, her hands across the top of her forehead. She knew she was going to try and .

"Jasmine," Gemma called. "Come on, let's go. We are needed here. We took an oath to help the sick and injured and that is just what we are going to do."

"What?" Jasmine gasped.

"Look at it," Gemma said. "Come on."

Jasmine went to run..

"Look," Gemma said. "Listen to me." Gemma put both her hands on Jasmine, locking her eyes onto hers. She tightened the grip on the top of her shoulders. "Listen," she said. Gemma looked at Jasmine. She watched as a small tear started to run down Jasmine's face.

"I can't do this," Jasmine cried.

Gemma watched as the light stream of tears ran down Jasmine's face. "You can do this," she insisted. Jasmine looked at Gemma. Gemma kept her hands on Jasmines shoulders as she continued. "We didn't spend four years at university to run when it got tough."

Jasmine looked at Gemma as she tried to hold her emotions in.

"Repeat after me," Gemma insisted. Jasmine nodded. "We can do this." Jasmine took a shallow breath.

"Hey," a voice shouted. "Come look at the news."

Gemma and Jasmine stormed into the staff room where a bunch of staff stared at the widescreen TV in the corner of the room. All the chairs had been taken by staff. Gemma watched the news channel.

"To the people that have just joined us, we are live from the news station here in Sydney to bring you this important news bulletin," the reporter started. "We are receiving reports of random acts of violence and mass murder all over New South Wales. Details are very sketchy right now, and there has been no statement released by the government or the police yet; however, we will continue to bring you information as we receive it by the minute and on the hour."

Gemma turned her head and looked at her colleague as she continued to listen to the news reporters.

"We have just been informed that we are going move to Canberra where Doctor Hoskins of the Australian Centre For Disease Control is going to brief us on the crisis that is gripping the nation as we speak."

Gemma watched as the camera switched to Doctor Hoskins. She watched as he looked over the top of his glasses down onto the A4 paper in his hand and started speaking.

"I'm Doctor Hoskins from the Centre For Disease Control here in Australia. As you are aware, Australia is currently experiencing an epidemic—the worst of its kind since the Spanish Flu epidemic of 1918 that left many thousands dead."

"Get on with it," a doctor requested. "What are we dealing with?"

"What we are dealing with here at the CDC is unknown," Hoskins stated, trying not to stutter. "Not even our top doctors and physicians know what it is fully. We are naming this virus 'virus Z.'" Now I know you all must be wondering why we are naming this virus Z," the doctor continued. "That is due to its uniqueness. There is no other virus like this out there. We have already searched and searched and have come to the firm conclusion that this is a completely new malady, and so we have named it 'Z.'"

"Great God!" A doctor exclaimed. "We don't even know what we are dealing with."

Gemma looked up as the reporter came over the news broadcast again. "We have just heard that Prime Minister Tony Brown will be making a statement any second from now," she announced.

The screen switched to the conference centre in the Parliament House. Tony Brown slowly walked out from the rear room. The cameras started flashing as questions were screamed at him by the journalists. Brown took a deep breath and began. "To my fellow Australians and to the people of the international community who have tuned to their news stations for this conference. It has been confirmed by the Centre For Disease Control here in Canberra that we are dealing with an epidemic—the first of its kind and one that is not known to mankind."

Gemma and the rest of the staff continued to stare at the screen.

"As any other World government would do, we have taken steps in an attempt to prevent the spread of this disease. As part of that, at 1600 hours, a national curfew will be imposed. All shopping malls, educational institutions, and any place with a large gathering of people are to be closed off until further notice. Go home, lock your doors and windows, and make your way to a hospital only if you are truly sick and in need of medical attention. I would also like to bring to the attention of world leaders that I have declared a state of emergency; military personnel are on their way to infected hot zones as we speak. Thank you, and no questions."

The cameras flashed away as Tony Brown walked into the back room. The doctor stood up.

"Come on, guys," he said. "We've got work to do."

Gemma pulled her mobile phone out of her pocket to see if Lewis had tried to contact her, but there was nothing on the phone. *'Please, Lewis. Please,'* she pleaded in her mind. *'Please still be alive.'* Gemma wiped a few tears away from her eyes. She walked over to the window and peered through the blinds into the faraway city. Gemma walked out of the nurse's station. She stopped when she heard her phone ringing in her pocket. She pulled it out to see it was her mom at the other end. She pushed the 'answer' button. "Mum. Are you okay?"

"Oh my God, Gemma, are you okay? How's Lewis? Please tell me both of you are okay."

"Yes, I'm fine," Gemma replied. "What's going on?"

"I don't know," her mum replied in tears. "We were out shopping in the town when people just started biting into each other. It was a sea of blood everywhere."

"Where are you now? Is Dad okay?"

"Yes, dad is."

"Listen, Mum, I know what you need to do."

"What should I do?"

Gemma was aware that one of the doctors was screaming for her to come over and assist him. "Listen," Gemma said again. "Don't stay at home. Get to dad's warehouse. You'll be safer there. I'll come and get you soon."

"Okay," her mum wept. "Please be safe."

"I promise I will," Gemma replied.

"Gemma!" a doctor yelled.

"Got to go, Mum. Sorry," she said. "Don't forget: Me and Lewis will get to you." Gemma put the phone down and ran over to the bed. "What have we got?" she asked the doctor.

The doctors looked down at the injured man. "Hit and run," the attending doctor said. Gemma looked down at the broken bones of the man.

CHAPTER ELEVEN

Military pilot Bradley McKabben looked out the front of his Black Hawk helicopter. Smoke spiralled up from burning buildings and vehicles.

"I can't believe it," he said. "It's like something we see in the movies." The first officer didn't respond as the soldier in the back of the helicopter stood up looking down at the street below.

"Listen up," James Hutchinson yelled. The group turned their heads and looked at their superior officer. "In two minutes we shall arrive at the hospital," he shrieked. "Our orders are to guard the hospital from all infected individuals. Only let people with no infections in for treatment."

The helicopter landed outside of the hospital. Hutchinson held onto his rifle and observed as yellow barriers were set up at the entrance to the emergency bay at the hospital.

"Move out," he yelled. "Surround the place. Come on, move it."

Hutchinson walked over to one of the officers and stood holding onto the shotgun that he had pulled from his police cruiser. "I need you and your men to only let people with injuries not related to virus Z into the hospital. Anyone who is infected must be immediately moved over to where my troops are setting up."

"Got it," the officer replied.

Two Black Hawk helicopters spun around heading back to Kingsford Smith where military operations were now running for the evacuation of New South Wales. Hutchinson walked into the ward looking at all the frightened faces. "Only non-virus-Z emergencies in here," he demanded.

"What?" the doctor asked.

"Those were our orders, sir. Sorry," James Hutchinson replied. "Orders from above." Hutchinson turned around and ran back outside. He watched the Black Hawk helicopters disappearing into the distance.

* * *

Lucas looked up and saw the entrance to his hotel coming into view. He placed his hand on his neck, still feeling the whiplash from the accident he had earlier. When he arrived at the entrance he was met by the manager in the galley.

"You okay, sir?" he asked. "What happened?"

"Back there, someone ran into the street. I swerved and hit a lamppost."

"Okay, come and sit down," the manager invited him. "I'll get you something to drink."

"No, it's okay," Lucas replied. "I'll be in my room, thank you." Lucas walked over to the elevator and reached into his bag for his room key. The elevator doors opened. He watched as people ran out of the with their bags packed. They were ready to leave.

"Are you leaving?" one man asked Lucas from outside.

"Maybe," Lucas replied. "Why?"

"Just watch out," the man replied. "My oldest son just got killed by one of them things out there."

Lucas watched as the elevator door closed. That was the last thing the man said to him. He could see the fear in his eyes. Lucas arrived at his room. He slid the card into reader, and his door opened. He walked into his room, putting his bag down next to his bed. He walked over to the balcony which overlooked the Sydney Opera House. Constant gunshots could be heard. Lucas turned around and picked up the TV remote. He turned to the news channel and listened to the broadcast.

"We are going to the Sydney Harbor Bridge, where reporter Anna Holt has some information for us," the reporter said in a controlled but panicked voice. "Anna, over to you."

Lucas sat on the edge of the bed as he listened.

"I'm standing here at the Sydney Harbor Bridge," Anna began, "where the Sydney Police have closed off the bridge in an attempt to prevent any of these things from entering this part of the city, in an attempt to save whatever hope this city has left."

Anna looked down the street. She saw several zombies running towards them. "Oh shit," Anna said.

Lucas continued to watch the screen.

"Anna, can you hear us?" the studio presenter asked.

Lucas watched as the camera pointed down the street. The zombies sprinted along the street towards the blockade.

"Anna, get out of there," the studio presenter said. "Come on, go!"

Lucas watched as Anna started to panic.

"Run!" the police officer screamed. "Just go, please!"

Lucas listened to the screaming as the screen went dead. The two studio presenters remained dead silent.

Juliana walked into the newsroom. She looked at the line of cameras and then at one of the female reporters. It was one of her friends that had just been killed. She jumped up from behind the TV set

"I'm sorry," she wept. "I can't do it."

"Hey," the producer shouted. "You can't do that!"

Juliana watched as the reporter stormed past her, wiping tears of fear away from her eyes.

"Juliana!" the producer ordered. "On. Now."

"Got it," Juliana replied.

Juliana slipped the earpiece into her ear. She leaned forward, looking into the camera. "We have just been informed that the chief of the New South Wales Police Department, Rolf Hepburn, is about to address New South Wales."

Lucas sat back as the screen switched to Chief Hepburn, who was sitting down in the chair in the media room of the new police station in downtown Sydney. Gunfire could be heard from outside of the station. His eyes kept darting towards the door after each and every shot. He looked over his glasses at the A4 piece of paper in his hand. which his speech was written on.

"As you are aware," Hepburn stated, "Australia—including New South Wales which is where I am broadcasting to—is going through a severe crisis. I am urging all people who are watching this broadcast to stay in your homes, follow orders from your local law enforcement officers, lock your doors, stay in a basement away from the windows, and watch all news stations for further updates."

Lucas perched back down on the edge of the bed. He looked up again at the news channel which had switched back to the newsroom.

"I have just heard that we are going across to Sarah Justins, our Canberra correspondent, for the latest news from Canberra." Reeves stated. "Sarah, can you hear us?"

Lucas watched as the picture changed to Sarah Justins. She was outside the Parliament House.

"Yes, I can hear you," Sarah said. "As you are aware, it has been confirmed now that the riots and the infections are not just happening in New South Wales; we have reports of disturbances here in Canberra and of mass disturbance in Perth. I have spoken to a few people who are fleeing their homes and seeking refuge with family and friends in small outback towns, away from the cities. Apparently, the rioters are attacking innocent civilians with the use of, well how shall I put this, biting"

Sarah turned her head looking at the Australian soldier as he stormed up to her.

"Sorry, Miss," he said. "Clear the area now!"

Lucas watched as the screen switched back to the New South Wales News office.

"We are going to be here twenty- four hours a day until the situation is resolved and Australia goes back to normal," Reeves stated.

Lucas reached over to the small case he had brought with him from the US. He rummaged through the clothes and pulled out a small silver box. He entered the code and watched as the top of the shiny box slowly rolled back, revealing a silver firearm with a few magazines. Lucas pulled out the weapon belt as well, putting it over his body and slipping the handgun into the pouch. The sun continued to shine in through the windows as a gentle breeze blew the curtains. He took one last look around his room before putting his jacket on and covering the weapon. Lucas walked to the front door, and he pulled it open, storming to the elevator. He hit the button, shuffling the pouch that was concealing the weapon.

"Come on, come on," He mumbled

The elevator dinged. He stepped back as the two doors opened. He walked in, looking at the screen on the wall, which was showing the news broadcast. He kept thumping the close door button. The doors shut and began to descend.

As the elevator opened, Lucas saw the hotel manager having a discussion with a woman. "I can assure you, madam," the manager said, "this will all be over in a while. The Australian police are very efficient when it comes to this kind of civil disorder."

"I'm sorry; I'm not staying," the lady said. "You have my card details. Charge it for however long I have been here."

The lady grabbed her case and headed towards the front of the hotel.

"Come on," she snapped at her husband.

"What's happening?" Lucas asked the manager.

The manager of the hotel hesitated for a few seconds but then told him the truth. "The whole country is breaking down. I'm sure it will be okay. Is your room okay for you, sir?"

Before Lucas could answer, he turned his head as two New South Wales police officers ran into the hotel.

"Need any help?" the officer asked.

"No, we are quite calm here," the manager replied. "Thanks all the same."

There was a sudden scuffle coming from the outside. Lucas saw the young porter, who usually helped people with their luggage, being bitten by one of the zombies.

"Shit," The officer said. The officer swiped his handgun he squeezed the trigger, launching the bullet. The zombie fell off the porter. The officer went and looked at the young porter, placing his hand onto the bite wound on his neck.

The porter was hunched over with pain. His teeth grit in pain as the officer kept his hand on the wound. The officer looked at the porter, keeping his sidearm out. All of the staff and guests in the hotel focused on him. He looked into the eyes of the officer. "Do it," he stuttered.

Lucas looked at the officer. His finger slowly edged towards the trigger again. He kept his eyes on the kid.

"Do it," he asked again. The porter kept his hand on the wound as he struggled to stand up straight. "Do— do," he panted. "Please"

The kid looked up quickly. His eyes shot open. He had turned. A few drops of blood started to run from his mouth. He just looked at the group as they stared at him. He was lifeless; not a memory of his life was left in him. The manager looked away in disbelief. The porter's eyes gleamed yellow as he continued to snarl at them. The kid screamed loudly and ran towards the officer.

The trigger was squeezed. The only sound in the hotel was of the gunshot from the handgun. The porter fell back onto the floor. His body twitched as blood ran out of the bullet wound onto the glossy floor.

"Do you want my opinion?" the officer said to the manager. The manager looked at the officer who was slipping the handgun back into the pouch of his belt. He waited for a few seconds. "Go home."

The manager looked at his staff as they awaited his order to leave. "Do it," he stuttered.

The staff left their positions. The manager began to walk towards his office behind the reception, keeping his eyes on Lucas. A scuffle was heard from outside. Lucas looked up as a horde of zombies ran up to the entrance to the hotel. Two of the zombies were the husband and wife that had left just a minute ago,

"Where did they come from?" the officer yelled.

The two officers swiped their handguns.

"Never." one screamed

Lucas spun around running towards the elevator. He hit the button to go down.. He watched as the two officers tried to fight the zombies from getting into the hotel. The top of the handgun pinged back. He didn't have time to reload. The zombie pounced onto the officer. Nothing could be done.

The manager watched in horror as his hotel was overtaken by the infected. He looked to see one standing next to him. "What!?" he said, gasping. "No!" The manager screamed as the female zombie lunged into his neck. Lucas heard a ping and looked over as the doors of the elevator opened. A zombie snarled, looking at Lucas.

"Oh shit," Lucas uttered.

The zombie sprinted over to the elevator as Lucas rushed into it, hitting the 'close door' button. He tapped it multiple times. The doors started to roll closed. Lucas reached for his handgun but didn't have time to use it. The zombie burst into the elevator. Lucas lifted his foot and pushed the zombie back away from the elevator. He felt the pure, utter strength of the creature as it continued to lunge towards him. Lucas power kicked the zombie out of the elevator. He held the 'close door' button in, refusing to let it go. Lucas watched as the doors sealed shut. Lucas fell against the wall of the elevator, placing his hand between his jacket, holding onto the shiny handgun as the lift descended to the lower car park of the hotel. Lucas ran out into the car park, noticing that all the vehicles were gone, including his. He had no choice but to go on foot from here.

"Bollocks!" he swore. He ran towards the ramp.

* * *

Elizabeth Wilson, wife of Roy Wilson, looked out of her bedroom window onto the well-kept housing estate. She looked out of the window as the once-friendly neighbours packed their camper vans and caravans, ready to flee into the outback. Elizabeth watched as the huge campervans rolled out of the driveways onto the main streets. She wiped a few tears away from her eyes when the house telephone started to ring. She got up quickly, thinking that it could be Roy on the other end.

"Hello," she panicked. "Roy, Roy, is that you? Please tell me you're still alive."

"Mrs Wilson," an unfamiliar voice said.

"Yes," Elizabeth said. "Yes, that's me. Who is this?"

"I'm with the investment group," he said. "I am here to evacuate you to a safe location away from Sydney, ma'am." Elizabeth didn't know what to say. "I need you to grab a few belongings and be ready to leave. We will be there in about two minutes,"

Elizabeth put the phone down, picked up her handbag and walked over to the drawers in the front room. She opened the wooden drawer pulling out the two passports. She looked out as a black jeep screeched to a stop. Two huge armed guards stepped out of the jeep walking up to the front gate, their weapons drawn, looking down the streets for zombies.

"Miss Wilson," the man demanded.

Elizabeth looked at the man. He had a bald head and an ex-security look about him. He was wearing a new tailored suit. There wasn't a single crease in his white shirt or black jacket. A jet-black tie was clipped to the top of his shirt. He looked through the dark sunglasses at her.

"Yes," Elizabeth said. "Yes, that's me what is going on."

"I'm here to get you to safety," he told her.

The man turned around looking down the pathway of her house. Not a speck of dirt could be seen on it. It had been laid recently. Elizabeth gently ran towards the front gate of her house. She looked at the other houses as youthful looters were entering them and taking anything that was worth money. Their faces were completely covered by the huge expensive widescreen TVs in their hands as they ran to the hijacked vans.

"Hang on, wait!" she demanded.

"We haven't got time," the man ordered, swiping off his glasses.

Elizabeth ran back into the house. She picked up a picture of her family on holiday in the Gold Coast; it had been taken only last year. She wiped a tear as she looked down at it, hoping that her son, daughter, and grandchildren were all safe. She hadn't heard from them since the infection had begun.

"Miss Wilson," the man yelled. "We need to go."

Elizabeth ran back out to the jeep as gunfire erupted. The looters dropped the TVs and other valuables as the chasing zombies entered the new housing estate. Snarls could be heard as the zombies ran down the street in packs, heading towards the looters.

"Shit! Run!" a looter yelled

Elizabeth looked at the pack of zombies as they ran after the looters. She watched as one kid fell to the ground. He couldn't have been any older than eighteen or nineteen. He spun around onto his back, trying to get up quickly as his onlooking friends watched as he was pounced on. The scream from him bellowed around the housing estate. He kicked his legs back and forth, and the blood from his wound spewed onto the street. Elizabeth watched as the kid's legs stopped kicking. The horde of zombies joined in on the feast. The van with the looted gear in it just pulled away from the dying teenager.

"Oh my God," Elizabeth gasped.

Elizabeth stood there, watching in horror. She couldn't take her eyes of the dying teenager as his body twitched in the middle of the street. A short snarl was heard. Elizabeth swung her head to see a sprinting zombie. The man at her door shot it straight in the head. Elizabeth placed both of her hands over her mouth.

"Get in," the man ordered. "Now!"

Elizabeth got into the jeep, slamming the door shut. She looked out of the back window at the zombies attacking the looters, who tried to run from the houses. The zombies then caught sight of the jeep.

"Go!" she yelled

The man slammed the accelerator down. The back wheels span as the jeep juddered. Elizabeth slipped her seatbelt on while looking out of the back window at the zombies.

"Shit," The man said. The jeep picked up speed.

"Where are we going?"

"Kingsford Smith Airport," the man replied.

"Why there?" Elizabeth asked. "What about my family and grandchildren?"

"It's been taken care of, ma'am, I need you to remain calm." The roads were very crowded as people were trying to escape the infection.

"What about my husband?"

"It's been taken care of," the man said again.

Elizabeth wiped a few tears away from her face as the jeep continued speeding down the main street towards the airport. "Please, God," she said. "Please."

* * *

Joshua Bryan, aged thirty-one, grasped the control stick of the jet-powered helicopter. He looked ahead, seeing the investment corporation building. He looked from the first officer, Jeff Goodfellow, who was employed by the Sydney Investment Corporation, to the shuttle staff around Australia and the other destinations across Australia.

"RPM match," Jeff stated.

Joshua didn't reply as he homed in on the huge skyscraper.

"Let's do this," he ordered, "and try and get out of the city."

"Agreed," Jeff replied

Joshua looked out across Sydney, seeing the smoke and muck flying up into the air from the explosions down below. He looked ahead at the Sydney Investment Corporation skyscraper. He slowly descended, looking at the giant 'H' symbol on the top of the building. The top of the pad was clear—not a soul was in sight.

"Let's get these people out of here." They touched down, looking at the back at the fire exit, waiting for the executives of the company to come out.

"Come on! Where are they?" Jeff begged.

Roy Wilson looked out of the window down onto the city, seeing the frightened people running everywhere from the chasing zombies.

"Sir," Chloe said. "We have to go. The helicopter has arrived."

Roy didn't respond. He picked up his jacket and put it on his body. He picked up his black briefcase and walked towards the door. Chloe was on her way to the fire exit on the roof. Roy looked into the huge office, knowing that he wasn't going to be returning for a long time. There was a sudden crash. He looked down the corridor, seeing a few of the zombies who had broken into the building.

"Come on," Chloe yelled from the stairs.

Roy started fast, walking up the corridor, looking back at the sealed door and seeing the zombies slam into it. He suddenly stopped.

"Shit," he gasped, looking at the fire doors.

Chloe looked back, seeing that Roy was heading back to his office.

"Roy!" Chloe screamed. "The helicopter is here."

"Go," Roy yelled. "I'm coming." Roy ran into his office. He sat down at the computer, trembling while trying to type.

"ROY!" Chloe screamed.

Chloe looked down the corridor at the door as it started to break away from the hinges. The huge panels of glass were starting to crack from the pounding zombies. Roy grasped the case in his hand. He struggled to breathe as the wooden door at the end of the corridor gave way. His palm was burning as he grasped the case. He ran along the corridor, panting for breath, his heart pounding in his chest with exhaustion and fear. He came to the stairs that led to the roof. He struggled to climb them as his heart pounded in his chest.

"Come on," Roy panicked to himself. "You can do this." Roy continued climbing the stairs towards the roof, where the helicopter was waiting for its departure. His grandchildren's laughs could be heard in his head as the zombies caught up with him. He listened to their unforgiving screams as they entered the stairwell. Roy suddenly stumbled, falling to the ground. The briefcase dropped, opening and releasing all of the files onto the stairway.

"Shit," he said. "No." He was suddenly pushed to the floor by one of the zombies.

Jeff looked out of his side window onto the fire exit of the Sydney Investment Group. The exit swung open. He watched as the small group of people ran over to the awaiting helicopter.

"Come on," Jeff yelled over the engines. Jeff signalled the group over to the helicopter. The executives of the Sydney Investment Corporation ran along the top of the skyscraper roof towards the awaiting helicopter.

"Come on, get in," Jeff demanded.

"They are right behind us," Chloe yelled. Chloe looked around. "Where's Roy?" she asked.

Roy then appeared from behind the fire exit door. He tried to close the door behind him but didn't have time to do it all the way.

"Roy, you okay?" the female asked. Roy couldn't answer. He was too out of breath.

"Come on," Joshua yelled.

Roy climbed into the helicopter. Jeff slammed the door shut. Before he got into the helicopter, it lifted off the pad. Jeff grasped the belt, pulling the door shut quickly. He sat back into the chair and looked down out of the side window onto the H-pad which was just below. They continued to ascend. Jeff and Joshua stared down onto the building, seeing the 'H' slowly disappearing under the zombies as they piled onto the roof. The helicopter turned.

"What happened?" asked Chloe. "Where did you go?"

Roy froze for a few seconds. "I transferred all of the company finances to the Hong Kong branch." Roy started to feel hot. "Where. . ." Roy panted for breath. "Where are we going?"

Jeff looked back at Roy, unaware of the bite on his arm. "To the airport."

"Why there?" demanded Chloe. "I thought all flights out of the country were grounded."

"They are evacuating from there."

"What about our families?" Roy asked. "Are they —they…?"

Jeff looked forward over the city.

"What about our families?" Chloe asked in anticipation.

"Already been taken care of," Jeff said. "The company's own security took care of them. They are there now awaiting us."

"Well, let's go," Roy demanded. Roy held onto Chloe as Jeff set course for the airport. Smoke gushed up from the streets where buildings and streets were burning. Petrol stations were on fire and huge billows of black smoke poured into the air as buildings ruptured into flames.

"We are safe for now," Chloe said.

Roy didn't answer. Chloe looked out the front window of the helicopter as the famous Sydney Opera House started to come into view.

"Hey, you okay?" Chloe asked Roy, trying to settle her nerves. Roy looked down at the floor of the helicopter. "Hey," she asked. "Hey, Roy, come on. We're safe now." Chloe looked at Roy seeing a small bit of blood dripping through his shirt. Her eyes opened. "You've been bitten!" she said.

"What?" Jeff asked. "I didn't quite catch that."

Chloe looked up as Roy started to lift his head. His eyes slowly opened. He looked Chloe in the eyes. She couldn't take her eyes of the yellow gleam of his. "Roy," Chloe said. "No, no, no! Not you! Please, God!"

Roy opened his mouth, slamming his teeth into Chloe's neck. Joshua looked into the mirror as he flew near the bridge. He looked at Chloe as she struggled to pull Roy off of her.

"Shit, no!" he gasped.

"Get him off her," he demanded. "Now! You know what happens after you've been bitten."

The rest of the group struggled to pull Roy off Chloe as blood gushed from her neck. It started to run out of her mouth, filling her lungs as well. Chloe struggled to breathe as Roy looked up. His eyes gleamed as he looked forward at the two pilots who looked back at him in horror.

"Shit," Joshua gasped.

Chloe looked up, her eyes gleaming. It didn't take long for the virus to take over her body. The rest of the investment group watched as Chloe and Roy dove onto them, taking chunks out of them. Within a few seconds, the whole investment group had been taken over by the Z virus. Josh looked back as Chloe and Roy dove into the flight deck of the helicopter.

"No, no, no!" Jeff screamed. He fell against the control stick of the jet-powered helicopter.

Joshua looked at Jeff as Jeff choked in his own blood. He looked at Chloe as he turned to the left very slowly. Joshua took his eyes off the control panel of the helicopter for a few seconds. He looked at her gleaming eyes. She just looked back at him. She gave a slight snarl. Her eyes locked onto him. Joshua held onto the control stick.

Chloe lunged for him. He screamed in pain as her teeth locked onto his neck. The nose of the craft pointed down as Chloe bit down into his neck. Blood rapidly spread out onto his pure white shirt. The four golden epaulettes were destroyed by his blood. He bent forward as the craft pointed down towards the Sydney Opera House. He lost consciousness as the helicopter fell from the sky. The people looked up as the helicopter plunged down towards the famous artifact. The wind blasted over the top the helicopter as Joshua tried to stay conscious. He looked out the front of the helicopter as it slammed into the opera house. He held his eyes closed, even though he was choking. The fuel tanks ruptured, causing a horrific explosion. The people screamed as the pulse ripped through the streets. The interior of the famous house slowly started to catch ablaze. The fabric seats quickly caught fire, and black smoke billowed up into the air as fire engulfed the building.

* * *

Elizabeth looked out the front of the jeep as it pulled up to the side entrance to the airport. Military personnel were everywhere. She looked up to see a private jet parked on the tarmac, ready to roll. The jeep screeched to a quick stop. Elizabeth looked up to see her family sitting by one of the jeeps that had picked them up a short while ago. Her granddaughter was clutching one of her cuddly toys. Elizabeth unfastened her seatbelt as the jeep pulled up next to the military personnel. Elizabeth stormed out of the jeep.

"Ma'am, you can't go there," the soldier ordered

"I want to see my babies."

"Ma'am," the soldier explained, "you can't go see them yet. I have to make sure you are infection-free." Elizabeth stood up straight as the soldier aimed the eye scanner at her face. A few long seconds passed. "Clear!"

Elizabeth sprinted from the jeep towards her family.

"Mum!" Her daughter, Susie, was in tears as her grandchildren came and hugged her. Elizabeth felt relieved knowing that her family was alive and well, but she was worried about her husband. "Where is my husband?" she asked one of the soldiers who was walking over to her. "I was told he was being evacuated by helicopter from the city center a short while ago."

"I'm sorry," the soldier said. "The helicopter that was carrying your husband and other employees of the corporation crashed about five minutes ago."

"What!?" Elizabeth gasped. "Nooooooo!"

"I'm really sorry," the soldier said, "but we have to go now."

Elizabeth and her family climbed onto the company's awaiting jet, which was ready to fly them down to Hobart. Elizabeth walked into the tight cabin and saw some of the other family members in the aircraft. The two engines at the back of the jet powered up to full. Elizabeth sat down as the new jet taxied quickly along the runway towards the active one. Only the few commercial airliners taking people to Hobart were leaving. Elizabeth hugged her family tightly as the jet pulled onto the runway and powered its engines up, lifting off the asphalt runway. Elizabeth looked down into the streets of Sydney. "It's okay," she said to her family. "We're safe now"

"Where's grandpa?" her granddaughter asked

Elizabeth didn't say a word as the jet climbed out towards the south.

* * *

Tony Brown stormed into his office after a brief toilet break. He looked at his staff, who were running around the busy building.

"Bring me up to speed again," he demanded. "Now."

"Sir," Thomas Legg said, stepping forward. "We need to evacuate you to a safer location."

"No," Brown snapped. "I'm staying here. Bring me up to speed, now."

General Kingsley stepped up. "Sir, the infection is spreading faster than we anticipated."

"What?" Brown snapped. "But you—?"

"I know," the General replied, "but look at this map."

Brown turned and looked at the map of Australia as it came up onto the screen in front of him.

"Please have a look at the country," General Kingsley said. "Tasmania is still infection-free, but as you can see, at the rate of the spread of the infection, we estimate that, within five hours, all cities will be gridlocked with these things."

Brown sat down onto his chair. His head pounded with pain. "Put the news on," he ordered.

"Sir?" Legg said in dismay.

"Just do it!" Brown snapped, swivelling on his chair to look at the news screen.

"As you can see," the reporter said, "here in Sydney, the police are starting to lose control of the streets. These zombies, or whatever you call them, are everywhere."

The scene suddenly cut away back to the studio. "I'm sorry for the sudden change of story," the studio presenter said, "but we are now going live to Leon Greendale for a special report."

The picture on the screen suddenly changed to a dirty old suburban town just on the outskirts of Sydney.

"This is Leon Greendale reporting live from Togala, about five miles outside of Sydney" He said. "I am here with a small group of people who want to remain anonymous."

Leon walked up to the youth, with balaclava covering his face, grasping a baseball bat that had an old, sharp, rusty nail sticking out of the end of it with blood stains on the point.

"Sir," Leon addressed him. "I understand you and some of your community are forming a vigilante group."

"Yeah," the youth replied. "All we are doing is sticking up for our community. The police are struggling downtown, and we haven't got much response out here. Tony Brown has just abandoned these small towns and focused his attention on the major cities, so this is what we are doing."

Leon held the microphone back to his mouth. Before he could speak again, he heard a sudden scream coming from behind him. He looked up, seeing a young female in her early twenties with a child in her hands.

"They are coming!" She yelled at the top of her voice.

Leon watched as the small group of youths grabbed their knives and other weapons.

"Go," the youth shouted. "Run! We will hold them off."

Leon watched as the youths charged into the group of zombies.

"Come on," the youths yelled. "Get out of here."

Brown watched as the youths started kicking the zombies to the ground.

"Back to the studio," Leon said. "I'm out of here."

Brown looked at the quiet room. "Release all inmates," he demanded, "ASAP."

"What?" General Kingsley asked. "Letting the scum of the country back onto the streets?"

"What other options do we have?" Brown inquired.

"Sir," a voice stammered, "Perhaps we should—"

"Release all inmates!" He screamed

"Yes, sir," Legg replied reluctantly.

* * *

Oscar Beuzeville walked onto the metal walkway that overlooked the prison.

"Attention," he said. "All of you listen very carefully."

Arron stopped talking and looked up at the prisoners. The prison went extremely quiet.

"I know a lot of you are extremely worried about loved ones in the country's current crisis," the guard said. "I can understand that." The prison continued to stay quiet. "As you can see, a lot of my guards have left as well to attend families. This will benefit you, I am sure. Under orders from Tony Brown and the Parliament of Australia, all of you are being released immediately to help fight off these infected people."

The prisoners and inmates started gasping and looking at each other.

"We're being let out, man," one of the other prisoners said to Arron. "This totally rocks." Arron didn't reply as he focused his attention on Oscar Beuzeville.

"This is the time for you to pay back the people and the communities you have hurt." Oscar looked down onto the gawking crowd. "I never thought I would ever say this to you people," he said.

The prisoners stayed silent. A pin could have been heard if it had been dropped. Arron looked into the eyes of Oscar as he put both of his hands onto the metal railing. He looked into Arron' eyes.

"Good luck," he said in a gentle tone. "There is a bus outside waiting to take you to the infected area of Sydney."

The gates rolled open, allowing the prisoners to be released. Arron got up, cracking his knuckles. "Right," he said. "Let's do this; it's payback time." Arron got up, looking at the guards as they led the prisoners through to the waiting inmate bus that would take them into Sydney Central. Arron walked through the corridors, looked out at the bus, and climbed aboard. There were no handcuffs holding his hands together—he was just plain free. The doors closed. The old, shiny, silver bus pulled out of the prison gates. Arron looked down the empty streets as the bus sped onto the road.

"Okay, listen up," a guard instructed them. "We are going to be downtown in about ten minutes. From there, you're on your own."

The bus entered downtown Sydney. Arron peered out of the dirty, stained barred windows. He looked onto the sidewalks of Sydney, trying to peer through the crossed metal windows. The bus pulled up next to some frightened people.

"Let's do this," a prisoner yelled.

Arron watched as one of the prisoners got up. He walked down the bus, followed by the rest of the prisoners. Arron looked out and saw an infected individual. He was just standing in the middle of the street, eyes gleaming yellow, as if wondering which individual to devour. "Come here, you fucker!" a former prisoner screamed.

Arron and the guard watched as the prisoner ran across the street towards the zombie. He kicked the zombie onto the ground and continued to kick away at his face. Blood splattered out onto the street as the zombie hissed, trying to get up again.

"Die, fucker!" he screamed down at the zombie.

Arron turned his head and looked at the guard. "Well," the guard mumbled. "This is how you guys wanted to live. It's all yours now. I've got a family to save—you know, the thing you never had respect for."

Arron watched as the prison guard turned around and left. "Cheerio," he said.

The guard got onto the bus as the prisoners split up and got ready to attack the zombies. Arron looked into the distance, to where the prison bus was disappearing. Freedom was his at last as he took deep breaths, looking at the dead infected person lying in the middle of the streets. Cars were rushing past in all directions. Arron heard a sudden scream. He turned his head to see one of the zombies biting into a male's neck, his frightened wife stood at a distance from him, hands flew up to her mouth, dropping the shopping bag.

"Help!" She screamed.

"Fuck it," Arron mumbled.

Arron ran over to the zombie. He placed his hands onto the belt of the zombie, ripping him off the man and kicking the zombie to the ground. Blood gushed out of its neck as he heard the bones snapping.

"Are you okay?" Arron asked the lady.

Blood was rushing down the man's neck. The female looked at Arron, who was still dressed in his prison robes. She then thanked him amidst tears.

The bitten man leaned against the lamppost.

"What's going on?" a passer-by asked. "Why have they released you?"

"To fight these things. I think the police are losing control," Arron replied to the person. Arron looked at the man and asked, "Are you okay?" Arron nudged the man. He watched as the eyes of the bitten man shot open, gleaming yellow, the veins in his face showing, blood running down his cheek. He turned and stared at his wife.

"What?" she screamed. "No, no, no! Not you!"

Before Arron could help, the man dove onto his wife, slamming his teeth into her neck. There was nothing he could do; it happened so unexpectedly. Arron looked around as people fled in all directions. The female gasped for breath as she fell to the ground. Arron looked around the streets.

"Arron," a prisoner said, "let's go." Arron didn't require any more prompting to run off into the streets.

* * *

Claire walked through the gate which led into the accommodation block of the university. It was a dangerous drive to the university, and it took a lot longer than was anticipated as the streets were blocked. She looked at the other cars and vehicles which left the university in hopes of fleeing the city from the zombies. She pulled out the electronic lock, opening the door. She pulled the door open. looking at the long line of flats lined up next to each other. Doors opened, and students came running out with bags packed.

"Claire," a voice called.

Claire looked up to see Tom. "Tom," she gasped.

Tom swung his head with fear looking at Claire. "Glad that you're alive. Have you seen the news? Tony Brown has put the country under martial law and state of emergency."

"I know," Claire replied. "The café where I work has been shut early, there is army in the city center and at the hospital, and those zombie type things are everywhere." Claire continued packing her small case.

"Look what we found at the mall," Tom said.

Claire looked down at a packed-up tent and camping supplies.

"You mean you looted from the mall?"

Tom looked up at Claire trying to break the guilty look on his face. "Yes… Well, never mind that," Tom said. "We're taking Ryan's truck and going to camp in the outback. It will be much safer out there until the city is safe again. Come with us."

It took a few seconds for Claire to make her mind up. "No," she said. "I'm going home."

"Claire," Ryan argued. "It's too dangerous outside. The highways out of the city are blocked." Ryan looked into Claire's eyes. "Claire," He began. "Listen, I won't try anything with you. Please"

Claire looked at Tom. "No," she said. "My family needs me." Claire turned and entered her small room. She picked up her bag with her laptop in and a few other things. She loaded them into the bag and ran to the front door, getting a glimpse of all the panicking students on the campus as they ran in all directions. Claire put her keys in her pocket as she ran down the stairs. She came to the bottom door, bumping into other people as they ran out. Claire ran to her car and opened the door of the old vehicle, wiping a tear away from her eyes, wondering which way would be the quickest from Sydney to Brisbane. She lowered the handbrake, slipping the car into drive. She caught a glimpse of Ryan's pickup truck in front of her. She watched as he pulled onto the road. Tom was in the back holding onto a baseball bat. She looked at the fear in people's faces as they sped out of the car park. Claire watched as Ryan looked into her eyes. Claire continued to follow the pickup truck through Sydney as Tom and a few fellow students sat on the back, holding onto a metal pole. She looked around all of the streets as people ran in different directions. It was a scary picture; all of the main streets were clobbered with people trying to flee the infected city. She followed the speeding pickup truck, using it as a clear sign ahead for her. Should she go into the outback with Ryan and Tom or take chance with the main streets and head back home? The thoughts were confusing as she looked at people fleeing the zombies.

"Shit," she gasped. Claire watched as Ryan weaved in and out of the cars that had piled up into each other, some with blood staining the windows. She felt her emotions turn when she wondered if her family was still alive.

"Claire!" Tom shrieked over.

Claire gently opened her window, looking into the side mirror to see what was behind her.

"Claire, please come with us. It's too dangerous out there."

Claire didn't reply. She looked over at the sidewalk seeing one of the infected individuals running over to Tom.

"Look," Claire warned Tom.

"What?" Tom frowned, leaning forward, trying to read her lips.

Tom swung his head to the left, only to see that the zombie was running along the side of the truck. He launched himself on top of Tom. Claire gasped with fear as Tom struggled to push the zombie off his neck as the zombie's teeth penetrated it. Blood gushed out onto the sidewalk. Ryan watched in a stupor as Tom collapsed onto the side of the road, blood rushing out the side of his throat.

"No," Claire wept. "I can't do this." Claire swung her car around the pickup truck, but she saw a few of the zombies attacking Ryan in the driver's seat of the old truck. Ryan and Tom, as well as a few of her university friends were now dead. Claire took no chances; she pushed the accelerator down, heading towards the main streets to get out of Sydney. She sped through the traffic, seeing police officers on the streets, trying to take control of the situation. Claire squinted her eyes and saw a roadblock ahead that had been set up by the police.

"This way! Come on!" an officer screamed. "It's safe beyond this point."

Claire watched the officer trying to get people into a safe zone.

"Come on, ma'am," he yelled. "It's safer beyond this point."

Claire looked out to the left, seeing one of the side streets. She swung the car to the left and sped along the street. She stared into the rear-view mirror, seeing hordes of the zombies running towards the police roadblock that had been set. Shooting continued from all corners of the city. Claire slowly turned her eyes in time to see someone standing in the middle of the street with gleaming yellow eyes. She swung her car to the left, slamming into the zombie. Claire yelped as the zombie grasped the front of the car. Claire suddenly lost control; she slammed the brakes on, slamming her car into a lamppost.

CHAPTER TWELVE

Lewis's eyes shot open with fright. He had been in a deep sleep, and the back of his eyes seemed to be burning. He turned his head and looked at the alarm clock, realizing that he had been asleep for most of the day and that it was already the late afternoon.

"Shit, how long have I been out for?" Lewis slowly rolled out of the bed, wiping his eyes. He had a slight headache as he stood up, feeling the blood rush from his head as he walked into the living area of his apartment. He stared down at the brochures for bigger housing sprawled about on the wooden table. The dinner plates were still on the table from the meal he had had with Gemma last night. Something caught Lewis's eye. He looked down and saw that the white wire had slipped out from the telephone. He leaned down and clicked it back into place. He picked his mobile telephone up of the table and saw that he had a number of missed calls from Gemma and from the police.

Lewis sat down onto the settee, but something outside caught his attention more. He looked over at the balcony door. He stood up as the breeze blew the clean nets around. He slowly pulled the door open, looking out onto the city. There were a lot of police sirens and noises. Lewis looked down into the street, seeing some people rushing to their vehicles. The sounds of gunshots seemed to be increasing by the second.

"What the hell is going on?" Lewis asked himself. He sat down on the couch, again picking up the television control. He pushed the small rubber button in. It took a few seconds for the wide-screen TV to power up. Lewis saw the New South Wales News Corporation on the screen. He couldn't believe his eyes when he saw the headline running across the bottom of the screen: 'VIRUS ALERT AUSTRALIA EMERGENCY.'

Lewis sat forward, looking into the clean screen as Juliana Reeves reappeared. "If you have just joined us here, we are on the air twenty-four hours in this emergency," Juliana Reeves stated. "It has been confirmed by the Australian Board of Health and Center for Disease Control that we are currently involved in an epidemic, the first of its kind."

Lewis sat back as the shooting outside seemed to be increasing by the second.

"The New South Wales police have advised everybody to stay in their homes and to follow the curfew ordered by Tony Brown. But what's this?" Reeves said as she put her hand into her earpiece trying to listen to the controller. "I'm now going to our Perth correspondent, Sarah Charleswin."

Lewis watched as the screen changed to the middle of Perth.

"What's the latest from Perth?" Juliana Reeves asked.

It took a few seconds for the words to come out of the reporter's mouth. "I'm standing here in Perth city centre's famous Murray Street where the police have completely lost control of the city," Sarah screeched. "I mean, words can't explain what is going on here."

Lewis watched as two policemen ran in front of her.

"Get away while you can," he demanded. "Get out of the city." The officer grabbed his handgun as two of the white vehicles pulled in front. The camera continued to point down the street as the running figures got bigger and bigger. Lewis watched in horror as the hordes of people were pushed to the ground before being eaten alive, in exactly the same way Bob was killed. Blood rushed into the storm drains as people continued to panic. The officer's weapon pinged back. He looked up as the zombie figure slammed his teeth into his neck. The reporter watched as the skin was ripped away from the officer's neck. The reporter looked up as the camera was dropped to the ground. Lewis watched in horror as the young female reporter was dragged to the ground by the zombies. He got up quickly, grabbing his car keys of the table. He glanced around the apartment, knowing he may never see it again.

Lewis ran down the stairs as his phone started to ring in his pocket. He took it out and saw it was Gemma. "Gemma," Lewis snapped. "Where are you?"

"Lewis? Oh my God, you are still alive! I'm still at the hospital," she burst out. "People are dying everywhere."

"Okay, okay," Lewis said. "Just stay calm. I'm going to come get you. We are leaving the city tonight."

"Okay," Gemma replied.

The phone went dead. Lewis ran down the stairs, feeling for his handgun in his pouch. He skidded to a stop, looking at the open glass door. He stormed out as he watched the cars speeding straight through the red lights.

"Lewis," a voice called. Lewis turned to see Jeff, his neighbour. "What the hell is going on?" Jeff demanded.

"I have no idea," Lewis replied. "It all just happened since I went to sleep."

"How's Gemma?" Jeff asked.

"She is still at the hospital. Where are you going?"

There was a short pause as Jeff pulled the car door open and got in. "I'm going to get Julie from her sister's. Then we are going onto Wagga Wagga," Jeff replied.

"Why there?" Lewis asked.

Jeff started to hesitate as he grasped his belongings. "I

can't say," he replied. "I shouldn't have told you. Good luck. Hope to see you again here, soon."

Lewis watched as the car pulled out of the parking space and then turned into the street. In the blink of an eye, one of the city buses slammed into the side the vehicle. Lewis watched in horror as two zombies ran over to the car, dragging Jeff out onto the street.

"No, no, no! Please!" Jeff yelled at the top of his voice.

Lewis watched one of the zombies sticking his teeth into Jeff and pulling him out of the car. "No!" Lewis cried. Jeff's screams were unbearable to listen to. Lewis slammed the accelerator down, pulling out of the car park. People continued running in all directions. Lewis sped through the city, heading towards the main police headquarters. He tried to blank out the screams from his fellow citizens as they were chased around by the zombie creatures.

"Help me," He heard. Lewis looked down at his phone. He took his eyes off the road for a second. He glanced up, seeing one of the city buses. It had overshot a red light.

"Shit," he gasped. He swerved the car, hitting the brake pedal down fully. The back wheels locked, and he lost control of the car, slamming into a lamppost.

Lewis opened his eyes to some tapping on his head. "Hey," an American voice was heard. "Are you okay, pal?"

Lewis looked at Lucas, who was leaning in through the window.

"Come on," Lucas ordered. "You have got to get out of here." Lucas opened the door of the smashed vehicle, helping Lewis out. Lewis shook his head reaching for his sidearm. He looked at the silver handgun Lucas was wielding.

"Where did you get that?" Lewis asked.

"I'm American; I was born with a gun in my hand," Lucas joked.

Lewis and Lucas ran along the pavement of the street, watching cars speed past them.

"Welcome to Australia. How long you been here?" Lewis panted.

"Arrived this morning," Lucas replied. "What a day."

"Yes, what a day," Lewis replied. Lewis skidded to a stop, looking down one of the side streets. He watched two New South Wales police cars surround a crashed vehicle.

"This way," Lewis ordered.

Lewis and Lucas ran over to the police officers. Ben Crayfellow spun around as he reloaded his handgun.

"Jesus, Lewis," Crayfellow exclaimed. "You startled me. I'm surprised you're still alive, man. The whole country has turned into a war zone with these things."

Lewis looked at the car in the middle of the street. He looked at Claire, the student gasping for breath.

"We'll get you out," Crayfellow reassured.

Lewis looked down the road and saw some of the zombies sprinting towards them, blood running out of their mouths, their eyes gleaming bright yellow.

"Positions," Crayfellow commanded.

"Get her out quickly," Lewis demanded. Lewis looked through the sight of his weapon, seeing the gleaming yellow eyes of the zombies running towards them. Lewis pulled the trigger, taking single shots at the zombies as the officers slowly pulled Claire out from the car.

"Are you okay?" The officer asked.

Claire wiped her face. "I'm okay. Just a sore neck, thanks."

Lewis saw they had gotten Claire out, but, unnoticed by the officers who helped her out, one of the zombies had run in from the opposite road.

"Look out!" Lewis shrieked.

The officer turned to see the snarling mouth of the zombie running up at him. He didn't have time to act. Lewis heard him scream. But it was too late; he fell to the ground, choking.

"Let's get out of here," Crayfellow suggested.

Crayfellow pushed Claire into his patrol car as Lewis and a few of the other officers jumped in. Lewis looked down at the dead officer as his eyes shot open, gleaming yellow, looking into the vehicle. He jumped up and ran after the police car.

"So, where are we going?" Crayfellow asked.

"Hospital," Lewis replied.

"Why?" Crayfellow asked.

"I need to get to Gemma," Lewis replied. "She called me a short while ago; they may need some more support down there."

Lewis looked out of the window, catching a glimpse of the Sydney Opera House in flames, as they passed through the streets of Sydney.

"Look at the opera house," Lewis said.

Ben looked through the window at the house.

"Iconic piece of history!" Crayfellow said. The officers looked sadly at the burning piece of history.

"So, what has caused this?" Crayfellow asked.

"I know only as much as you do," Lewis replied. "All I know is that other cities in Australia have tried to evacuate but were overrun by these things."

Crayfellow pulled the handbrake up, skidding around the corner. "Sorry," he said. "Always wanted to do that."

Lucas looked out as the main police headquarters came into view in the far distance. The yellow barriers were pulled back. Ben pulled the handbrake up, looking down the main street, still seeing cars rushing back and forth in the dimness of the evening.

"Claire," Lewis said. "Get inside and find some help."

Claire ran up to the gate and walked in, looking at the clean, well-kept path of the new station. Lewis looked to see a grey van turn up. It skidded to a stop next to the other patrol vehicles. The siren was switched off, but the blue and red lights remained on like a signal to say there is civilization left at the station. Lewis looked at an elderly officer. He was grasping a G36 machine gun, with a helmet on and covered from top to bottom in body armour. He strolled towards the group.

"Jackson," a voice called. "Nice to see you again."

Lewis turned around and saw Mike Needleson, his friend who worked for the tactical support unit.

"Hello, Lewis," he replied. "Missing out on all the fun, aren't you?"

Mike looked around at all the New South Wales police officers who were standing by the barricade. He turned his head to see Ben.

"Hello, sweetheart," Mike said. "Nice to see you, too."

Ben looked at Mike. "Okay, girls, if you'd like to go take a walk inside and let my boys take over," he suggested. "I think there are some chocolate fudges left in the lounge if Jackson hasn't pigged them all. You need to keep your energy up because I know times are hard for you sweeties."

"Hey, fuck you, man" Lewis joked.

Crayfellow walked forward towards Mike. "I'm glad you find this amusing," he said to him.

"What's that, darling?" Mike asked Ben.

Ben looked at Mike. "It's a shame that my training didn't start earlier," Lewis replied to Mike.

"What's going on?" Needleson asked. "Do you know of any more news on this Z virus?"

"Z virus?" Lewis asked in a shocked dead voice.

"Yeah. Z virus," Mike replied. "Doctors and scientists at the Australian Centre For Disease Control have been analyzing this new virus and have got no name for it, so they have just thought, 'fuck it,' and called it 'Z.'"

Before the conversation between Lewis and Mike Needleson could go any further, a shot was heard. Lewis grabbed his handgun when he saw two of the zombies running towards them, snarling, with blood dripping out the fronts of their mouths.

"Take them out, boys," Mike commanded.

The two officers took the running zombies out. Lewis

looked into the west, seeing that the sun had almost gone down.

"It will be dark soon," Lewis stated. "What we doing after leaving the city?"

"Are you mad?" Mike said. "It's not just the big cities that are infected. The whole damn country is being taken over by these things."

Another shot was heard. Lewis and Mike swung their heads, looking down the road to see a huge horde of the zombies running towards them.

"Shit," Needleson gasped. "Position, boys."

Lewis watched as the heavily-armed officers took position, looking through the sights of their weapons.

"Jackson," Needleson yelled. "Feel free to participate."

Mike handed Lewis a SPAS-12 shotgun from the armoured van behind him. He ran up to the white police car.

"Awaiting orders, sir," a voice yelled.

Mike Needleson looked at the zombies as they sprinted towards the police station. Then he looked to the left at the crowded police station. "Fire!" he screamed.

The officers opened fire on the sprinting zombies as they came up the road.

"Come and get us!" one officer yelled.

Lewis looked through the sight of the SPAS-12 shotgun, squeezing the trigger. The shell launched from the barrel of the weapon, blasting the zombies in half. Bits of intestines landed on the street as the chasing zombies continued to arrive in hundreds.

"There are far too many," Lewis shouted.

"Never too many," Mike replied. "Have some fun, boys."

Mike turned, looking at Ben.

"And girl," he then said.

The officers continued to open fire on the zombies as the sun almost finished going down in the west. Lewis felt the SPAS-12 shotgun push his body back as the zombies sprinted towards the police blockade. Lewis looked into the wing mirror of the cruiser. He swung his head around to see one of the military attack helicopters. It swung behind the roadblock. He took his eyes off the road ahead for a minute. He looked at the launchers mounted on the underneath of the helicopter. He squinted his eyes looking to see a few small sparks shoot from behind the back of the launcher,

"Shit," he uttered under his breath

The two rockets launched from the sides of the helicopter. The jet stream of smoke was blasted out of the back of the two rockets heading towards the oncoming zombies. Mike swung his head, looking at the rockets zooming towards the oncoming zombies.

"Shit," he yelped. "Everybody down!"

Lewis looked at Ben as he stared at the incoming rockets. "Ben, get down!" he ordered. Lewis pulled Ben to the ground. The rockets that were shot overhead slammed into the street, blowing some of the zombies into pieces. Large chunks of asphalt blew up into the air. The helicopter continued to hover behind the roadblock. The machine gun started to spin.

"Stay down, people," Needleson ordered

Bits of body parts were flying everywhere. Blood rained down onto the street, followed by the golden shells from the machine gunshots. The helicopter suddenly swung around, heading away from the police station.

"That's slowed them down," Lewis said to Ben

Mike slowly got up after the rapid gunfire

"Jackson," Needleson yelled. "Are you okay?"

"I'm fine," Lewis said. "Ouch, fuck, that hurt."

"Thanks for that," Ben said.

"Not a problem," Lewis replied

Mike looked at Ben. "Are you okay, sweetheart?" Mike asked. "Do you need a plaster for that?"

Ben looked at Mike. He focused his attention back down the street. He saw more zombies charging towards them. "Shit!" he exclaimed.

"Keep going," Lewis ordered.

The sun continued descending. Soon, the streetlamps would be on.

SYDNEY HOSPITAL

The officer looked up the street as he stood guarding the barrier to the hospital.

"They are coming!" a woman yelled, running past the officers. "They're coming!"

The officer looked down to see the gleaming eyes of the zombies as they sprinted towards the checkpoint, blood from the innocent victims of their attack rushing from their mouths. Some of the infected were soldiers.

"Oh shit," he mumbled. "Contact."

The two soldiers behind him spun around, kneeling by the white police cruiser and looking at the sprinting zombies.

"Stand by," he yelled.

The zombies slowly came closer and closer to the hospital. The road was full of them. They charged towards the entrance of the hospital. There was nowhere to run.

"Fire!" the soldier ordered. Exactly at that moment, the police and military opened fire on the running zombies. The hordes seemed to be increasing by the minute as people ran past the barricade and into the hospital.

"Get out of the way!" The soldier yelled. "Get out of the way!" The soldiers and police struggled to shoot in between the running people.

The people in the hospital looked down out of the window, seeing the glowing eyes of the zombies heading towards the hospital. The gunfire was intense. The people knew they were running out of time. Gemma listened to the rapid gunfire from the outside looking out the window as the police and military fired on the zombies. No matter how much the police and army tried, the zombies went on, arriving in large numbers. Soon, they would be out of ammunition.

"There are too many," an officer yelled.

Gemma stood by the window, continuing to look up at the attacking zombies, some of which were nearly reaching the blockade.

"Gemma," Jasmine called. Gemma turned her head and looked at Jasmine as she ran up to her. "Grab your keys," Jasmine demanded. "Let's get out of here."

"What?" Gemma gasped. "We can't leave everybody."

"Come on," Jasmine yelled. "This place is finished; let's get out of here."

Gemma ran to her locker and pulled her car keys out. Jasmine was looking out the window in horror as the zombies were breaking the barricade to the hospital. Gemma followed Jasmine along the corridors towards the exit to the staff car park. She kicked the door open, looking out at her car, which was still parked in the same spot. She hit the 'open-door' button in as the zombies ran into the car park. Gemma trembled when she put the keys into the ignition of the new car Lewis had bought her for her birthday. She pushed the brake pedal down, setting the car into reverse. She pulled out of the parking spot, slamming into the lamppost behind her. The yellow registration plate fell to the ground as she sped to the exit. Jasmine looked into the mirror.

"God, that was close," Gemma said. Gemma listened to Jasmine as she broke down into tears by her side. "Hey," Gemma said. "Don't worry. I'm scared, too." Gemma continued speeding up the road away from the hospital. She stared into the mirror as the huge building disappeared.

Lewis and Mike Needleson continued shooting at the running zombies.

"Getting low," Lewis stated.

"Me too," Mike replied to Lewis. "But having fun."

"Do you take anything seriously?" Ben asked

"Nope," Mike replied. "I'm too old for that."

One of the officers turned his head around, looking down the street. He saw the yellow glowing eyes of the zombies. "They are coming from the rear," he shouted.

Mike Needleson turned around to see more of the zombies running towards them from the rear. "Cover the rear," Mike yelled, tapping Ben's bum.

A few of the officers kneeled on the middle of the street as the zombies were attacking from all directions. No matter how many they took down, the zombies still seemed to be coming. Mike looked down as he loaded one of the magazines into the G36. He listened to the constant shooting of the officers. He looked up into the sky and saw one of the news helicopters above the station.

"Shit," he mumbled under his breath. Mike walked to his van. He stepped into the back, looking at the TV on the wall. He saw a bird's eye view of the police station. He watched as the camera suddenly shifted its focus to the street ahead of the station. Mike gently shook his head when he viewed the oncoming zombies. He realized there was to be no end to the fight in the near future.

"Sir," Mike said into the radio.

Commander Rolf Hepburn picked up the radio, looking out onto the street outside, "Go ahead, Needleson."

"Sir," Needleson said again. "There are too many of them. I don't think we can hold them off for much longer."

Commander Hepburn put the radio back down onto his desk as he walked back over to the window. He let his breath out when he saw the shooting starting to slow down as his officers were running out of ammunition. He looked over his shoulder and saw the radio still on his desk that was linked to all the police radios within the city. He reached over and picked it up. He grasped to it, still listening to the rapid gunfire.

"Fall back," he commanded. "Fall back."

"Shit," Lewis gasped. He looked down at the SPAS-12 shotgun and saw he was out of shells.

"Right, everybody," Needleson yelled. "Inside. Inside now. Come on, shift it." Mike watched as the officers started running through the gate into the police station.

Lewis held onto the SPAS-12 as he ran up to the new silver gate.

"Come on, move!" Needleson shouted above the clamour.

"Ben," come on," Lewis said. "I'm not losing you."

Mike Needleson watched as a few of his officers were dragged to the ground by the attacking zombies.

"Come on, Mike!" Lewis cried.

Mike and Lewis slammed the gate shut. His eyes opened with disbelief when he saw one of the officers who had been attacked getting up, with yellow, gleaming eyes, running towards the gate.

"Damn! Fuck it!" Mike yelped.

Lewis looked at Mike as he stared through the metal poles of the gate at the snarling zombies.

"Come on," Lewis said.

Mike and Lewis ran up the concrete path towards the police station. Lewis looked as hordes of zombies started crowding the outside of the gate, slamming against it. Lewis and Mike slammed the two brown doors shut.

"Well," Ben Crayfellow said. "Now what?"

"What can we do," Mike Needleson said in exasperation, "other than wait until more help arrives?"

"There won't be any more help," an officer said.

Before a conversation could ensue, Lewis stepped in. "I need to get to the hospital," Lewis said. "I need to get Gemma."

"I think it came under attack," a voice said.

Lewis swung his head. "What do you mean?"

"It came under attack a few minutes ago," the officer explained. "We heard it over the radio, and I think it may be on the news."

"I need to get there," Lewis insisted "I know she is still alive."

"She's as good as dead, man," the officer snapped back at him.

"Hey," he shouted. "You take that back."

"It's as good as true."

Lewis went for the officer. Rolf Hepburn walked into that area of the station, seeing his officers arguing and yelling at each other.

"Enough!" he screamed. "All of you!" Lewis and the officer stopped fighting instantly. "May I remind you what is going on in this city?"

"What's going on, sir?" Crayfellow asked the chief.

"I don't know," he murmured weakly.

"What about the army?" Lewis asked.

Hepburn looked at Lewis. "What about them?" Rolf replied. Rolf kept his hands behind his back, slowly strolling away from the onlooking officers.

"Listen," he snapped, spinning around on his toes. "Sydney is the only city left that has some kind of civilization. Adelaide, Brisbane, Wagga Wagga, Perth, Canberra—all gone, finished, no one left alive."

"All of them?" Crayfellow couldn't believe what he just heard.

"Yes," Rolf screamed. "All of them. All I know is that the military were evacuating via Kingsford Smith Airport to some location, and that is all I know."

Lewis watched as the chief walked off. He was reaching for his firearm. Lewis turned and looked back at the group. "Well," he said. "What do we do?"

"We get to the airport," Crayfellow replied.

"After the hospital," Lewis said.

Lewis and the rest of the group jumped when they heard a sudden gunshot from the other room. Crayfellow began to walk to the room.

"Leave it," Lewis said. "He's dead."

"Why did he kill himself?" an officer asked.

There is a silent pause from the group.

"The convoy he sent to pick up his wife and daughter. . ." the officer said. The officers knew the response. "They lost contact a short while ago."

Lewis walked into the rest area of the station. He sat down, switching on the TV. He looked to see Julianna Reeves on the screen.

"Is there anyone there?" she asked. Lewis looked at the screen, hoping it would switch to the hospital. Nothing. "I have just been told by my producer," Julianna Reeves slowly said, "that we are going off the air to the emergency broadcast system. All I can say to the people who have stayed with us throughout this crisis is this: Good luck and God bless you. I'm Juliana Reeves."

Lewis watched as the screen switched to the Emergency Broadcast System. The group stayed quiet. Mike was staring at the emergency system, leaving the G36 by his side.

"Right," Lewis said. "What shall we do? To the hospital?" The group of officers stayed quiet. "Well, let's get down there," Lewis suggested. "What's the armoury like?"

"Out," Mike said. "So, if I were you boys, I'd make all rounds count—one shot to the head, that's it."

Lewis felt the pouches and realized he had a few magazines left.

"What about the evidence room?" an officer suggested. "Anything in there we can use?"

"Out," Crayfellow said.

The group went quiet.

"Well," Needleson said. "Let's get out of here and get down there where we are most needed."

Lewis and Ben jumped at a sudden bang. It seemed to be coming from the main gate to the station.

"Now what?" Mike Needleson asked.

Ben, Lewis and Mike walked over to the main entrance, looking out of the glass windows out onto the two huge, metal gates. Lewis squinted his eyes. He looked to see the rhino.

"The fuck?" Mike gasped

The rhino continued to slam into the wall that surrounded the gate. Tiny chunks of concrete were falling to the ground as the rhino charged at it. Its eyes were gleaming yellow.

"What do we do?" asked Mike.

Lewis watched as the rhino slowly turned around and walked away from the gates.

"I think he has gone," Ben said.

It went quiet for a few seconds. Lewis watched in horror as the rhino slammed through the gates. The infected stormed the grounds.

"Everybody," Needleson ordered. "To the garage. Let's get out of here."

Lewis reloaded his handgun, looking at the zombies who were running towards the building.

"Come on, Lewis," Ben demanded.

Lewis turned and ran with the group through the station. He heard the glass smashing behind him as the zombies broke in. Blood was staining the floor as they entered the stairway that led downstairs.

"Lewis, come on!" Needleson screamed. "I will still want you on my team when this is over."

"I'm coming."

Lewis and Ben entered the underground garage. They saw there were only two cars left, but it was enough for the small group to make it to the hospital and try to support the last of the remaining survivors. Lewis threw the keys over to Crayfellow as he sat in the driver's seat.

"Come on, girls," Needleson ordered.

The zombies slammed into the entrance door of the underground garage.

Lewis stepped into the back seat, reloading the firearm. He looked out the back window as the other officers got ready in the car behind.

"Okay," Lewis said. "Shall we roll?"

Ben pushed a small button on the dashboard. The huge

black gates rolled open, allowing them to leave. Lewis looked out of the window into the dead street at the rear of the station.

"Come on, fucking thing," Lewis snapped.

Crayfellow rolled out, pulling onto the street. He kept the accelerator down, but he soon saw something out of the corner of his right eye. He looked at the huge horde of zombies who sprinted towards the car. Ben slammed the accelerator down fully as the second car continued to follow them. Blood smeared onto the window. Claire hunched away as she looked into gleaming eyes.

"Jesus," Ben said. "Look at them." Ben kept the accelerator down as the two squad cars fled the police station. Lewis looked out the back window as they sped from the police station.

CHAPTER THIRTEEN

Juliana stood up, looking at the fear expressed in the cameraman's face as they had switched over to the Emergency Broadcast System.

"I'm out of here," he said. "My family needs me; that's if they are still alive!"

Juliana didn't reply as the once highly-motivated team fled in all different directions of the studio. The lights shut off, one after the other.

"Juliana," a voice was heard calling her. Juliana looked over seeing Katherine Hope. "Come on, let's go," she said.

Juliana ran through the news studio, looking in at all of the empty offices. No staff were running around; there were just empty seats where people once used to sit and work.

"Come on," Katherine yelled.

Juliana ran through the empty studio. "Wait," Juliana yelled.

"What?" Katherine enquired.

Juliana ran to her seat. She picked up her side bag, looking at the small digital camcorder.

"Come on," Katherine said. "Let's get to the airport if that's where they are evacuating from."

Juliana followed Katherine to the car park of the news

studio. Katherine unlocked her car, looking around the streets. She saw an occasional car whizz past. Juliana put her seatbelt on as the car pulled out of the car park. The roads were empty for a change, and so was the pavement.

"What shall we do?" Katherine asked. "Go straight to the airport or go home and get our belongings?"

Juliana looked out the front of the car again. "Let's just get home," Juliana said. "Then, if the state is bad, we go straight to the airport and get out of here."

Katherine nodded as she sped through the streets. She turned to her left. "Hey, wait," she said "Just checking. . ." she said. "Something." Katherine turned onto a road that ran to a school. She looked to see a school bus that had bent around a lamppost as it was pulling out of the high school. Smoke was hissing from the engine, blood stained the sign on the side of the bus. The two red lights on the top were starting to fade away.

"The hell?" Katherine said

Juliana pulled out her small digital camcorder. Katherine and Juliana stared at the bus as they drove past the burning school. Katherine looked into her rear-view mirror as she continued to pick up speed, heading towards the airport. Juliana took one last look into her side mirror as she closed her digital camcorder. She saw one of the zombies out on the street. Katherine was still staring into the rear-view mirror. She couldn't take her eyes of the school for some reason which was unknown to Julianna.

"Look out!" Juliana yelled.

Katherine looked up and saw one of the zombies in the middle of the street. Katherine slammed on the breaks. The front wheel of the car turned to the right. Juliana grasped her seatbelt as the car slammed into a tree on the sidewalk. Katherine lifted her head.

"You okay?" Katherine asked.

"I'm fine," Juliana replied. She turned her head to the left and yelled, "Look out!"

Katherine looked out the right-hand window and saw the zombie. It was a young boy, around fifteen, still in a school uniform with his tie half-undone and his eyes gleaming yellow. He was just looking at her.

"No," Katherine pleaded. "I love you."

The fist of the young boy slammed through the window. Juliana wept as the glass window was ripped from the rubber sockets surrounding the windows.

"Come on," Juliana yelled.

But before Katherine could undo her seatbelt, the zombie leaned into the car and slammed his teeth into her neck. Juliana looked back when she heard the scream from Katherine. She stared at the long river of blood rushing down her neck as her eyes slowly closed.

Juliana looked back down the street, seeing more of the zombies running towards the crashed car. Juliana held onto her camcorder as she ran along the sidewalk into one of the alleyways away from the crash scene.

* * *

Prime Minister Tony Brown stared out of his office window. The moon gleamed down. Not a cloud was to be seen in the sky. There was a sudden knock on the door. He slowly turned around, looking at the white door.

"Come," he ordered.

Brown had been looking out of the window at the news helicopters as they flew around the city, taking pictures and broadcasting them to the world.

"Sir," Thomas Legg intervened.

"What?"

"Sir, we need to evacuate you to a secure location," Legg stated.

"No," Brown insisted. "I want to stay. What's the status of the country?"

Legg paused for a few seconds and then replied reluctantly, "Not good, sir."

"Well, give me the details."

"Sir, it is too dangerous for you to be here. Infection levels in Canberra are extremely high, almost critical. We have set up a command post in a secure location for you. Your family is already there waiting for you."

Brown reached up and pulled the curtains across. He picked up his bag and, escorted by Legg and a few of the Australian Army personnel, walked through the Parliament House.

"This way, sir," a soldier gave directions.

Brown watched as the side door to the house was opened. He felt the cool summer night air blow onto his head as a jet-powered helicopter touched down on the helipad in front of him. Brown, Legg, and the Australian troops ran across the grass towards the helipad, but something caught Brown's attention. He looked over towards the two front gates leading to the building. He started in horror at the zombies trying to break through the huge gates, their eyes gleaming yellow. The gate gently rocked back and forth.

"Oh, dear God!" Brown exclaimed.

The soldiers couldn't hold the gate closed. The zombies burst through, one after the other.

"Get on the chopper," Legg yelled. "Them things are coming."

Legg watched as the door was sealed shut. He sat down next to the prime minister as the helicopter lifted off the helipad in the middle of the parliament compound. Brown watched in horror out of the window as the zombies sprinted across the well-cut lawns towards the helicopter as it lifted off the pad heading away from the Parliament House. Brown looked down out of the window as they passed over Canberra. He looked down at the streets as the zombies ran in all directions while police cars were barricading the streets, trying to prevent the infection from spreading, but nothing seemed to work.

"The curfew failed," Brown said. "If only people had listened to me! If they had stayed off the streets, we could have eradicated them things by now."

"You did all you could, sir," Legg tried to console him.

"It took us so quickly," Brown remembered. "We estimated twenty-four hours before it got to this level of infection."

Legg didn't know how to reply.

"What's the current status with the safe zone at Hobart?" Brown asked.

"The American Air Force has flown some supplies and troops there, and it's been deployed as we speak," Legg reported. "But we have yet to confirm that the rest of Tasmania is infection free."

"What about the evacuation of New South Wales and Sydney?"

"We currently have troops that are evacuating via Kingsford Smith Airport," Legg said, "but. . ."

"But what?" Brown inquired.

"The evacuation is still on," Legg stated, "but it is very slow due to the amount of aircraft and flight crew that are operating. The New Zealand Prime Minister is sending over one of their 777s to help evacuate its own people back to Auckland. Then they will be quarantined until they are certain they are free from infection."

"How long until we get to this place of safety?" Brown asked. "I want to see my family."

"Not too long, sir."

Brown took another look out of the window as the helicopter sped over Australia, heading into the Pacific Ocean and leaving the burning country behind him. The lights from the cities and the only few remaining survivors slowly disappeared. Brown loosened his tie as the helicopter powered towards the ocean.

* * *

Captain David Stanfield, an ex-New Zealand Air Force pilot, looked out the front of the Jet New Zealand 777 jet as the Australian coastline came into view. It was not long before they would be able to land. First Officer Jacob Palacios, also an ex-military pilot, looked down at the flight management computer as he programmed the route to Kingsford Smith airport.

"I want everyone up here now," David Stanfield ordered. Stanfield watched as the cockpit door opened. Carly Parkinson, the chief cabin attendant, looked down at the flight crew as the aircraft started its descent into Sydney.

"Okay," Captain David Stanfield said. "We land in just under the hour. The moment we land, we get to the gate and get out of there."

"What about fuel?" Carly asked.

"We have enough," Captain Stanfield stated. "I bought extra."

Chloe felt the aircraft gently start to bounce as they passed through a light cloud. Captain Stanfield was looking out the front of the aircraft as Australia started to come into view on the horizon. Some of the city lights were still on.

"I still can't believe what is happening," Carly said.

"Carly," Stanfield called her attention. Chloe turned to the captain. "I don't know how many people we are getting out, so go and prepare the cabin for a full load—I mean standing as well."

"Got it," Carly said. Carly turned around, walking back into the cabin of the huge wide-bodied jet. She looked at the cabin crew who were waiting for the orders from her.

"Okay," she said. "Let's do this."

Captain Stanfield looked forward again as the lights from the destroyed cities slowly started to get brighter.

•　•　•

Brown looked down out of the window of his helicopter as his party approached the HMAU frigate ship. He looked down at the single helicopter pad on the back of the ship. The lights flashed on and off as it touched down with a bump. The door was opened from the outside. Brown still felt the rushing air from the blades above as they powered down.

"Hello, Mr Prime Minister," a sailor said. "Can I get you anything?"

Brown didn't reply as he was escorted down the metal stairs into the ship, to be greeted by Captain Kirk Henderson.

"Mr Brown," Kirk said.

Brown looked across the ocean seeing nothing but water. "Yes," Brown said.

"Would you follow me, please?" Kirk directed him.

Brown looked up as one of the sailors scanned his eyes. "What are you doing?" he snapped.

"Just precautions sir," he replied. "You're clean; you can go through."

Brown walked through the ship, escorted by Captain Henderson.

"In here, please," Kirk directed again.

Brown walked in to see all the generals and doctors from the CDC there. But something else captured his attention. He turned his head and looked at the display board next to him where he saw a huge map of Australia. He stared at the red dots scattered about the map.

"What's that?" Brown demanded.

General Kingsley stood up with his laser pen, pointing at the map of Australia.

"As you can see," he explained, "the only place that we have direct contact with is Sydney. The rest of the cities and towns have all gone out of contact."

"What's the state of Sydney?" Brown asked.

General Kingsley took a deep breath before he replied. "It's not going too well. We have the airport secure, but the evacuation is going very slowly."

"I know," Brown said. "Legg told me. I want all military personnel who are still out there to head directly to the airport and assist with the evacuation. Also, get onto neighbouring nations if they can provide aircraft capable of landing at Hobart Airport."

"Right you are, sir," General Kingsley said getting up.

There was a knock on the door. Legg stood up, walked over to the metal door, and pulled it open.

"Daddy," a voice echoed.

Brown looked up and saw his daughter running to him in a pink dressing gown. "Hey, sweetheart," Brown said softly. The people looked at the prime minister as he hugged his daughter. "Where's your mummy?" he asked.

Tony Brown then saw his wife standing outside, weeping, trying to keep her emotions hidden from her daughter, trying to hide the fear from her. "Listen," he said. "I need you to be a good girl and go look after your mummy for me, please. Daddy is really, really busy today."

"Why are we here, daddy?" she asked. "Am I still going to Charlie's party tomorrow?" The room went dead for a few seconds. "She's my best friend. I love her to bits," she said cheerfully.

"I know you do," Brown replied. "Go on and look after mummy for me, please."

"Okay, daddy," she said.

Brown took a deep breath, watching as his daughter ran out of the room. He shuffled the collar of his shirt. "Okay," he said. "Carry on"

* * *

Lewis stared out of the front of the white police cruisers as they both turned up outside of the city hospital. Lewis looked up at the old-fashioned building. No one was around; the place was completely deserted. Some of the lights were out in the building. The emergency generator was dying out by the minute. Lewis stepped out of the cruiser, looking down the empty streets. The yellow barricades sealed the roads off. Blood stained the police lines. A few of the blue and red lights were on. They were the only things lighting the barricade. Mike looked at the blockade vehicles.

"You," he ordered the officer The officer swung his head, looking at Mike and awaiting his orders. "Get them lights out"

"Sir," he replied.

Lewis watched as the officers cut the blue and red lights to the cars. It went dark where they were standing.

"Let's do this," Lewis said.

The group stood quietly. "We'll stay," one officer said. "In case we have to make a quick getaway."

The officers waited by the car as Lucas, Jackson, and Crayfellow entered the hospital. The automatic doors slowly slid open. Claire was by Lucas's side. Lewis grasped the handgun and slowly walked through to the automatic door. Lucas pushed them open further for Claire.

"Are you okay?" he asked her.

Claire could only nod as they progressed further into the deserted hospital. Lewis pulled the torch out of its pouch. He clicked it on. It was the only thing that could be heard as they walked along the wooden floor. Looking at the tiny drops of blood on the floor, he kept the torch on the ground, staring at the drips of blood as they started to get bigger. His eyes were locked onto the wooden floor of the hospital. The tiny drops of blood he was weaving in and out of a second ago turned into a streak. Claire heaved, looking at the stretched river of blood on the wooden flooring. It was struggling to dry up without the light from above. A few flickers could be seen from the Emergency Department ahead

Needleson followed Lucas and Crayfellow as they entered the department. The green curtains from the medical bays have been ripped off their plastic hooks. Blood had stained them. A handprint of blood was running down onto the floor.

The once white and black tiles were now red, a river of blood running in between the cracks like a river. Slowly running into the ward, Lewis took his attention away from the gore of the hospital. He looked at the four corners of the hospital, each one leading to different wards of the hospital.

"Right," he whispered. "Let's split up."

Mike looked down the corridor. He shone the torch down the dark corridor, looking at the wheelchair that had been slammed into the lower glass window. The wheels were bent from where it had fallen onto its side.

"You go that way," Lewis said to Needleson. "Meet back at the entrance in ten minutes."

"Got it," Mike replied. Mike reloaded the G36 and crept along the empty corridors of the hospital

"The rest of you," Lewis said. "Stick with me."

"Why don't we split up?" Lucas asked.

"We stick together for now," Lewis replied. "Maybe when we go upstairs we will."

Lucas, Claire, Crayfellow, and Lewis walked into the ward. Blood stains were everywhere. It looked like a battlefield. The once pure, white bedsheets were now a pure red from blood that flowed from injured and infected. Bullets lined the floor. Lewis turned the corner, searching for the staff locker room. He peeked in through the glass window before walking in to see a static television. He slowly opened the wooden door. Lucas and Claire walked in behind him. Lewis looked at Gemma's locker. It was open with nothing in there worth taking—just a picture of her and Lewis stuck to the back of the locker.

"Anything?" Lucas asked.

Lewis stayed dead silent for a second, just staring at the picture of him and Gemma. "Nothing," he finally said.

The TV was static; nothing was being broadcast. Lewis walked over, picking up the remote. He flicked through the channels, looking at the static picture. Lucas looked up at the ceiling.

"Wonder how he is doing."

Mike grasped to the G36 as he crept through the empty corridors of the hospital. "Anyone there?" he asked. "Hello?" Mike continued to search the empty wards of the city hospital. He turned his head into one of the wards, catching a glimpse of someone. He looked to see a doctor, aged around thirty-five, looking out of the window onto the dark, dying city. Blood was on his scrubs. He was just standing there, looking out into the city.

"Doc," he said. "It's okay; you are safe now. Come on, we are evacuating to the airport. We'll get you out. We need all the help we can get."

The doctor spun around. Needleson looked in horror at the snarling doctor who had blood running out the side of his face with gleaming yellow eyes. The doctor snarled as Needleson squeezed the trigger of the G36. The doctor fell against the window. Mike Needleson reached for his radio.

Mike spun around to see a large group of zombies standing there, looking at him with yellow gleaming eyes. They were wide open, not blinking at all.

"Oh shit," Mike said. Needleson squeezed the trigger, just standing there. Lewis looked up, swiping his handgun. The shooting stopped suddenly.

"Fuck it," Lewis gasped. "Come on, Claire." Lewis opened the door and was followed by Claire. He looked at the zombies running down the aisles towards them. "This way."

The officers outside of the hospital frittered about as the shooting continued from inside the hospital.

"Let's get out of here," the officer said.

The two officers looked at each other, seeing the zombies running towards them.

"Let's go. Come on," the officer shouted.

Lewis froze as he watched the two officers dragged to the ground by the snarling zombies. He looked back and forth;

the only way out was down the sidewalk to the car park. Lewis ran along the pavement keeping his eyes on Lucas, Claire, and Crayfellow. Lewis heard the scream from the two officers as he ran along the pavement. Lucas spun around looking through the sight of the handgun. He pulled the trigger trying to slow down the chasing zombies. Lucas felt his bag slipping off his shoulder. The old, tatty bag slipped off his shoulder, slamming into the ground.

"Fuck, no." Lucas stopped in his tracks.

Lewis looked back, seeing that Lucas had dropped his bag. "Leave it," Lewis yelled.

Lucas stopped picking up his bag. He launched it over his shoulder.

Lewis shot at the zombies, stopping them from ripping Lucas to pieces. "Down here," Lewis ordered.

The group ran down a set of steps. Lewis looked out and saw one of the city ambulances in the middle of the car park. Its back doors were open, and there were blood stains on the ground.

"Get in that," Lewis ordered.

"Lucas, in that," Crayfellow said.

Lewis stopped shooting at the zombies as they fell down the stairs running into the car park. He stumbled back, feeling something caught on the bottom of his shoe. He kicked over a registration plate. He looked down and saw that it was Gemma's.

"Gemma," he uttered.

"Lewis!" Lucas screamed. "Come on, man!"

Ben hit the accelerator as Lucas reached out, grabbing onto Lewis's arm and hauling him into the back of the ambulance.

Crayfellow gasped, "That was close."

Lewis let his breath out and stammered. "Gemma is still alive."

"What?" Crayfellow asked. "How do you know that?"

Lewis continued to take deep breaths as Lucas sped along the road, away from the chasing zombies.

"Back there," Lewis panted. "I found her registration plate on the ground."

"Do you think she has gone to the airport?" Lucas enquired.

"Yes," Crayfellow said. "She must have gone there knowing that is where you would be."

"Well, let's get to the airport then," Lewis stated.

Ben pushed the accelerator down as they headed towards Kingsford Smith Airport.

CHAPTER FOURTEEN

Carl Farrington entered the Mayor's office in Hobart. He didn't even knock. "Mayor West?" Farrington asked. West slowly turned around in the chair to face him. "I have some information for you."

West sat down onto his desk, looking up at the emergency broadcast system that was still being broadcasted in Australia. After a moment, he said, "Let's hear it."

Farrington sat down on the chair in front of the mayor. He pulled out a map of Hobart. He rolled it out across the desk. He reached over, picking up one of the black marker pens. Mayor West watched as Farrington drew a thick black line around the entire city.

"The city is completely contained, sir. Our troops have sealed all exits. The only way into the city is across the Tasman Bridge. Here." West watched as the bridge was circled, plus the dot as well. "That is the only way in and out of the city for the time being," Farrington said.

West stared down at the circled map. "What about people on the other side of the bridge?" West asked.

"The only people we are letting in are people who have residence within the city," Farrington replied. "The Hobart Police have set up a team letting people into the city only when they have cleared the medical screening, but anybody with medical or military experience is being fast-tracked."

Farrington reached over, picking up the remote to the TV that was on the mayor's desk. He switched the channel over. "We managed to get some news crew over here," Farrington said, "and have set up a channel broadcasting just to Tasmania."

West looked at the TV as it showed the Tasman Bridge. Military vehicles blocked off the bridge, allowing only very few to enter the city.

"Please return to your homes," The load speaker said. "Only people with military, police, medical, and emergency service training are to approach the main gate."

West shook his head, seeing people trying to get into the city away from any possible infection that could be within Tasmania.

"Are you going to open the city again?" Mayor West asked.

"Not for a long time," Farrington replied.

There was a knock on the office door. "Sir," a soldier drew his attention.

Farrington looked at Mayor West "Excuse me," he said. Farrington got up, heading towards the entrance to the office. He left the map of Hobart on the desk in front of the mayor, the pen nib pointing at the city centre. Mayor West looked out of the window, down onto the street below. One of the military jeeps turned up to take Carl Farrington somewhere within Hobart. He slowly pulled the blinds down, sitting at the desk to take one last look up at the news screen in front of him.

* * *

Lewis looked out of the vehicle, scanning the streets ahead. Only very few lamps were on, but something else captured Lewis's eye. He looked out of the right-hand window, seeing one of the city shopping malls. It was complexly dark. Not a living soul was around.

"Hey, stop," Lewis said to Ben.

Crayfellow hit the brakes slowly stopping the ambulance. Lewis stepped out of the vehicle, down onto the ground. He swiped his handgun, looking over into the city shopping centre car park. He looked at the military jeeps and other vehicles in the car park, with their doors open and blood splattered onto the windows. A few golden bullet shells were on the ground. He saw a car slammed into a tree. He walked over to it, looking in through the broken windows and glass scattered about. He looked at the back, seeing the registration plate had fallen off. He slowly strolled around to the front. A slight hiss could be heard from the engine. He quickly looked over his shoulder, swinging his head down to the front of the car. He shone the small torch on to the front of the car. It was Gemma's. He looked away, back at the military jeeps.

"Keep your eyes open," Crayfellow ordered swiping his handgun. He looked around the empty car park seeing some of the Australian Army vehicles scattered about.

"What were they doing here?" Crayfellow asked.

Lewis looked around at the barriers that had been set up. "Evacuating to the airport," he said. "This was one of the extraction zones before the back streets and housing estates were overrun by them things."

"Do you reckon they are at the airport?" Claire asked.

Before Lewis could answer, a horrific yell was heard. Lewis looked up and saw the infected running towards them. "Oh, fuck," he gasped.

"Jesus," Crayfellow exclaimed. "There are thousands of them."

Lewis looked over at the Shopping Centre. He knew they wouldn't have time to get back in the ambulance and get away.

"Inside," he yelled "Get to the mall."

The group ran across the car park towards the entrance to the mall. Lewis ran up the concrete ramp.

"Get the doors open," Lewis yelled as he kneeled and started shooting, trying to slow the screaming zombies down. It wasn't working. "Come on," he yelled

"It's locked," Crayfellow yelled in a panic.

Lewis spun around. "Move!" he yelled. Lewis shot the lock of the mall doors. Claire yelped at the gunshot. Crayfellow pulled the door open to the huge Sydney shopping centre.

"Come on, come on," Crayfellow shouted. "In!"

Lewis got up, running through the open door to the centre. "Get them doors sealed," he yelled.

"With what?" Crayfellow panicked.

The zombies slammed into the doors of the shopping centre. Lewis looked to the right and saw a suit tailor shop. It hadn't been looted out. Hanging outside was a belt stand. "Shit," he gasped. "Hold them doors." Lewis ran over and picked up the leather belts off the stand. He ran back over looping the strong leather material through the shiny door handles, pulling them closed. Crayfellow helped to seal the doors closed as the zombies banged on the glass doors. Blood was drying on the clean glass.

"Come on," Lewis said. "Let's get out of here. Try and find a rear exit to get back to the ambulance." Lewis ran through the centre, followed by Lucas and Claire. There was a sudden cracking sound. He skidded to a stop and looked back. His eyes opened wide only to see that the glass doors were starting to crack.

"Fuck," he gasped and looked around.

"Where's the back exit?" he asked.

"This way," Crayfellow replied, pointing.

Lucas ran with Claire as they stared into the empty shops from which all the merchandise had been looted out, Lewis ran into a clothes shop. The other side led to the back exit. He skidded to a stop, holding onto the handgun. He looked through the sight. He jumped when he saw a figure. He continued staring through the sight.

It was Gemma. She just looked at him as he looked down the top of the handgun down towards her.

"Gemma," he gasped.

"Lewis," Gemma burst out.

Lewis lowered the handgun. "I knew I'd find you in here," Lewis said.

"What do you mean?"

"Every time I lose you in here, I always find you in this spot," Lewis replied.

Lewis flashed back to when he used to bring Gemma here shopping. He flashed back to her walking around the clothes with Jasmine as happy female shoppers strolled around, clutching onto their paper bags. Now, memories of people running with fear. A small shadow started to appear from where the changing rooms were.

"Get back," he ordered. Lewis grabbed onto Gemma's arm, pulling away and still holding onto the handgun. Lewis stared through the sight. He watched as Jasmine slowly walked out of the changing room area. She looked to see Lewis standing in the middle of the shop, looking down the handgun at her.

"Lewis," Jasmine called in joy.

Lewis lowered the handgun again. "Jasmine," Lewis replied

"Only just," she replied.

Crayfellow entered the shop looking for Lewis. "Lewis," Ben said, "We have to go."

The cracking of the glass got louder and louder by the second.

Lucas looked at Ben. He shrugged his shoulders, still holding onto the bag. Lewis heard the glass shatter from the quiet shop. Lewis looked through the centre. He squinted to see one of the signs. It pointed to a fire exit.

"This way," he ordered. "Gemma, go!"

Lewis looked back, seeing the shadows of the undead, on the ground, as they were heading towards the shop. Any second now, they would appear. It happened quickly. Three of them entered the shop, their teeth and voices snarling. Lewis spun around and ran out of the shop. He looked ahead to see some stairs. Ben was at the bottom awaiting him.

"Come on, Ben" Lewis ordered.

Ben climbed the stairs, but his foot lost its grip. He slipped, twisting his ankle. "Agggggh!" he screamed in pain "Fuck me!"

Lewis stopped as he heard the scream from Crayfellow, who now lay half-way up the stairs with his hands on his ankle. The zombies sprinted towards him. Lewis started running down the stairs.

"Jackson," Crayfellow yelled. "Leave me!"

"No!" Lewis said. "I'm not leaving you!" Lewis tried to pick up Crayfellow. "Come on," Lewis said.

"Jackson, go," Crayfellow demanded. "I'll hold them off. They need you."

"I'm not losing you."

"Lewis, go!" Ben screamed the order

Crayfellow reached into his pocket and grabbed the keys to the ambulance. "Now, go," Ben demanded again. Ben started to open fire on the zombies.

Gemma waited at the top of the stairs with Lucas and Claire, who were looking down as the zombies sprinting across the glossy floor towards them. "Come on!" Gemma screamed.

Crayfellow swiped his handgun, taking single shots at the zombies as they ran towards him. He fired the last round from the magazine. He reached for his pouch to see if he had any left in the magazine pouch. "Come on," he pleaded, shuffling the pouches and pockets around. There were no magazines left for his weapon. He eyes opened in fear as the zombies dove onto the ground, biting into his neck. He felt the bloody teeth of the zombie bite down into his neck as he started to choke. The rest of the attacking zombies were all trying to get a piece of him. Blood ran down into his lungs as his eyes closed.

Lewis and Gemma came to the exit of the centre. "Now where?" Gemma asked.

Lewis held onto the keys that Crayfellow threw to him. "This way," Lewis said. "Claire, stay with Lucas."

They arrived at the fire exit. Lucas pushed the handle down. The door wouldn't budge. "It won't open," he said.

Lewis stormed up behind the group, kicking the door open. He left the mall, looking out onto the empty child's play area that was next to the building. He looked back into the mall. The zombies arrived at the top of the stairs. Lewis could only stare into the store. He looked at a male zombie who was dressed in a suit, with blood staining the sky-blue shirt and his tie half-undone from where his body heat increased when he was bitten earlier in the day.

Lucas swung his head, looking to see Lewis, who was just standing there, looking into the mall, dazed. The zombie snarled, sprinting towards the fire exit. Lewis slammed the door shut, trying not to make as little noise as possible. He made sure it was locked and couldn't be opened.

"Come on," Lewis ordered. "Move it!" Lewis and Lucas ran ahead, holding onto their handguns and sneaking up the side of the shopping centre towards the front. Lucas looked back at the fire exit, waiting for it to swing open. Lewis peeked around the corner towards the front of the store. The coast was clear. The ambulance was still parked where they had left it a few minutes ago. He stared into the distance, continuing to keep his eye on the mall, seeing if they were waiting for him—or for the fire exit to open. Lewis stood by Gemma's side, holding onto her arm tightly as they snuck through the carpark looking towards the front entrance, seeing that the zombies had made their way into the huge building. Lewis ran across the carpark with Gemma and

Lucas. He opened the two back doors, helping Jasmine in, but something caught Lucas's attention.

He saw that the zombies had made their way around to the other exit and had caught up with them. Lewis slammed the key into the ignition. The ambulance struggled to start. "Oh no," he gasped. "Come on, start, you little fucker. Start!" Lewis struggled to start the ambulance but at last succeeded in starting the engine. Lewis slammed the accelerator down.

Gemma and Jasmine watched as one of the zombies climbed onto the back of the ambulance. Gemma watched as it banged his head into the back window, which was slowly starting to crack. The zombie's cheek skin was starting to peel as it pushed its way through the double-glazed glass.

"Lewis!" Gemma screamed.

Jasmine hunched up into the seat as Claire crawled to the back.

Lewis looked at the cracking glass in the rear-view mirror. "Can you find something to hold onto?"

"Why?" she asked.

"Just do it!"

Gemma looked at the group and saw they all were holding onto something. "We're holding on," she yelled

Lucas pulled out his handgun. "Now," he said, "I'm going to enjoy this." Lucas frowned as Lewis pushed the accelerator down to full. He looked over as the speedometer started to increase. He felt the G-force pushing him into the back of the seat as his hands grasped the steering wheel.

"Just a bit more, please," Lewis said. The speedometer hit seventy. "That'll do nicely."

Lewis reached down, wrenching the handbrake up, he swung the ambulance to the left. Gemma watched as the zombie flew off, slamming into the ground. The wheels smoked, and the smell entered the vehicle through the broken window.

"Yeah," he yelled. "Proud to be an Australian!"

Lucas looked at the zombie rolling off the street. "Now where?" Lucas asked.

Lewis froze for a second, watching the ambulance pick up speed again. "Let's just get to the airport," Lewis said, "and see what's going on there and try get to the evacuation site."

"Do you reckon New Zealand is the place we are going?" Lucas asked.

"No other country is going to allow us, as the whole of Australia has been quarantined—no one in or out," Lewis said. "Let's just hope there is somewhere else—some Pacific island they are using."

"Somewhere with cocktails and a beach," Luas laughed.

Lewis looked up at the street signs that pointed to the airport.

* * *

Kingsford Smith Airport was full of people trying to get into a plane and be evacuated to Hobart. Machine guns were mounted on jeeps as the crowds of people pushed to enter the terminal.

"Keep in line," the soldier ordered.

People continued to push and shove, eager to get onto a plane and out of the city. Lewis looked up, seeing a military blockade. He saw the spotlights shining into the air as armed jeeps and soldiers stood, guarding the entrance to the airport that had been set up for the evacuation of the city.

"This appears to be the place," he said.

Gemma smiled, looking at Lewis as the soldier at the gate put his hand up, stopping the vehicle. Lewis opened the door, looking down the road. He could see the two green Humvee jeeps positioned there guarding the entrance to the airport, machine guns mounted on top. A few survivors going through the scanners to ensure they were free from infection. He looked to see Dylan Blackwater, a man he had served with in the Australian Army a few years before he left.

"Hey, Dylan," Lewis shouted.

Dylan looked up quickly to see Lewis running towards him. "Hey Lewis," Dylan said, "Long time."

Lewis ran up to Dylan.

"Glad you are still alive," Dylan said, shaking his hand

"Me too," Lewis replied. "What the hell has caused this shit?"

"I know only as much as you do," Dylan replied. "All I know is, one minute the cities are normal, and the next minute they have blood-thirsty zombies running around them after you."

"I'm surprised Sydney has anybody left alive!" Lewis replied, "Our police station was overrun a while ago, before I found Gemma at the mall."

"There's not many left alive," replied Dylan. "Canberra, finished. Perth, fucked. Adelaide, finished. Brisbane, all gone, finished."

Gemma walked over, her arms folded, shivering as Lucas stood next to her.

"Who's this?" Dylan asked.

Lewis looked at Gemma. "Oh," Lewis said. "Gemma, meet Dylan." Gemma smiled. "My fiancée," Lewis replied. "Gemma, I served with Dylan."

"How long did you serve together?" Gemma asked.

"About two years," Lewis replied.

Claire walked forward, looking at Dylan. "How are we getting out of here?" Claire asked.

Lewis and the group saw a passenger aircraft that had just taken off from the airport.

"So, flights are still running then?" Lewis asked.

"Only a few," Dylan replied. "We have the aircraft, but not the pilots. But the air force is sending some of theirs over as well to help extract to the evacuation point."

"Where's that?" Lewis asked.

"Hobart."

"Hobart?" Gemma enquired. "Why all the way down there?"

"It's the only place that is free from infection," Dylan said. "So, when you look at it, it is an island, away from the mainland, free of infection—and a new dawn begins for Australia, hopefully."

"How's the evacuation going?" Lewis asked.

"Not good, man," Dylan replied. "Follow me."

Dylan held onto his M16 machine gun. Gemma watched as Lewis and Dylan walked up some metal steps leading to the top of the wall that had been set up around the airport.

"Hey, where did you get that?" Lewis asked.

"What?"

"That," Lewis said, pointing at the M16.

"Oh," Dylan said. "The Americans dropped some extra firepower for us to help fight these things, but I think a lot of the supplies and troops have been sent to Tasmania to assist our boys and girls down there."

Lewis and Dylan came to the top of the stairs overlooking the airport. Lewis looked ahead, down onto the overpass which led over to the airport. There was a huge drop below it. It added to the height sensation. Troops dotted the bridge.

"See for yourself," Dylan said.

Dylan handed Lewis a pair of binoculars. Lewis grabbed hold of them, looking across towards the airport. He couldn't believe his eyes. He focused the binoculars until he saw the terminal building of the famous Kingsford Smith Airport. Long lines of shuffling people were trying to get into the terminal to get on an aircraft and leave the country.

"Jesus!" Lewis mumbled "I'm surprised there are this many left alive."

Lewis handed the binoculars back to Dylan as he walked over to a map of the airport on the desk next to him.

"The airport is completely contained by these walls," Dylan said. "The only way out is across this overpass, along this road, and out this terminal."

"The only way?" Lewis asked.

"Yes," Dylan replied. "The only way out of Australia."

"How long until you seal the gate?" Lewis asked.

"Once we can guarantee everyone beyond these doors is safe," Dylan replied. "Let's just say we are here for a long time."

Gemma walked up to Claire as she held onto her side bag which contained her laptop and other amenities.

"You okay?" Gemma asked.

Claire nodded as she trembled with fear, standing by the gate. She saw Lewis and Dylan walking down the stairs.

"I believe New Zealand is sending one of their jumbos over to get some of their people out," Dylan said, "but as you were saying, due to the location of Hobart and the insufficient air transport, the evacuation of Sydney is going to take a long, long time."

"Why Sydney?" Lewis asked. "Why didn't they evacuate Perth and the other cities?"

"It took us by surprise, this Z virus," Dylan said. "Before we knew it had happened, once great cities had already turned into battlefields with the undead. Because Sydney was the only highly-populated area left, we were ordered to evacuate Sydney to Hobart—well, whoever was left."

Lewis looked down the road to see some lights coming.

"Oh, God," Dylan said.

"Got more company," Lewis said.

Lewis watched as one of the city public buses pulled up to the gate. Dylan grabbed his M16 while walking up to the doors. He saw the old driver, still in uniform. There were frightened passengers in the vehicle.

"Is there anyone on this bus showing symptoms of infection?" Dylan shouted.

The group stayed quiet as Dylan looked down the long bus at the frightened people.

"Okay. One at time, you will need to pass a medical

screening; then we can evacuate you," Dylan ordered. "Please make your way to that gate."

The group started getting up as Lewis, Claire, and Gemma watched the people walk over to the medical detectors which were set up by the gate. Dylan walked up to Lewis as the people went through the gate, one after the other, being cleared of infection.

"So far, so good," Dylan said. "What about you? Are you going through?"

"I'm police," Lewis said. "I have no choice but to stay."

"I'm a nurse," Gemma said. "I can help."

"No, you can't," Lewis replied. "You're pregnant."

Gemma stepped forward. "Hang on. We can't go."

"Why?" Lucas asked.

"My parents are hiding in a warehouse just outside Melbourne," Gemma frittered.

Dylan looked up after hearing 'Melbourne.' "I'll get a message to control," Dylan said, "and maybe see if there are any units left near Melbourne."

Lucas looked down the road and saw some running figures coming towards them. It was a small group of gleaming eyes that were starting to get bigger by the second.

"Shit," Dylan said. "Positions!"

"Gemma, go," Lewis snapped.

"What?" Gemma asked. "What about you?"

"Don't worry about me," Lewis replied. "Get Claire, Jasmine, and yourself out. Lucas, that's your job."

"Sir. . ." Lucas replied.

The last of the people from the bus were scanned by the troops as the zombies slowly started getting closer and closer to the military gate. Lewis held onto his sidearm, looking through the sight.

"Lewis," Dylan yelled. Dylan threw one of the M16s through the air. Lewis caught the weapon as a utility belt with some spare magazines was thrown over as well. Gemma stayed, looking back down the street at the glowing yellow eyes of the running zombies. Gemma stood there while Claire pulled her along, with Jasmine close behind.

"Come on," Claire pleaded.

Lewis and Dylan opened fire as the two troops on the heavy machine guns mounted the Humvee. The soldiers at the scanners continued scanning the last few people as they passed through onto the overpass. Gemma looked back after she was scanned.

"Lewis, you are next," Dylan ordered.

Lewis went through the scanner and saw that he was clean. Dylan ran through, followed by the rest of the troops. He opened a small side door on the gate by lifting the red lever up. The huge, black gate slowly started to roll closed as the two remaining soldiers ran through after jumping off the Humvee, taking shots at the zombies. Dylan heard a sudden jerk. When he turned, he saw, to his utter shock, that the two gates had failed to close, still leaving a gap.

"Oh, fuck, no," he yelled. "Come on, fucking things!"

Dylan ran up to the power box as Lewis assisted with the shooting of the zombies as they continued running towards the gate.

"Come on, push them," he ordered

The soldiers couldn't budge the gates. They were locked open.

"Fuck it," Dylan mumbles. "Fall back!" The soldiers ran back along the overpass. "Let them have it!" Dylan ordered, yelling.

The group opened fire onto the running zombies. They seemed to keep coming, one after the other.

"Bring back memories?" Lewis asked Dylan

"Hell, yeah," he replied

Lewis continued to shoot at the hordes of screaming zombies as they sprinted over the overpass.

Dylan looked ahead. There were too many of them to hold back. "Shit," he uttered. Dylan looked to see his troops were running low on ammunition. "Fall back," Dylan ordered. "Fall back now. Move it, boys."

Lewis and Dylan ran along the overpass, turning around and shooting while running backwards. Dylan reached for his radio. He swiped it from the pouch, looking at the running figures. "Need as much help at the end of the overpass as possible," he requested. "This is urgent."

Lewis looked in the direction of Lucas, Gemma and Claire. "Come on," he scolded them. "I thought I told you to go."

"I'm not leaving you," Gemma insisted.

Dylan looked ahead, seeing the other side of the overpass. He saw some red and blue lights. Six police cars sped up towards the entrance to the overpass. They skidded to the right, trying to help block the road. Dylan pulled out his radio.

"I need an airstrike!" he demanded into the radio. "ASAP. The overpass leading to the airport."

"T-minus three minutes," the operator replied.

"We haven't got three minutes," Dylan screamed.

The zombies sprinted across the overpass towards the shooting officials. Lewis looked through the sight, trying to help slow the zombies down as they waited for the air strike to happen.

"Where is that airstrike?" Dylan yelled into the radio.

"T-minus two minutes," the radio operator said.

"Two minutes," Dylan yelled. "We can do it, boys."

Lewis continued shooting at the zombies, slowly putting them down, one after the other.

"Lewis, just go," Dylan demanded. "We can hold them. Get Gemma and the rest to safety."

Lewis swung his head, looking at Dylan as he loaded the last magazine into the underneath of the M16.

"What?" he gasped. "You sure?"

Dylan looked Lewis in the eyes. "I'm sure."

Lewis got up. He and Dylan palm-slammed each other.

"Oh. Lewis," Dylan yelled over the gunfire. Lewis stopped. "Lewis," Dylan said again. "If you can't get out via the airport, if you can, get to the Davenport ferry in Melbourne by tomorrow at twelve; there is another way out of Australia."

"Why there?" Lewis yelled.

The zombies continued to pour onto the overpass.

"The navy are going to stop there tomorrow morning at twelve, and that's the last pickup. After that, there are going to be no more rescues. You got it?" Lewis nodded. "Now, go."

Lewis ran down the street, looking ahead at Claire, Gemma, Jasmine, and Lucas.

Dylan heard his M16 suddenly click. "Shit," he gasped. Dylan pulled out the radio. "Where is that airstrike?"

Before the operator could return the call to Dylan, she heard some horrific screams from the group at the airport.

Lewis looked back along the overpass, seeing that the zombies had broken through the police and military barricade. "Shit," he gasped. He looked down over the side of the overpass. It was a short drop, but they could make it.

"Gemma," Lewis yelled. Gemma looked back at the zombies as Lewis looked down onto the grass patch below. "We've got to jump," Lewis said.

"What?" Gemma gasped. "We'll never make it."

Lewis looked back up the overpass, seeing the zombies getting closer and closer by the second and the snarls getting louder. The airstrike was still nowhere to be seen.

"Lucas," Lewis yelled. "You go first and catch the rest, one after the other."

"Understood."

Lucas sat on the side of the overpass. "Here goes. . ." Lucas slid off the side of the overpass. He landed on the grass. He looked through the sight of his handgun. Not a living could be seen.

"Send them down," he yelled up.

"Okay, Gemma," Lewis said.

Jasmine panted for breath, looking at Gemma. "I'm right behind," Jasmine said. "Go on, you can do it."

Lewis helped Gemma up onto the side of the overpass as the zombies ran closer and closer. All the troops and police at the bridge were now dead. Jasmine looked back as Lewis got onto the overpass.

"Okay. On three," Lewis said.

Gemma nodded, wiping a few tears away from her face. Lucas looked up as Gemma sat down, getting ready to jump.

"One, two. . ." Lewis said. Lewis shoved Gemma off the side of the overpass. He then helped Claire down off the overpass in the same way. Then, he looked to Jasmine, who was staring in horror at the zombies as they sprinted down the overpass towards them. Lewis helped Jasmine onto the side of the overpass as Gemma was helped up by Lucas down below.

"Are you okay?" Lucas asked Gemma.

Gemma replied with much relief. "Yes, I'm fine." Gemma looked up at Lewis and Jasmine as they stood on top of the overpass.

"Okay, Jasmine," Lewis said. "Let's go." Lewis leapt off the side of the overpass as Jasmine stopped, looking down onto Gemma. Lewis landed on the ground, looking up, seeing Jasmine still standing on the side.

"What?" Lewis gasped. "Jasmine, come on!" Jasmine just stood on the overpass road looking down at the group and trembling with fear.

"Jasmine," Gemma yelled. "Come on, you can make it." Gemma looked at Lewis. "She is scared of heights."

"What?" Lucas asked, looking up at her.

"Jasmine, come on," Lewis pleaded with her.

Jasmine continued to look down at the group. She turned her head, seeing the zombies as they arrived at the lower part of the overpass. Jasmine looked ahead towards the airport. She stepped down off the side of the overpass.

"Jasmine!" Gemma screamed.

"Gemma, no!" Lewis said.

"Jasmine!" Gemma yelled up again.

"Gemma!" Lewis said. "If any of them things are near, they will hear."

Gemma frittered about. Jasmine looked back as she ran along the overpass. She stumbled to the ground, with the zombies diving onto her. Gemma and Lewis heard her screams.

"Gemma, come on," Lewis pleaded. "We have to get out of here."

"No," Gemma yelled. "Jasmine. . ."

"Gemma, come on," Lewis said. "She was dead before them things caught up." Lewis pulled Gemma along, followed by Lucas and Claire. The road was nearly empty with just a few cars scattered about it. Lewis held onto his sidearm looking ahead down the road, into the distance. He watched as a small light started to get bigger. It was the airstrike. He looked about back and forth for somewhere to hide from the pending explosion that was about to occur. The F-35s swooped down towards the bridge as the zombies ran across the overpass. The people at the airport did not have a chance whatsoever to get out of the country now. The underneath of the jet opened. The two sidewinder rockets blasted from underneath. Lewis skidded to a stop. He blinked as the missiles passed his head, heading for the overpass.

"Down!" Lewis screamed

"Claire, get down!" Lucas ordered

Lewis helped Gemma to the ground. The two rockets slammed into the concrete bollards holding the pass up. The explosion blasted over the top of them. Flumes of dust and muck blew up into the air. Lewis felt small bits of asphalt and muck land onto his head. He watched as the asphalt road caved down onto the road. The zombie figures slid down the road as it caved in onto the road below. Lewis started to stand up. He watched as the zombie figures, one after the other, tumbled down onto the road. He re-focused his attention on Gemma.

"Hey, you okay?" he asked her.

Gemma got up off the road, looking at the dust ahead as it started to settle. The overpass continued to cave in in front of them.

"What about the people?" Claire asked.

Lewis stood up straight, staring at the small flume of dust that had started to roll towards them. The bridge had been blocked from sight for a few seconds. Lewis stared into the dust, reaching for his sidearm. His eyes squinted. He watched as three zombies blasted through the dust towards the group. "I knew that would happen," he said.

"Come on," Lucas ordered.

The group turned around and ran down the street.

The people at the airport listened in fear as the shooting stopped. The last thing they heard was the explosion from the airstrike. The zombies sprinted down towards the terminal.

"They are coming," a voice yelled. "Run."

"Hey," a soldier yelled. "You can't go through."

People were pushing their way into the airport terminal, screaming. The New Zealanders were boarded onto the 777 jet that had been sent over from Auckland.

"Come on. Move," the soldier ordered.

The soldier looked down the jetway, seeing more people running towards the aircraft. "It's full," he shouted at them. The soldier turned his head as the cabin attendant swung the door shut.

"Shit," he gasped

Captain Stanfield looked out the side of the cockpit window as the terrified people ran into the terminal. "Let's get out of here," he said.

The two engines were fired up as the solider on the ground pushed the aircraft back from the stand. Stanfield pushed the throttles forward, quickly taxying towards the runway. The zombies attacked the airport from all corners. All of the corners had been breached.

"Shit," Stanfield gasped as he grasped the control stick, turning the aircraft's nose wheel.

"Where we going?" the first officer demanded.

"Zero-seven," he replied

"What?" the officer gasped. "To the short runway?" Stanfield looked out the front window at the chasing zombies. "Okay," he said

Stanfield picked up speed, heading towards runway seven. The zombies filled the taxiway ahead. "Shit," Stanfield gasped. He saw an early entry point for the runway. "Fuck it," he yelped pulling onto the runway.

"We'll never get off the runway in time," the first officer insisted.

"Kingsford Smith tower," Stanfield said. "We are out of here."

"Zealand Two-one-two," the controller said. "What—Oh, no, no! Help, help, help!"

The captain closed his eyes, hearing the screams from the controller. "I think that's our clearance," he said.

Stanfield pushed the two brake pedals down, setting the take-off thrust. The aircraft started to shake as the engines continued to power up. Stanfield watched as the runway started to fill with the zombies. He released the brakes, feeling the extreme G-force as they started to pick up speed. The take-off was sluggish; it was taking a bit longer for the aircraft to pick up speed because of the extra fuel he picked up in Auckland. He looked down at the speedometer as the aircraft continued to pick up speed. The first officer looked ahead, seeing the zombies getting closer. They were nowhere near the rotation speed. Captain Stanfield just stared down at the avionics as they passed one hundred knots.

"Sir, we're not going to lift off in time," the officer said

"Yes, we will." Stanfield stared down at the speedometer,

grasping the control stick. The red lights came into view indicating they were near the end of the runway.

"Sir!" the first officer yelled.

"Fuck it!" Stanfield yelped. Stanfield reached over, grabbing the flap lever. He lifted it, putting it to full. The flaps lowered down slowly. They entered the end of the runway. The lights beamed red.

"Thirty degrees," the first officer screamed.

"That will do," Stanfield replied pulling the control yoke back. The extra flap and lift helped pull the jet off the runway. "God, that was close."

The huge jet climbed into the clear night sky. The moon gleamed down as the jet turned to the right, heading east towards Auckland. Sydney slowly got smaller and smaller. People stared down out the windows onto Sydney as the few gleaming houses started to get slammer and smaller, disappearing as they pulled out over the Pacific Ocean.

* * *

Lewis looked down the side street. They managed to get off the highway a minute ago, away from the chasing zombies. He grasped the handgun, looking to see the car park of a local food store coming into view. He looked at the dark, gloomy building. There were no shoppers—just an empty car park with a few carrier bags blowing around it. The occasional trolley squeak was heard as it wheeled across the car park.

"In here," Lewis said. "Let's get undercover."

"Then what?" Gemma asked.

"We'll see when we get inside," Lewis replied. He looked around the empty car park. Shopping trolleys were littered all over the place. There was also spilt food, trampled-on eggs, and some tins. Claire looked at one of the trolleys. Blood stained the gleaming metal. She started to gag.

"Hey," Lucas said. "You okay?" Claire continued to stare at the blood covered trolley. "Come on," he ordered.

Lucas pulled Claire away from the trolley as Gemma looked through the automatic doors. No one could be seen. Lucas peered over his shoulder, looking into the dead carpark, watching the small plastic carrier bag slowly blow across the car park and into the distance, slowly disappearing from sight.

"Is it safe?" Gemma trembled.

Lewis looked forward again, through the automatic doors into the dark shop.

"Well, there's only one way to find out."

Claire stood by Lucas. Lewis put his hands in between the two rubber grips, slowly sliding the doors open. "In," he whispered. "Fast."

Lucas entered the store first as Lewis covered the rear, looking down the streets for zombies. The coast was clear. Lewis walked back into the store and then sealed the doors closed, looking around all the empty aisles which had been looted out. Lucas walked over to the counter and looked at the very few tins of food that were left. He reached his hand and picked up a small, silver tin. He turned it and saw that it was just ordinary cat food.

"Ha," Lewis said. "Even cat food had been looted; people must have just come in and grabbed whatever they could without even taking a second to think." Lewis turned around as Claire walked next to Gemma.

"Are you okay?" Gemma asked, trying to calm Claire's nerves. Claire nodded.

Lewis stood by the open door, looking towards the front exit of the store. He placed his hand on the sidearm, ready to swipe it. "Okay," Lewis said. "Stick together. Try and find some water or something."

But before the group could walk off in different directions, a light crash was heard; Lewis and Gemma started in its direction. They looked into the dark stock warehouse. L Lewis continued to stare at the open door leading into the stock warehouse. He walked in, looking at the shiny trolleys slammed into each other, some with food on them.

"What is he doing now?" Claire asked Lucas.

"He's just making sure the place is secure before we rest," he replied.

Lewis entered the rear stock room and saw that it had also been looted out, leaving no food or drink. He heard a slight stumble somewhere deep in the interior of the warehouse. He grasped the handgun and the torch firmly, and he crept along the dirty floor. Lucas entered the warehouse and was soon close behind Lewis.

"Wait here," Lewis said. "Stay with Gemma and Claire."

Lucas turned around, heading back into the store.

"Hey," Lewis snapped, looking out of the warehouse.

Lucas turned around.

Lewis signalled Lucas to look around the store as he went further into the rear. He could hear his boots scrape along the cold concrete floor. "Hello? Anyone here?" he asked. Lewis continued looking through the sight of the handgun, still grasping the torch and shining it on the looted-out cages of food.

"Don't shoot." There came a tired voice.

Lewis swung his head, looking down the top of the gun through the sight. Lewis looked down onto a middle-aged man who was quite shivery and nervous.

"Don't shoot," he said again. "Please, don't shoot. I'm not one of them things."

Lewis lowered the handgun, switched the torch off, and helped the man up. Lewis looked at the blue uniform and the Australian Railway Company logo on the waistcoat.

"Who are you?"

"Name's Eric."

"Hello, Eric," Lewis said. "Welcome to our friendly little group."

Eric stumbled up and slowly staggered through to the main shopping area.

"Who's this?" Lucas asked.

Lewis looked at Eric and said. "Guys, meet Eric. Eric, they are Lucas, Claire, and Gemma."

Eric looked at Gemma and Claire as they stood in the middle of the store floor. "So, how are we getting to the airport?" Eric asked. "I heard they are evacuating people from there," he said as Gemma stormed away into the aisles of the store, wiping tears away from her face.

"Gemma," Lewis said.

"What?" Eric said. "What did I say?"

Lucas walked over to Eric and placed his hand on his shoulder. "The airport was overrun a while ago," Lucas informed him. "She lost one of her friends there."

Eric looked over at Lewis as he hugged Gemma. "Look, I'm—"

"It's okay," Lewis said to Eric. "You didn't know."

Gemma and Lewis walked back to the group a few minutes later.

"What do we do now?" Lucas asked. "Stay here?"

"No, we can't stay here," Lewis replied. "Way too dangerous. Our best bet is to keep moving and try to get to Hobart."

"Hobart? Why all the way down there?" Eric wanted to know.

Lewis folded his arms, looking over again at the front entrance to the store.

"So," Lucas asked, "what do we do?"

"We get to Melbourne," Lewis replied.

Eric looked up when he heard Lewis speaking about Melbourne. "Hey," Eric said. "I'm a train operator. I was due to take the thirteen-thirty to Melbourne."

"Melbourne?" Gemma said. "That's where. . ."

Lewis swung his head looking at Eric. "Are the lines still in operation?" Lewis demanded.

"They were closed down when the infection of these things was spreading," Eric stated.

"No! What I mean is, do the lines still have electrical current running through them?" asked Lewis.

"Yes, they do," Eric replied. "The army was going to use them as a way of evacuating the main cities into the outback away from infection. Well, the train I drive isn't electric, its diesel."

"All right," Lewis said. "Suppose you come with us to the main railway station, and we find you a train. Could you take us to Melbourne?"

"Well, yes, I can. Why all the way down there?"

"Because her parents are hiding out in their warehouse," Lewis said. "And from there, we can get to a safe zone."

"What safe zone?" Eric asked.

"Hobart," Lewis explained.

Eric looked shocked.

"The Australian Navy is going to stop at the Davenport ferry in Melbourne and then will move to Tasmania," Lewis said. "So, we had better make haste."

"Well, let us get out of here," Eric supported it.

"How far is the main station from here?" Lucas asked.

"About six miles," Eric said.

"Well, we had better get going then, hadn't we?" Lucas replied.

There was a sudden crash from the main entrance. Lewis spun around. He swiped his handgun. Zombies were slamming into the strong glass automatic doors, trying to get in, with gleaming yellow eyes focusing on the group.

"Shit," Eric panicked. "What do we do?" Eric looked back into the warehouse.

"Lucas," Lewis said. "Get Gemma, Claire, and Eric out through the back fire exit and wait for me out there."

Lucas led the group into the warehouse. "Look—the fire exit," Lucas said. "Come on, go." Lucas led the group through the warehouse, grasping the weapon in his hand. Lewis was slowly walking up to the front door of the store, looking at the blood-thirsty zombies outside banging on the glass, trying to get in. He took a shallow breath, looking at the handprint of blood as it is smeared down the front of the door, drying at the same time as well.

"What are you thinking?" Lewis asked.

The zombies continued to bang and thump on the door. Blood was spread across all of the glass panels.

"What are you saying to me?" Lewis said under his breath. Lewis looked up as the glass on the sealed automatic doors started to crack. "Shit, I'm out," he said.

Lewis spun around and ran along through the empty aisles of the shopping centre as the zombies broke through the glass. He watched as the glass cut their faces, ripping skin off onto the glass. Lewis came to the warehouse, running out towards the fire exit. He slammed the door shut, knowing it wasn't going to hold closed.

"Lewis!" Gemma shrieked.

Lewis could see Gemma, Claire, and Lucas by an alleyway entrance leading into the back streets of the empty housing estate. He ran up to them. "Come on," he ordered

Lewis peeked around the corner of the alleyway entrance. The zombies ran out of the store's back emergency exit. They stopped, looking around. Lewis continued to observe them as they snarled. They slowly turned around, running back into the store. Lewis ran up the alleyway.

CHAPTER FIFTEEN

Tony Brown sat down at the desk, looking up at the screen of Australia. He had been on a short break outside of the ship. He stared up at Sydney as it was the only city left with some form of civilization. Brown rubbed his hands and asked, "How is the evacuation going from Kingsford Smith Airport?"

Before General Kingsley could reply to the question from the PM, one of the sailors entered the ship's command room. He didn't even knock. He just burst in, as the information was emergent.

Brown looked at the sailor as he whispered into the general's ear. "You can speak up," he insisted.

The sailor didn't respond to Brown as he stood up straight. He turned around and left the command room. Kingsley looked over at the prime minister.

"What?" Brown asked. "What is it?"

General Kingsley stood up. He rubbed his uniform flat as he stood up, looking down onto the prime minister. Brown watched as he started to scratch the back of his head, looking away, breaking the eye contact.

"What?" Brown asked again. "What is it?"

Kingsley looked up. "I'm sorry, sir," he said. "Kingsford Smith was overrun a short while ago."

Tony stared in disbelief. "What?" he gasped. "No."

"Apparently, sir, we believe the entrance gate to the airport jammed open when they came under attack," Kingsley replied. "And—and. . ." Kingsley looked at the prime minister as he sat down onto the swivel chair. His fists started to turn white with blood constriction. He banged his hands on the table. General Kingsley turned around and pushed a key on the keyboard. He watched as the last red dot which showed Sydney's location disappeared. The screen went blank.

"You did everything you could, sir," Kingsley assured the prime minister.

"I don't want to hear it," Brown snapped.

Brown got up and stormed out of the control room on the HMS frigate. He pulled his tie off and threw it onto the ground. He walked up the thin corridors of the ship, heading to the private quarters where they were waiting to see him. All the sailors stood with their backs to the wall, allowing him to storm past them. Brown arrived at the door. Two sailors stood guarding the entrance. He gave a gentle tap on the door. His wife slowly got up off the bed walking up to the door. His daughter was sitting on the bed. She was humming, colouring in a picture. His wife slowly walked up to the door, looking through the small spy hole and seeing Tony, standing there, with no tie on, just looking at the door waiting for her to open it. She knew something was wrong because he wouldn't have knocked otherwise. She turned the handle, opening the door. He still just stood there, his arms shoulder-width apart, just looking at her. The top button on his shirt was undone. He just stared at her, looking at her eyes. She started to shake her head, she knew it had to be something to do with Sydney. She placed her two hands over her mouth.

"No," she whispered. "No."

Tony's facial expressions changed; his upper body started to relax.

"No," she said again.

Brown entered the room. He looked at his daughter lying on the bed and colouring the picture.

"It's Charlie's party tomorrow," she said looking down at the book. "Am I going to go?"

Brown looked up to see one of the sailors standing outside the room. "Sailor, can you take my daughter and get her something to eat, please? I think she is really hungry, and she has been a very good girl."

"Certainly, sir," the sailor replied. "Come on, let's go get you a drink."

Brown watched as his daughter slowly walked out of the living area. The metal door was closed after them. "We lost contact with the Sydney evacuation team thirty minutes ago," Brown said remorsefully. "We tried but just lost complete control of the situation." Brown hugged his wife as tears started to run down the side of her face.

"Well," she sniffled. "What next?"

Brown didn't hesitate to speak for a second. "We stay here, where it is safe. However, we did manage to evacuate a lot of people to Hobart. The Americans are still sending troops and resources there as we speak."

"That's some good news," his wife cried.

Tony looked up as his wife continued to cry into his arms. "It's okay." He tried to comfort her.

"No, it's not okay," she replied. "Our friends, her friends and family, are all dead."

Brown didn't know how to reply. "I'm going to find out who caused this horrific attack and make sure they pay," Brown insisted. "I promise you that. No one dies in vain in my country." Brown let his wife go. "I've got work to do," he said.

"Tony, no," she wept. "Stay with me, please."

"I've got a job to do," he replied. "I need to go and check

on the status of Tasmania and Hobart. Plus, I have got to speak to world leaders."

She gently nodded, watching him turn around. He opened the door, looking at the two sailors guarding the entrance. He stormed down the corridors.

* * *

Lewis poked his head out of the alleyway entrance. He looked into a house. The roads were empty, and there were no cars in the driveways. Food and paper lay scattered about everywhere. Toys littered the streets, dropped by the frightened children. Lewis saw visions of parents trying to drag their children to safety.

"God, look at this place!" Gemma said to Claire. Claire didn't reply. Gemma walked close to Claire, looking at all of the empty houses.

Lewis walked up to the driveway of a house. The light had been left on. He walked on the gravel, trying not to make it crunch. He walked up to the window of the front room. He peered through the gap in the curtains, catching a glimpse of the flickering static television. No more news broadcasts were on. He pictured the family out of his imagination in the house: the toddler sitting on the white plastic mat, playing with toys; the young mother walking around the house on the phone, chatting and awaiting her husband to come in from the outside; the sun shining in through the window as the mother continued to walk around.

"Yeah, he is fine," she replied. The mother walked over to the toddler. She reached down, picking him and putting the phone back to her ear. "Yeah he's fine," she replied again "He is out back gardening. It relieves pressure from the job he does"

She turned looking to see Lewis looking through the window. "I've got to go," she said. "I have a police officer at the window." The lady walked over to the window. "Lewis," she said

Lewis frowned, hearing Gemma's tone of voice.

"Lewis" the mother said again.

"Lewis," Gemma said.

Lewis jumped out of his dream, seeing Gemma standing next to him. He didn't hear her walk up to him. No crunching of the stones was heard. Lewis took another look through the window into the house. The living room was dark. Kids toys were everywhere. Drawers were flung open with utility bills on the floor.

"Come on, let's go," Lewis ordered.

Lewis turned around, looking down the street. The streetlamps were still running. The street has a slight bend to it. He couldn't see around it.

Lucas walked over, still grasping the bag over his shoulder. "So," Lucas began. "You know these streets; where is this railroad station?"

Lewis looked at Eric. "Not too far," Eric replied. "We're about five miles from the city center now"

"Shall we roll, then?" No one replied for some time.

"We go to the station," Lewis said at last. "Get on a train, get to Melbourne, and then to that last navy pickup and, hopefully, live a peaceful life."

Lewis kept his hand by his handgun. He looked at some of the other houses on the estate. A small cabin bag was lying in the doorway of a house. Blood had covered it. The handle was still in the up position. Lewis looked away, trying not to go back into one of the daydreams he had had only a minute ago. He started to focus his attention on Eric.

"So, how long is it going to take to get to Melbourne?" Lewis asked Eric. Eric continued walking along the pavement, looking at the streets ahead of him. "Eric?" Lewis asked again.

"Huh, what?" Eric replied.

"How long does it take to get to Melbourne?" Lewis asked again.

"Oh, about nine hours direct full speed, but depends."

"Depends on what?" Lewis persisted.

Eric took a breath. "If the points are wrong," Eric said gloomily, "we are going nowhere."

"Why is that?" Lewis enquired.

"Because if it is on the wrong line, it is not going to its destination. There is a control room at Sydney central station. I can set the points from there for the whole track—with some luck."

"That had better be our first stop then," Lewis decided.

Lucas looked over at the other side of the street. He looked to see some yellow barriers that had been set up by the police. One white patrol car was parked behind the barriers. Lucas slowly walked over, looking at the clean, white New South Wales police cruiser blocking the street. Golden bullet cases lined the middle of the street. Lewis walked up to the vehicle and looked in the front, by the driver's seat. He opened the doors, pulling down the dashboard. No weapon, nothing. Not even a spare magazine.

"Nothing," Lewis said sadly. "Not even a spare magazine."

Lucas reached in and pulled out one of the police radios. There were two of them.

"I'm channel seven," Lewis said, throwing one over to Lucas. "Just in case we get split up or can't speak too loudly."

Lucas saw the key in the ignition. He slowly reached for the ignition to see if they could drive to the train station. Lewis looked at the dashboard and saw the siren. The lights were switched to the 'on' position.

"Hey, wait," Lewis insisted. Before Lewis could prevent it, Lucas turned the keys in the ignition. The lights and sirens of the vehicle were switched on.

"What?" Lucas screamed. "Shit, no!"

The blue and red lights gleamed through the street. The sirens screamed as well. Lewis looked up into the distance, seeing the glowing yellow eyes of the zombies as they ran towards them.

"Turn them off," Lewis commanded.

Lucas reached in, shutting the engine down. The lights continued to run. He looked up, seeing the gleaming eyes of the zombies.

"Move it," Lewis yelled. "That way!"

Lucas ran along the pavement.

"Lucas," Lewis ordered. "Go that way. I'll slow them down."

"Got it," he replied.

"Lewis," Gemma called

"Gemma, go," he insisted

Lewis turned around, looking at the small group of zombies as they ran towards them. He swiped his handgun, looking through the sight and taking single shots at the zombies, one after the other. Lewis spun around, running into the housing estate. He looked to his right, where he saw one of the zombies running towards him. He saw that the top of the handgun had pinged back; he was out of ammunition. He reached into the pouch, feeling for any magazines. He had none left. "Shit," he gasped.

Lewis reached for the extending baton. He swiped it from the pouch, flicking it out. He had one chance at striking. The zombies snarled and ran towards Lewis. Lewis heard a shot. He watched as the female zombie fell to the ground. He swung his head to the left to see somebody whose face was completely covered in a balaclava. The person in the balaclava pulled the trigger again. Lewis squinted his eyes closed as the bullet travelled past his head, slamming into a zombie that was behind him, about to attack. Lewis looked down at the two dead zombies on the ground. He saw two clean shots, direct to their heads.

"This way," the shooter directed.

Lewis ran through the streets towards a city bus. Zombies were charging in from the other streets.

"Come on," the voice yelled. "Get this thing moving!"

Lewis dove into the bus. He looked out of the window to

see the glowing eyes of the zombies as they ran closer and closer to them.

"Drive!" the person yelled.

The bus slowly started to roll as the zombies chased after them. Lewis sat back against the window, looking out onto the snarling infected.

"Are you okay?" Lewis asked Gemma.

Gemma nodded, wiping a few tears away from her face. "Oh, God, I want to get out of here," she cried.

"Hey," Lewis said. "It is going to be okay."

The zombies started to disappear as the bus picked up speed. Lewis got up, walking down to the front of the bus. "Thanks" Lewis said. "For back there."

"Not a problem," the man replied. Lewis watched as the man ripped off his balaclava. Lewis couldn't believe his eyes; it was Arron Philips—the man who had tried to kill him a few years ago, when Bob had saved Lewis's life.

"You?" Lewis snapped pointing the firearm at Arron as he continued looking up the main street out the front of the bus.

"It's okay," Arron said. "You can kill me if you wish; it saves me doing it later."

Lewis lowered the empty handgun, slipping it back into the pouch as the bus continued along the streets.

"Here," Arron said. "Take these." Arron handed Lewis a few magazine clips.

"Just in case," Arron said. "If you do want to carry out my wish and take revenge for Hudson's death, be my guest."

Lewis looked into the window, seeing a reflection of the rear. He turned around. A huge man was slowly walking towards him with anger in his eyes and tattoos covering his arm. He was grasping a blood-covered pickaxe. Lewis got up, reaching for his sidearm.

"Leave it," Philips ordered. "He's okay."

The huge man walked backwards and sat back down on his chair.

"So," Lewis said to Arron in a monotonic voice. "They let you out to try and fight the infected?"

"They sure did," Arron replied.

Gemma walked down to the front of the bus. She wanted to be with Lewis. "Who is this?" she asked.

Lewis looked forward at Arron as he stared out the front of the bus.

"It is okay," Arron said. "Tell her. I don't care anymore."

"Gemma. . ." Lewis hesitated for a few seconds.

"Tell her," Arron insisted. "Somebody else to hate me!"

Lewis looked down towards the front of the bus, looking at the streets ahead. "He was the one who tried to kill me that time," Lewis said. "You remember, when Bob saved me."

"What?" Gemma gasped.

"He was the one who tried to kill me a couple of years ago," Lewis said again. "You remember, when Bob saved me."

The bus swung to the left.

"So Mr Philips," Lewis said.

"Yes, Mr Jackson?" Arron replied.

"Don't get smart," Lewis replied. "Where are we going?"

"See for yourself," Arron replied.

Gemma and Lewis both looked up to see the city scrapyard. Lewis squinted at the two huge gates which had slowly started to open. Someone stood on the fence overlooking the city. He was holding onto a baseball bat. A number of bin-fires dotted the yard. People were hiding inside scrap cars, away from the zombies if they broke through the barriers. The bus stopped, and the engine shut down. Only the crackling of fires could be heard from the metal bins.

"What is this place?" Gemma asked.

"I don't know," Lewis said, "but I am going to find out." Lewis walked down to the front of the bus as the metal gates were closed. Sydney disappeared behind them. He stepped down from the bus onto the bumpy ground. Gemma stood by

Lewis's side as Lucas held onto his bag, looking around the yard. The night sky was clear. Stars shone down on Australia. Lewis looked up at the backstreet gang members, who were holding on to cricket bats and other similar weapons. They were all gang members. Some were armed with bats that had huge, rusty nails sticking from them while some held knives, and still others had anything that could be used to fight the zombies.

A female figure sat in with the group of people. She squinted her eyes. She looked in disbelief. It was Juliana Reeves, She was sitting in the corner, trying to keep her head down and out of the way. She slowly lifted her head and saw Lewis storming through the yard.

"Oh my God!" Juliana gasped.

She quickly got up and started walking quickly over to Lewis as he kept his eyes on her.

"Great," he mumbled. "Her."

"What?" Gemma asked, trying to keep the conversation going.

"She was at the hearing today about Bob's death," Lewis replied.

Juliana walked up to him. "You're Lewis Jackson?"

Before Julianna could continue the conversation, Lewis replied. "Yes, that's me."

"I was at. . ."

"I know," Lewis interrupted. "I saw you."

Juliana went quiet for a few seconds.

"Broadcasting twenty-four hours," Lewis said.

Juliana started to turn on her shoes, trying to distract Lewis after what he had just said to her. "Oh, that," she said. "Sorry—under orders."

"So, why did you go off?" Lucas asked as he stood there.

Juliana started to stutter. "Orders."

Gemma stuck to Lewis as he walked into the scrapyard. People were hiding inside burnt and rusty vehicles. Gang members and backstreet people were looking out into the dark streets for zombies.

"This way," Philips told Lewis.

Lewis didn't reply to Arron's order. He followed him into a corner of the scrapyard. He looked to see a figure, sitting down, surrounded by a few of the gang members. They were standing by his side, just awaiting his orders, scared to say 'no.' Lewis blinked. He stepped to the left, allowing the light from the bins behind him to show the figure's face. He couldn't believe his eyes. Leif Dasinger was sitting down on a chair in front of him.

"You?" Lewis asked and looked at Leif Dasinger.

There was a short pause before Dasinger spoke. "Well, well, well. Officer Lewis Jackson," Leif Dasinger spoke monotonically. "We haven't spoken in ages. I heard about Officer Hudson this very morning; what a pity!"

"So," Lewis said. "Where have you been hiding all these months? Every cop in the New South Wales division has been looking for you."

Dasinger shrugged his shoulders. "I've been around"

"Many drug runs lately?" Lewis asked. "Any more people you extorted for money? I bet the list goes on!"

"Well, quite a lot," he replied. "But that's all in the past now, Australia is a totally different country now."

"How can you sit there and say that?" Lewis asked.

Gemma walked over to Juliana Reeves, still keeping her eye on Lewis. Julianna had her small camcorder out, filming the conversation between Leif Dasinger and Lewis in the distance.

"Hey, what are you doing?" Gemma asked.

Juliana snapped the camcorder screen that she was holding. "Oh, this? Just taping a few bits to put to good use—that's if any of us make it out of here alive," Julianna replied to Gemma slipping the camcorder back into her bag.

"How did you find this place?" Gemma asked.

Juliana stayed quiet for a few seconds before replying.

"When New South Wales News went off the air, we decided to evacuate and leave it to the emergency broadcast system.; I and a colleague left the studio, but we came under attack by these things not long after we left."

"Zombies?" Claire said.

Juliana held a sarcastic smile when she looked up at Lewis. He was still talking to Leif Dasinger.

"So," Dasinger said. "What are you going to do to me, Mr Jackson? Radio for some backup?"

"What do you mean?"

Leif Dasinger stayed quiet for a few seconds. "Well, now that you have got me, are you going to arrest me and take me to the station? Oh, but I heard that place got overrun a while back."

Lewis looked over at Gemma as she stood by Claire and Lucas. "No, I'll wait until Australia has reopened, and then I am going to come and hunt you down," Lewis said.

Gemma stood by the metal wall of the scrapyard, looking up at one of the gang members as he stood up on the set-up tower, watching the streets for any zombies. He just stared out into the distance. He held a baseball bat with a small rusty nail sticking out of its end.

Gemma suddenly felt some vibrations beneath her feet. She looked down at the ground as the vibrations got heavier by the second. "Can you feel that?" she asked.

"Feel what?" Lucas asked.

"That," she replied.

Lucas stood still looking down at the ground. He could feel the small vibrations in the ground starting to get heavier by the second, too. Lewis peered over his shoulder, at Gemma as she stared down at the ground.

Lewis stormed over to Gemma. One of the gang members looked down at the ground, feeling it vibrate as well. He walked over to a small hole in the metal wall that had been drilled. He peered through it.

"What is that?" she asked again.

"Shhhh."

"What?" Gemma asked

"Shhhh," he snapped louder.

Lewis arrived at Gemma as the gang member snapped at her. "Hey, don't shush her like that," Lewis snapped.

"Listen," the gang member ordered.

Lewis pulled his handgun out before walking over to the fence of the yard to peep through the hole. Lucas stood behind him, trying to catch a glimpse of the outside. He felt the ground vibrate gently beneath his feet. Gemma looked through the tiny gap in the fence, seeing an object suddenly appear in the distance. It had a slight yellow gleam.

"What the. . . ?" Lewis gasped seeing a single glowing, yellow eye. The light from the scrapyard shone down showing the figure of a rhino. Lewis squinted his eyes, to see the bullet holes in the side of the rhino's body where service personnel had tried to kill it. His eyes opened wide. The animal stopped in its tracks, looking over at the scrapyard unaware of the presence in the yard.

"Stay very quiet," Lewis said.

The gang member looked down at the rhino. Lewis stared at the Rhino as it started to look away from the scrapyard. It just stood there, steam rushing out of its nose. Lewis trembled, staring at the zombie as the gang member sat above on the tower. The rhino scoffed along the ground.

"Come on," Lewis pleaded.

The Rhino started to slowly walk away from the scrapyard, unaware of the people looking at him. Lewis looked up at the gang member. He held onto his handgun as the animal slowly strolled away. The gang member slipped his handgun back into his pocket. He reached down for the bat accidentally knocking it through the metal pole. Lewis looked in horror as the bat tumbled, rotating in the air, from the top of the tower slamming into the ground. The clunk echoed around the empty streets. It continued to bounce onto the concrete ground.

The rhino looked back quickly. It saw the gang member, standing on the tower. Lewis stared through the hole.

"Shit," The gang member panicked.

Lewis watched the gang member look through the sight of his handgun.

"No!" Lewis called.

The kid opened fire onto the rhino. The Rhino looked over and up at the gang member as he looked through the sight of the handgun again.

"Lewis," he called, trying not to yelp. But it was too late. The member squeezed the trigger in. He launched the bullets one after the other. The rhino scoffed his hoof along the ground and then charged towards the scrapyard.

"Shit!" the gang member gasped. "Everybody back!"

The rhino slammed into the metal wall. The gang member tumbled from the tower, landing outside the compound. He landed on his stomach, feeling the pain rush through his body. He struggled to stand up as the Rhino slammed back into the compound, eager to break in. The gang member slowly staggered up off the ground. He had twisted his ankle and could hardly walk. He staggered along. The rhino stopped, looking to the left, seeing the staggering man. The rhino then turned, strolling towards the gang member.

"No, please!" The gang member pleaded.

The rhino knocked the man to the ground with his head. The man looked up at the rhino as it stopped, looking down onto him. The rhino opened his mouth, and he bit into the gang member's neck, crunching down onto him. Lewis looked away. Lewis then looked at the rhino as it started headbutting the wall, trying to get in. Gemma ran over, looking at the bits of muck fall onto the ground.

"What is it?" Lucas asked.

"Wait and see," Lewis replied.

Gemma held onto Lewis as the rhino continued to slam into the wall of the scrapyard. A light roar could be heard from the rhino as it suddenly went dead. Only the sound of a few bits of wall could be hard as they fell, hitting the ground, along with the crackling fires as people hid inside the burnt cars, trembling with fear. Lewis looked at the wall, ignoring the gang and prisoners behind him. He just stared at the wall. It was dead silent. He heard a crash. The rhino slammed through the wall. Lewis jumped as smoke and bits of debris were thrown toward him.

"Gemma, down!" he shouted. Lewis helped Gemma down.

"Claire, down!" Lucas ordered. Lucas covered Claire as the bits of concrete wall hit the ground.

Lewis swung his head, looking back at the rhino as it stormed into the scrapyard. "Shit," he gasped. People were scared for their safety as it had now been compromised. The rhino charged towards the shooting gang members. Gemma watched as they were launched over the fence into the outside of the complex. The rhino had made a huge hole in the wall that zombies were sprinting through into the complex.

"Shit," Lucas screamed. Lucas pulled his handgun out of his pocket. He looked through the sight, taking shots at the glowing eyes as they ran towards the scrapyard. Lewis looked at Eric.

"Eric, on the bus," he ordered. "Now."

"Got it," Eric replied.

Lewis took shots at the snarling zombies as they entered the yard. He swung his head around, looking to see Leif Dasinger. He had a machete in his hands as was wearing a leather vest with the top undone. He grasped the plastic end of the weapon. He swung it around, slamming it into the neck of a zombie.

"What's the problem, Lewis?" Leif asked. "Things getting a little too tough for you now?" Leif swung the machete again, slamming it into the zombie's head. He ripped it out of the head, looking at the stream of blood and brain tissue as it ran out of the creature. He stood there with his arms apart, clutching the machete.

The rhino was strolling around the yard as the people fled. It turned its head, looking at Leif as he stood there, looking eye-to-eye with Lewis. Lewis looked at the rhino as it turned around without making any noise at all. It breathed out gently.

"Come on, Lewis," Leif said. "Come and arrest me."

Lewis looked at the rhino, still peering over his shoulder.

Leif looked forward at Lewis. He knew Lewis was looking at something, but he didn't know what. He stopped and slowly turned around. There, standing behind him, with its eyes gleaming yellow, was the Rhino. Leif started to panic as the creature edged closer and closer to him.

Leif looked at Lewis. "Shoot it," he said.

The rhino continued to slowly take one step closer to him at a time. The rhino snarled. Lewis watched as it reached out, slamming its mouth into Leif. Leif screamed in pain as the teeth sank into his side. The rhino picked Leif up. Leif dangled in the rhino's mouth. He fell back, struggling to breathe as the Rhino bit down onto his body harder and harder. Lewis could hear the bones crunch and snap as Leif was slammed into the ground of the scrapyard. His body splattered blood.

"Lewis!" Gemma yelled.

Lewis looked over at the bus. Gemma was waving him over. He looked back, seeing the wave of zombies sprinting towards the scrapyard.

"Time to go," he said.

Lewis ran over to the bus. He dove in through the open doors.

"Come on, let's go," Lucas screamed in panic.

Arron slammed the accelerator down fully, and the bus slowly started to roll towards the opening in the scrapyard. Gemma looked out the back window, seeing the rhino rip Leif into pieces.

The rhino turned its head as the bus started to pick up speed, rolling away from the scrapyard. It charged up the street after the bus.

"Holy shit," Lewis gasped. "Can't this thing go any faster?"

Arron looked into the side mirror at the chasing rhino as it charged up the street after the bus. It slammed into the side of the bus. Claire fell off the seat as Lewis swiped his handgun. He looked through the sight, pulling the trigger. The bullets penetrated the tough skin of the rhino but seemed to have no effect. Juliana filmed the event on her small camcorder.

"Lewis," Arron said, drawing his attention. Lewis ran down the bus as Arron struggled to keep it straight along the bendy road. "Take the wheel."

"What?" Lewis gasped.

"Just do it," Arron replied. "I have an idea."

"For God's sake!" Lewis mumbled.

Arron got up out of the seat. Lewis jumped into the driver's seat, keeping the accelerator down. "What are you doing?" He asked.

"I'll show you," Arron yelled. "Trust me."

"I don't," Lewis mumbled looking ahead into the streets.

Arron searched for the emergency exit in the middle of the bus. He kicked the door open when he found it.

"What are you doing?" Lewis asked again, this time in terror.

Arron climbed onto the top of the bus as the rhino continued to slam into it. Arron kneeled, making his way along the roof of the bus, trying not to fall off the side as the rhino chased after them.

"That animal doesn't give up" Lewis moaned. Lewis looked forward along the road, seeing some vehicles scattered about. He knew he had to weave in and out of them, but it was going to be hard to keep his speed up to maximum. "Hang on, Arron," Lewis yelled.

Lucas leaned out of the window, knowing that Arron didn't hear what Lewis had said. "Bro, hang on!" he yelled.

Lewis started weaving in and out of the cars in the middle of the street. Arron skidded along the top of the bus towards the rear as Lewis continued weaving in and out of the burnt-out vehicles.

"Lucas," Arron yelled. Lucas leaned his head out of the broken window. "When I say, shoot shit face there."

"Got it," Lucas replied, "Why?"

"Just do it."

Arron kneeled, trying to keep his balance, feeling the air rush through his uncut hair. "Hey," he screamed to the rhino. He hung over the end of the bus. He reached into his pocket, pulling out a grenade. The rhino caught up with the bus again. "Chew on this!" Arron yelled, throwing the grenade into the rhino's mouth. "Now!" Arron screamed at Lucas.

Lucas swiped his handgun and took shots at the rhino.

Lewis looked into the mirror as the rhino backed off. Then, he saw the grenade erupt. The rhino staggered about in the middle of the street. It slowly fell to the ground as Arron swung in through the broken window. Lewis looked at the dead creature as they continued along the street.

"How did you get a grenade?" Lewis asked.

"Thought I'd save it for a rainy day," Arron replied with a smile.

Lewis didn't reply as he looked down the street heading into the city centre. He looked out the window onto the dead body of the rhino as it lay in the middle of the street.

"Where are we going?" Gemma asked.

"Train station, then down to Melbourne""

The bus continued along the street.

* * *

The 777 jet cruised along at thirty-eight-thousand feet. The cabin was quiet; not a person was speaking. The sounds of screaming and running people could still be heard. Captain Stanfield stared out over the dead and dark Pacific Ocean, as they left Australia behind them. The once great nation was now in pieces.

The chief cabin attendant, Carly, walked to the back of the plane. She looked at a small group of people who had congregated at the back toilet. She walked to the small group of people as they stood there. "Are we okay?" she softly asked. Everyone stood quietly. She tried to break the silence. "That man has been in there an awfully long time," she said. She was scared to knock. "Hello?" She whispered. She tapped on the door. Nothing was heard in return. She looked at the onlookers as one of the soldiers arrived at the back of the plane.

Carly slipped the key into the lock. She slowly pulled the lock, hearing it click. She opened the door. The soldier stood back. The onlookers could only stand and watch. Carly slowly pulled the door back. Only a squeak could be heard. She looked down onto the toilet, seeing a man. He was older, with dark hair, wearing a shirt and dark trousers—an everyday man. He was holding onto a cross, gently rocking back and forth, not letting go of the cross. The soldier looked through at the man as Carly slowly edged closer to him.

"Hey sir," Carly whispered edging into the toilet. She tapped the man's shoulder. "Sir," she said.

The man quickly lifted his head. His eyes shot open with his eyes gleaming yellow. A slight snarl could be heard.

"Move!" the soldier screamed. The soldier grabbed hold of Carly, pulling her away from the toilet door.

Carly fell against the side of the cabin. The man dove out of the toilet. The soldier lifted his hands up stopping the zombie as he dove onto him. The zombie lunged and the soldier fell back pulling the trigger. The bullets fired out of the magazine, piercing the side of the aircraft. The people screamed, looking at the back of the aircraft.

"What's going on?" a passenger asked in alarm as the cabin started to fill with a light haze.

"What the. . . ?" Captain Stanfield shouted.

"Depressurizing," the first officer replied.

"Oh, no," the captain screamed. "Come on, let's get down."

The aircraft pitched down as the two pilots finished putting on their oxygen masks. Carly crawled out of the way.

"Help," the soldier yelled over the lack of oxygen

Carly turned to see the rifle on the floor where the soldier had dropped it. She crawled over, looking at the fighting zombie as he tried to plunge his teeth into the soldier's neck, watched by the terrified people. Carly picked the rifle up off the floor. She looked through the sight, struggling to see through the light mist that had filled the cabin but still catching glimpse of the zombie's gleaming yellow eyes as he continued to try to bite into the soldier's neck.

"Shoot him!" the soldier yelled. "Come on!"

Carly trembled as she held onto the rifle. She felt her heart pounding as the soldier was losing grip. The mist had started to clear. Then, a sudden shot was heard. The soldier looked up as the zombie fell off him, rolling onto its side. Carly looked back and saw one of the other soldiers still looking down the scope of his gun at the zombie.

"Thanks," the soldier said.

"I'm sorry," Carly cried, grasping the gun

The soldier looked at her and consoled her. "It's okay."

Carly watched as the soldier stormed off down the aisle of the aircraft, ignoring the people's demands for answers.

"Everyone stay in your seats," he ordered. He went to the cockpit and asked, "Are you guys in here okay?"

"We're fine," Captain Stanfield replied, breathing normally again. "What the hell is going on back there?"

"Don't ask," the soldier advised. He turned around and headed back into the aisle of the aircraft. "Get the body moved," he ordered. "Anyone who needs the toilet is escorted, you get me?"

Captain Stanfield looked out the front of the jet.

"Do you think we'll make it to Auckland?" The first officer asked.

"Yes," the captain said. "That's why I took on extra fuel."

* * *

Carl Farrington walked out of the tent in the centre of Hobart. He looked up, seeing one of the buses arriving with refugees from Sydney. "How many we got?" he demanded.

"One-hundred-and-eighty," the soldier replied. "That's that last of them, sir."

"What?" Farrington gasped. "What happened?"

"The airport was overrun," the soldier said. "I'm surprised you didn't know. That's it. Australia is gone. Finished."

Farrington didn't reply as the individuals slowly stepped off the bus.

"I saw Sheila just before we left," Farrington heard someone say, "I think she will be on the next plane."

Farrington looked away. He simply couldn't tell the people who were waiting in the tent for the next plane to arrive that there were no more aircraft on the way to Hobart. Farrington took a deep breath. He walked up to the tent, taking a glimpse of the clear night sky as the moon shone down on the city. Not a cloud was in the sky, and it was very cool. Farrington entered the tent, looking at the people sitting on the benches. They looked at him as he grasped his rifle.

"When's the next bus due to arrive?" somebody enquired.

Farrington took a deep breath. "Can I have your attention please?" he said. The tent went so quiet that you could hear a pin drop. "I'm sorry to say this," Farrington said, pausing.

"Well?" a man said. "What is it?"

"Kingsford Smith. . ." Farrington struggled to say. There

was another pause. "Was overrun a short while ago. I'm sorry, but there are no more planes."

"What!" A lady screamed aloud.

"I'm sorry," Farrington said again. He watched as the screams of emotional pain from the people rose to a crescendo.

He spun around, walking out of the tent and towards one of the jeeps parked there. He beckoned the driver to bring the jeep, and when it came, he said, "Mayor's office." As the jeep sped through the streets Farrington wondered how he was going to break the sad news to the mayor.

He jumped out of the jeep and entered the office. He slowly walked up the stairs and knocked on the door. West's eyes shot open. He had been half-asleep. His wife and daughter were playing with his grandson in the corner. His grandson was just sitting there, unaware of what was going on in Australia. What kind of world was he going to grow up in now that this had happened?

Farrington knocked again on the door, this time a bit louder.

"Come," West ordered.

Farrington walked into the office. "Sir, I need to speak to you," he said.

Mayor West turned, looked at his family, and nodded at his wife.

"Come on," she asked. Mayor West watched as his family walked out of the office, slowly closing the door behind them.

"What's the news?" West questioned.

Carl sat down on the chair. He looked into the tired eyes of the Mayor and said slowly, "Sydney airport was overrun. There are no more aircraft coming."

"What?" West asked. "No, no. That airport was filled with soldiers."

"I'm sorry," Carl replied. "It is true, sir. Tasmania is what is left of Australia."

Mayor West looked down. Then he asked, "How's the island sweep going?"

"So far, good," Carl replied. "None of my teams have come across any cases of infection."

Mayor West looked down again. A small tear ran down his face.

"I'll contact you if we have any news," Farrington replied.

West nodded as Carl got up and left the office. West couldn't wait for the door to shut. He felt his tears run down his face as he placed his head on the table in front of him. He reached over and pulled one of the tissues out of the box as his wife and daughter walked in.

"Oh, Pete," his wife wept. West stood up as his wife and daughter landed in his arms.

CHAPTER SIXTEEN

Lewis looked up at Sydney's central train station, Arron Philips by his side. "Right," Lewis whispered. "Let's do this. Eric, you stick close."

"Yes," Eric said. "I want to get out of here, too."

Lewis took one last quick look around the outside of the once-busy train station.

"Where's this control room?" Lewis enquired.

Eric pointed to one part of the dead train station. "See that part of the station? It's up there."

Lewis looked at Eric and said, "Well, we had better move it, then. Philips, you're with me; Lucas, you are with the rest."

"Got it," Lucas replied.

Lewis looked back, seeing Juliana with the camcorder open and running again. He turned his head forward and walked up to the shiny silver doors of the train station, staring at the blood-stained handprint on the front of it. He pulled it open, hearing it squeak. The ticket machine was covered in blood, and there were blood-stained shoeprints on the ground.

"God!" Lewis mumbled. No one was around in the station. Eric led the way towards the platform where the train should still be waiting to go down to Melbourne.

"There," Eric pointed. "That's the train I was due to take."

Juliana was still filming the train station. Lewis looked along the platform for any zombies that could be around. Luckily, the station was completely deserted.

"Lucas," Lewis said. "Get everyone on that train and stay down and out of sight."

"All received," Lucas directed them.

"Lucas," Lewis said again. Lucas looked at Lewis. "Sweep the train," he ordered. "All corners and rooms."

Lewis then looked at Eric. "Where's this control room?"

"This way," said Eric. "It's back upstairs."

Lewis looked at Gemma. "Come on," he snapped. "And you, Arron."

Arron looked at Lucas as he followed Lewis and Eric. Lewis walked with Eric back into the station. Arron stayed close behind.

"Over there," Eric said.

Lewis looked over towards a door in the far corner of the station. Eventually, they arrived at it. It was a long walk over to the door. Lewis looked at the door. It was reinforced.

"Let's see if I can remember the code," Eric said.

Lewis kept his back to the door, looking around the blood-splattered, stinking station.

"Damn it," Eric swore out of the blue. "They have changed it since I last used it."

Lewis looked around the station as Eric continued to fail to unlock the door.

"Shit," Eric said, trying the code again. Again, he failed, and he cried in disgust. "Oh, fuck it!"

Lewis looked around the empty station. "How long ago did you work in the control station?" He asked.

"About three years ago," Eric replied.

Lewis looked up at the ceiling of the station. "I think they may have changed it since then," he said.

"Stand back," Lewis ordered nudging Eric out of the way. He aimed the gun at the lock and squeezed the trigger. The shot shattered the lock but echoed around the empty station. Eric jumped, and Lewis spun around, looking around the station. The coast remained clear.

"What was that?" Lucas asked over the radio "Lewis, you okay, bro?"

"It's nothing. Don't worry," Lewis replied. "Keep your eyes open and stay down."

"Got it," Lucas agreed.

Lewis and Eric entered the corridor. Lewis slowly closed the door behind him, moving the cleaners' trolley to stop it from drifting open with the breeze.

"This way," Eric said. Lewis followed Eric through the thin corridors of the train operation control room.

"Here it is," Eric said at last. Lewis opened the control room door. He and Eric walked in and looked around the empty control room. "Here," Eric pointed.

Eric sat down onto the swivel chair and looked up at the line of monitors showing the tracks and signals. "Let's hope there is still power," he said. Eric pushed a few switches on the control panel. The lights came on. "Thank God."

"Get to work," Lewis urged him. "Make it quick."

Lucas looked around the empty train. It was so silent that you could hear a pin drop. Gemma looked down at her phone and saw that the signal was still out. Lucas looked at the poster on the wall of the train. He slowly turned his head, looking out of the window onto the other platform of the station. He looked at the white poster advertising a new health pill. He watched as a small dark shadow passed over the front of it. It was moving. Lucas slowly turned around, looking out the window of the train. He felt his heart pounding as he stared out at one of the zombies. Its head was down, and so it didn't see them.

Claire looked up. She took a deep breath. Lucas grabbed

Claire's mouth. "Shhhhhhhh," he whispered. "Get down now. All of you. Do what Lewis said."

Gemma and Claire got down onto the floor of the train. Lucas reached for the radio. He peered up, seeing more of the zombies invading the platform. Juliana reached into her bag, pulling out the small camcorder. She lifted her body, slowly pointing the camcorder towards the window to film the zombies as they staggered through the station towards the stairs.

"Get down," Lucas ordered Julianna. "If those things see you—"

There was a sudden stumble.

"Shit," Juliana gasped.

Lucas looked at Juliana as one of the zombies turned its head and slowly staggered up to the side of the train.

"Shhhhh," Lucas said to the group. He and the rest of the group listened to the snarling zombies as they looked through the window of the train.

"Lewis," Lucas whispered into the radio.

"What is it?" Lewis answered.

"Got a problem,"

Lewis looked down at the radio. "Surprise me,"

"Got some zombies outside, bro."

Lewis let his breath out, looking over at a TV monitor on the wall. Somehow, the system was using backup power. He stared at the crowd of zombies looking into the train.

"Shit," Lewis exclaimed. "Eric."

Eric looked up at the screen. "Holy!" Eric gasped, looking at the monitor

Lewis looked up at the gathering of zombies on the platform. They were walking in from the line. "Lucas," Lewis snapped. "Get Gemma and the rest to the front of the train."

"Understood,"

Eric finished setting the points and signals for the straight trip to Melbourne.

"How long does that thing take to start up?"

"About a minute," Eric replied.

"We may not have a minute," Lewis said. "Could you instruct Lucas and make him start that thing up?"

"Yes," Eric replied. "It's quite simple."

"Lucas," Lewis said. "Get into the front of the train."

"All received," Lucas said. He kept his head down, heading into the cab of the train. "Okay," Lucas whispered. "I'm here."

Eric looked up at the screen, seeing more of the zombies enter the platform from the other stairs. "Okay, Lucas," Eric said. "On the main dashboard, you'll see a shiny, silver key." Lucas looked around the cab of the train, seeing the shiny key still in the ignition. "Turn it to position two," Eric instructed.

"Got it," Lucas replied. Lucas turned the silver key to the right twice and watched as the power surged through the train.

"Okay," Eric said into the radio. "That's the electric running. Now, turn the key back to position one and push the red button in next to the dashboard; that will start the locomotive engines."

Lucas followed Eric's instruction carefully. The generators of the train powered up. The zombies snarled, running towards the train. The noise seemed to be attracting them.

"Done," Eric said. "And the points are done as well. We can leave."

"Well, let's go," Arron said.

Arron, Lewis and Eric walked out of the office. They arrived at the office door. Lewis moved the cleaner's trolley out of the way, looking into the empty station.

"How long did you say it would take to get to Melbourne?" Lewis asked.

"If we don't stop, about nine hours," Eric replied. "It's usually eleven hours."

"What?" Arron gasped.

"I know. Sorry," Eric replied.

Eric, Lewis and Arron walked over to the stairs leading

down onto the platform where the train was running and waiting, ready to go. Lewis sneaked down the stairs, looking onto the platform and seeing the zombies looking into the train. He slowly walked back up the stairs towards the group.

"Okay," Lewis whispered. "Arron, you go with Eric over the bridge and cut across the track and get that thing moving."

"Got it," Philips replied. "What about you?"

"Don't worry about me. Just get going," Lewis replied. "Eric, the instant you get in that cab, hit it."

"Will do," Eric said.

Lewis watched Arron and Eric sneak away towards the bridge leading over to the other platform. He peered around the corner, watching the zombies as they stared into the carriages of the train. Lewis peeked his head around the corner from the bottom of the stairs. He looked across the platform to ensure that Arron and Eric were in position and ready to run across the track and climb into the train.

Then, Lewis took a deep breath. "Hey!" he screamed. "Hey, look! It's me! You know, the poor bastard!"

The zombies snarled, looking over at Lewis by the stairs. They started sprinting towards him. He spun around, running up the stairs as Arron and Eric ran across the track.

Eric climbed up the side of the train, followed by Arron. He swung the door shut. He sat down into the seat, seeing Lucas by the door. Eric slowly started pushing the power stick forward. The train slowly started to roll out of the station.

Lewis ran down onto the opposite platform. The zombies ran down the stairs as the rear of the train rolled out of the station. Lewis jumped down onto the track, hearing the zombies running in from behind him. Lewis leapt, grabbing onto the train as it continued to pick up speed. He felt the vehicle pulling him along as he hauled his body up. He grasped the pole as the zombies slowly started to disappear from sight and their bodies slowly got smaller and smaller as the train picked up speed, heading out of the city.

"Jesus," he panted. "That was close. I'm getting too old for this, shit."

The radio in his pocket went static for a few seconds as he regained his breath. "Lewis," Lucas said over the radio, "Lewis, can you hear me?"

"Yes," Lewis said at last. "Yes, I can hear you."

"Oh," Lucas said. "Thank God. Man, where are you?"

Lewis grasped to the back of the train. "I'm just hanging around," he replied. Lewis took a few deep breaths. He managed to open the back door. He held onto his sidearm with paranoia. He walked down the aisles of the train. It was empty. There were no personal belongings or blood stains inside. He peered into all the rooms. They were empty. He strolled through the train towards the front. He looked ahead to see Gemma. She lifted her head.

"Lewis," Gemma whimpered and dove into his arms.

"I'm okay," he said. "Just another day, really."

"I'm glad you found that amusing," Gemma stated.

Lewis looked around the front of the train. "Where's Arron?" he enquired.

"He is up in the front with Eric," Lucas replied.

Lewis nodded after Gemma had finished hugging him. The train picked up speed as it made its way through Sydney, ready to go into the outback and down towards Melbourne. Lewis walked into the front car of the train, looking for Eric and Arron as they sat in the cab. Eric was observing the tracks ahead.

"You okay?" Lewis asked Eric.

"Bit shaken after that ordeal, but I'm okay, really." Eric switched on the lights. He slowed the train down, looking ahead along the track. Lewis and Arron also looked ahead to see that it was completely blocked by the infected.

"What should I do?" Eric asked, looking at Lewis.

Lewis let out his breath, looking down as Eric held onto the power lever. "Is that your throttle?" he asked.

"Yes," Eric replied. "Why?"

Lewis leaned over pushing the throttle to full.

"What are you doing?" Eric asked.

"You'll see," Lewis said. "If you don't like blood, close your eyes." The train quickly picked up speed, heading towards the zombies as they stood there, watching the train, heading towards them. The zombies snarled as the train slammed into them. The crunches from the groaning creatures could be heard as blood splashed onto the front window.

"Ouch!" Lucas said.

Juliana closed her eyes when she saw the huge splash of blood slamming into the front of the train.

The train gradually slowed down as it joined the main line heading south towards Melbourne.

"We take turns sitting with Eric. The last thing we want is him falling asleep," Lewis proposed.

"I'll take my turn first," Lucas said. "Then you will, Arron?"

"Got it," Arron accepted.

"Then me," Lewis agreed.

The group went quiet as Sydney disappeared behind them and the train hit full speed.

Lewis walked into the first-class carriage, looking for Gemma and Claire. "Okay," Lewis said. "Arron and Lucas are going to be keeping an eye on Eric while he takes us down to Melbourne. Then, it's to your dad's warehouse and then to the Davenport ferry where we should be in time for the last navy pickup."

Gemma smiled as Lewis leaned against the side of the train wall. "Lewis," Gemma said. "Take a good rest."

Lewis walked towards the bedding area of the first-class coach. He slowly lay down on the clean bed, closing his eyes and falling asleep without delay.

* * *

Lewis opened his eyes as the train changed lines. The shudder made him jump. He slowly sat up, rubbing his eyes after the sleep.

"Gemma," he mumbled. "You okay?" But there was no answer. He got out of the bed and walked out of the carriage. He called Gemma again, but still, there was no answer. No one was around. Lewis walked forward to the front of the train. Still, no one was around. At last, Lewis came from to the coach and saw Eric still sitting in the main seat, staring into the night.

"Eric, where's Gemma?" Eric didn't reply. "Eric?" Lewis said a bit more loudly, trying to grab his attention. Then, he placed his hand onto Eric's shoulder. Eric turned his head, snarling. Lewis stepped back upon seeing Eric's glowing eyes and the drops of blood running down his mouth.

"Eric!" Lewis yelped. "No! How did they get you?"

Lewis spun around, looking for Gemma. "Gemma!" he shouted. Lewis stopped in his tracks in the carriage. He looked into the glowing eyes of Bob. Gemma and Lucas were behind him and Arron further down the coach with Juliana next to him.

"Bob," Lewis said. Lewis looked up as Bob shot forward at him.

Lewis jumped as he opened his eyes to a slight beam of morning sunlight. "Gemma?" he called.

Gemma quickly got up from the seat outside of the cabin where she had been asleep as well. "Lewis," she answered. "I'm here."

Lewis coughed. "Is Eric okay?" he asked.

"Yes, he is fine," Gemma replied.

Lewis continued to cough. "What time is it?"

Gemma looked down at her watch. "It's 7:00 a.m. Did the sun wake you up?"

"Yes, a bit." Lewis replied.

Lewis put his hand down onto the sidearm before getting up and heading into the front of the train. "You okay?" he asked Eric.

"I'm fine, thank you," Eric replied. "Making time nicely. Let's hope there is fuel at this next station. We will be there in a little while."

"How long does it take to refuel the train?" Arron asked.

"Not long," Eric replied. "It should have been done back at . . . but . . ."

"Never mind that now," Lewis said. Lewis looked out of the window as the sun continued to climb. He stood next to Lucas, who was looking into the dense outback.

"Here we are," Eric called.

Lucas and Lewis jumped up as they rolled towards the station. The platform was deserted. Gemma looked out of the window as they rolled into the station. No one was around. Eric put the brakes on, shutting down the engines.

Lewis swiped his handgun as he leaned out of the door. "You two stay here, okay?" he asked Gemma and Claire. They didn't reply as Lucas, Arron, and Lewis jumped down onto the platform. Just a gentle breeze could be heard.

"Okay," Lewis said. "While he refuels us, you two go and find some supplies."

"Got it," Arron said.

"Back here in ten," Lewis ordered. Lewis then turned to Eric. "How are you doing?" he asked.

"All good here," Eric replied. "However, there isn't much fuel, so we won't have enough to get to Melbourne, but it will get us a lot closer."

Arron saw a small coffee shop. He slowly opened the door, walked in, and looked at the overturned chairs and seats. The power had gone out. All of the drinks were now warm. Arron picked up a bottled water from the counter, looking out of the window on the train as it sat still at the station. He walked towards the door, catching a glimpse of the warehouses on the other side of the train station. It also seemed to be empty, with no one in sight. There was no heavy machinery, lifting equipment or sounds of people shouting at each other. Arron walked back along the platform towards Lewis and Eric as they continued to refuel the huge train.

Lucas walked into the station ticket office. No one was there, either. He heard a crash from behind him. He spun around, looking at the door leading into the ticket area. He pulled out the shiny, silver handgun, still holding onto the bag on his back. He slowly walked up to the door, placing his hand on the shiny handle. Lucas opened the door.

He jumped, seeing a cat run out. It turned around, looking at him and hissing. Lucas smiled, but as he turned his head, he was terrified to see a zombie charging towards him. Lucas didn't have time to aim the handgun. He fell back, slamming his head into the door of the train station. He looked up, seeing Lewis run in with his extending baton drawn. Lucas slowly got up, as Lewis slammed the baton into the head of the zombie. Blood was rushing from the zombie's ruptured skull. The zombie fell to the ground, but Lewis held onto the baton. Then he turned around, helping Lucas the rest of the way up.

"Thanks," Lucas said.

"No problem," Lewis replied. "Next time, be more alert." Lucas brushed some muck off his bag. "Come on," Lewis said. "There is no one here."

Arron looked around the station. He heard a shuffle coming from behind him. He slowly turned around, looking through the metal fence. "How much more time will you need?" he asked Eric

"Not much. Only about five minutes more. Then we will have enough to get near Melbourne," Eric replied.

"Eric," Arron whispered. "Switch them pumps off and slowly get back onto the train."

"Why?" Eric stood up, turning around and looking at the metal fence that faced the car park of the station. Eric and Arron stood up straight, looking at the gathering of infected people, all of whom were looking down at the ground.

"Where did they come from?" Eric wondered.

Arron turned back, looking at Eric. "Does that really matter right now? Cut the pumps and get on the train, but don't start it."

"Got it," Eric replied.

Arron slowly reached into his trouser pocket, pulling out the radio. "Lewis," he whispered.

"Go ahead," Lewis replied into the radio.

"Got a problem," Arron said.

"What's up?" Lewis replied,

"No biggie."

"What?" Lewis asked.

Arron looked at the dazed zombies as they looked at the ground. The gate leading into the station was open. Lewis walked out onto the platform of the long station. He saw Arron putting his hand up, telling the couple to slowly walk forward together. Lewis looked through the silver fence, listening to the groaning zombies, bumping into each other, heads still facing down onto the ground.

"Shit," he mumbled. "How's the fuel?"

"Just a tiny bit more. . ." Eric replied.

"Can it go any faster?" Lewis asked.

"No," Eric whispered. "We still won't have enough to make it to Melbourne anyway."

Lewis started to hesitate. He looked at the gathering zombies groaning as they continued shuffling into one another.

"Eric," Lewis whispered. "That's enough."

"We won't make it to Melbourne," Eric replied. "We could run out way before we hit the city."

"Shit," Lewis gasped.

Eric looked down at the fuel gauge. "About three minutes," he said.

"What?" Lucas gasped.

Lewis saw Gemma stepping down from the train. "Gemma," Lewis whispered. "Get back on the train." Gemma looked with fear through the metal fence onto the car park of the station. "Gemma," Lewis whispered again. Gemma slowly walked backwards onto the train.

"Done," Eric said.

"Good," Lewis replied. "Get them out, and let's get out of here." Lewis looked onto the gathering of the zombies.

"Shit," Eric mumbled.

"What?" Lewis asked.

"It's stuck," Eric replied.

Lewis spun around, walking up to the side of the train and looking at the two pumps stuck inside the train. Lewis slowly walked over to Eric. He kneeled, pulling on the two tubes. "Oh, fuck," he mumbled. "Come on, you little shits!"

Lewis looked over the gate that led onto the platform. The zombies were still gathering around the fence. He slowly walked up to the open the gate, looking down at the zombies. They were all staring down at the ground, unaware of the group on the platform. Lewis reached down, pulling out his handgun. Lewis felt the hot metal burn the palm of his hands as he started to slowly pull it close. A slight creak was heard from the gate's hinges. Lewis squinted his eyes closed. The zombie in front of it snarled. His heart pounded as it slowly started to look down again towards the ground.

Lewis looked up as the fuel pipes were pulled away from the side of the train. Lewis reached for his radio. "Arron," Arron looked over at Lewis as he stood by the gate. "Tell Eric to start the train when I say," Lewis demanded.

"Got it," Arron replied.

Lewis continued to hold the gate to the platform as Arron entered the train, looking at Eric as he sat down in the driver's seat, exhausted from all the driving he had done that day.

"When I say," Arron ordered, "start this thing up."

"Will do," Eric replied.

Lewis continued to look at the motionless zombies staring at the ground, bumping into one another. Lewis pushed the side button in. "Okay, now," he ordered. Lewis grasped the metal gate. He looked up as the puff of dark black smoke billowed out of the top of the diesel locomotive. Lewis slammed the gate shut as the group of zombies looked up at him. He slid the bolt across.

"Lewis, come on!" Gemma yelled.

Lewis looked at the zombies as they climbed onto the metal. It slowly started to sway back and forth; it was not going to hold.

"Lewis!" Gemma screamed.

Lewis shook his head as the fence started to break away. He stepped aboard the train, pulling the door shut behind him

"Go, go, go, go!" he yelled to Eric.

"Okay, okay," Eric replied. "I'm going." Eric pushed the power stick forward.

The fence collapsed and the snarling zombies ran towards the train as it rolled out of the long station. "Christ, that was close!" Lewis exclaimed as the train continued to pick up speed.

"Next stop; Melbourne," Eric said.

Lewis entered the front of the train. He looked at Eric. "Hey, man, you okay?" he asked.

"I guess so," Eric replied, "but really tired. I could use a cup of coffee."

"I'll get that," Lewis replied.

Lewis left the cab of the train. "Lucas," he said. "Please join me for tea duties."

"Right, boss," Lucas replied with a smile.

Lewis and Lucas walked to the small kitchen on the train where the stewards would prepare drinks for the customers.

Lucas walked in, looking at the paper coffee cups all stacked up next to each other. "Do you want one?" he asked Lewis.

"Yeah, go for it," Lewis replied. "Might as well."

Lucas smiled as he opened the small coffee sachet, pouring the coffee into the cup. "Eric!" Lucas called. "You take sugar?"

"No, thanks!" Eric yelled back.

Lewis leaned against the door of the kitchen, looking at Lucas as he prepared the drinks.

"What shall we do when we get to Melbourne?" Lucas asked

"Get to her dad's warehouse," Lewis replied. "Then, make our way to the Davenport ferry, and then we are out of here!"

"So, what are we going to do at the station? Find a ride?" Lucas enquired.

"Of course," Lewis replied. "Her dad's warehouse is about a twenty-minute drive, providing the roads are clear."

Lewis felt the train pass over the points as the sun shone in through the window. "We haven't had much time to talk, have we?" Lewis asked.

"No," Lucas replied.

Lewis watched as Lucas finished making the coffees. "We haven't spoken much since we first met at the car crash," Lewis said.

"Oh, I see," Lucas replied. "What you want to know?"

"What were you doing here in Australia before all this happened?"

Lucas put the cup down onto the shiny side and emptied the sugar sachets into his cup.

"A well-earned vacation."

"Holiday?"

"Oh, yes," Lucas replied. "I'm not going to be forgetting this one!"

"I think a lot who got out will be saying the same thing. You're not the only one," Lewis replied to Lucas, as Lucas handed him his coffee. "What were you doing before you came here?" Lewis queried.

"Working. So, I booked my vacation."

Lewis continued to dig for information from Lucas as he slurped the coffee from the paper cup. "What do you do?"

"Security."

"Security?" Lewis asked.

"Yep," Lucas replied. "Work at a downtown mall. I was considering looking for a job down here. Would be nice for a change of scenery, but I don't think I will be returning here for a long, long, long time."

Lucas picked up the cup, looking up at the clock on the wall.

"What will you do when you get back to Honolulu?" Lewis asked.

"Sell my story to the press and make some extra money, clear off a few credit card bills. You know what I mean. Then get wasted every night."

"As you do before an apocalypse," Lewis stated.

Lewis smiled as they walked into the cab of the train, looking at Arron as he tried to keep Eric awake. "Eric," Lewis said. "Drink this. It will help keep you awake, man."

Lucas handed Eric the coffee cup. "How long now 'til we are at Melbourne?" Lucas asked him.

Eric looked down at his watch. "Providing all the lines ahead are clear, we should be in Melbourne in about three hours, going at this speed all the way. We have knocked about three hours of the normal timetable so far."

Lewis looked down onto his watch. "That gives it two hours until the last navy pickup."

"If they get here," Lucas said.

"Eric, are you okay?" Lewis asked.

"I guess," Eric replied.

Lewis turned around and walked out of the cab. He walked back into the carriage where Gemma and Claire were.

"We are going to go get your mum and dad," he said. "Then, it's off to Hobart where we will be safe, I promise."

"I hope they are still alive!" Gemma murmured.

"I do, too," Lewis replied to comfort her. "And then we can get out of here, down to the Davenport ferry and get picked up by the navy." Lewis leaned against Gemma. He was still very tired. Melbourne was slowly getting closer and closer. He closed his eyes as he was starting to fall asleep again. The coffee hadn't helped at all. The time went by slowly for the anxious group.

CHAPTER SEVENTEEN

In just under an hour, they would be in Melbourne. Lewis looked up at the clock on the wall of the train. He knew they would be arriving at Melbourne soon. "Okay," he said, "listen up."

Arron got up from the seat in the cab where Eric was. "Carry on," he told Eric. "I'll be back in a second."

Lewis watched as Arron entered the front coach of the train. "Okay," Lewis said. "We are almost at Melbourne. When we get off the train, we must stick together. We're not going to make it to the main station because of the fuel."

"You bet," Juliana said. Juliana reached into her bag, pulling out her camcorder, ready to film the group getting off near Melbourne

"Okay, everyone," Lewis said. "Take a break. Reserve as much energy as you can because we won't be resting until we get to the warehouse once we're off this train."

Eric stared out the front of the train as he continued along the track as the train had hit full speed again. He started to feel tired after the continuous drive without any breaks.

Lucas came in and sat next to him. "Hey, you okay, man?"

"Fine," Eric replied. "Can you get me another coffee, please?"

"Sure, man," Lucas replied. "Keep rolling."

Eric looked back as Lucas got up and left the cabin. Lucas walked through the train, seeing Lewis and the rest of the group relaxing in an attempt to regain as much energy as they could before they arrived in Melbourne.

"Is he okay?" Lewis asked Lucas.

"He is. I'm just going to get another cup of coffee for him," Lucas responded.

"I'll come with you. The last one didn't wake me up that much."

Something suddenly caught Eric's attention. It frightened him as he continued speeding along the track. "Oh my God!" he gasped.

Lewis heard Eric's cry as they continued walking down towards the kitchen area of the train. He turned and ran back into the cab. As soon as he got there, he saw Eric slamming the red plunger down. He grabbed onto the metal pole, looking out the front of the train at a truck that had gotten caught on a level crossing.

"We are not going to stop in time!" he screamed.

"Fuck it," Lewis said. "Everyone to the back now."

"What?" Lucas asked.

"No time," Lewis yelled. "Get them to the back. Eric, come on."

Aaron ran out of the cab, running down the train as Eric held onto the red plunger.

"Come on," Lewis called.

Eric and Lewis got up and ran through the main train towards the rear coaches. The front of the train slammed into the truck on the track. The main train veered off the track, running onto the side of the steep drop, the ground being turfed up by the front of the train. Soon, it skimmed down the side of the long drop into the forest and shrubs below. The train continued to turf up the ground below as the chasing carriages pushed it along the ground. Eric lost his grip, falling back into the front of the cab.

"Jesus Christ!" Lewis yelled.

The train continued sliding along the ground with Eric in the front of the train.

Lucas opened his eyes and looked at Gemma. "Are you okay?" he asked. Gemma rubbed her head as Lewis crawled over to her. "Ouch," he moaned. "Fuck it, I'm getting too old for this kind of shit."

"I'm okay," Gemma said. "How about you?"

Claire opened her eyes, looking out the window of the train into the light forest. A gentle stream ran into the train from the small river outside as it ran through the broken window of the carriage. The cool water splashed her face as she slowly got up.

"Eric," Lewis yelled. "Are you okay? Can you hear me from there?"

Juliana started to slowly come around after the crash. She looked at her bag as her camcorder hung out of it. She slowly got up, looking at Claire as she stood up looking down at the cool water from the stream as it ran into the train through the broken glass windows.

"Is it okay?" Claire asked Juliana.

"I guess so," came her weak reply. Juliana switched the camcorder on to test whether it still worked. Lewis staggered up and slowly walked into the front of the train, looking at the sparks from the generators. He saw Eric lying on the ground, blood rushing from his head.

"Eric!" Lewis said, shaking him, "Eric, come on! Please!" Eric didn't move even after being shaken. "Come on!" Lewis cried again.

Lewis lifted Eric out of the control wheel of the train, seeing that the force of the crash had killed him. There was nothing he could do for him. "Shit," he mumbled to himself. Lewis got up, paying his last respects to Eric, and then he walked back into the other coaches.

"Is everybody okay?" he asked the group.

"We are all good back here," Lucas replied. "How's Eric?"

Lewis didn't respond to the question. "Come on," Lewis snapped. "Let's get out of here."

Lewis kneeled, looking out of the broken window as the water from the stream trickled in. He turned and looked at Claire and Gemma. Claire was using the stream water to wash away the blood from the small cut on the top of her head.

"Are you okay?" Lewis asked Claire.

Claire nodded as Lewis crawled out into the stream, feeling the cool water rush over his face from the gentle current that came over the stones. Lewis looked around. The area was clear. He grasped his sidearm, watching Claire and Gemma crawl out through the broken window of the carriage. Juliana was standing there, filming the train wreckage. The front of the train was smoking.

"Come on," Lewis snapped. "Let's get out of here in case that thing blows!"

Lewis led the group along the slow-running stream, away from the train. He looked back at the front of the train. It was quite a distance away now; even if anything happened to it now, they would be safe.

"Okay, take five minutes," he said. "Let's clean ourselves up before we go on."

Lucas looked over, seeing something over the edge of the stream. He slowly walked over, looking at a campsite that had been set up. Lewis looked over as Lucas arrived at the tent. Some burnt food was still in the metal tin. No one was around. It was completely deserted.

"Wow," Lucas exclaimed. "Think we hit the jackpot with this, guys!"

Lucas kneeled and saw some open food pockets sprawled about.

"Guys, we got food here," Lucas said. "Let's gear up and move on after we have washed up."

Claire and Gemma walked over, looking down at Lucas as he pulled out the small chocolate bars from the wrappers. He placed the bar into his mouth. The sugar boosted his energy as he looked across the gentle stream. Only the sound of the running stream was heard as it passed over the stones. The water was clear as crystal as it continued to pass over the cobbles. The silence and trickling of the stream was broken.

"What have we got?" Lewis asked.

"Just your ordinary campsite," Lucas replied. "Dig in; there is plenty of food here."

Lewis walked over to the tent. He peered in, looking at the ruffled-up clothes. No blood stains.

"What do you think happened to them?" Lucas asked.

"Who?" Intervened Lucas

"The people who were here?"

"No idea," Lewis replied.

Lucas sat down, overlooking the stream. He picked up the small stone next to him, flicked his wrist, and skimmed the stone along the surface of the stream watching it bounce across the surface. He watched it disappear. Claire and Gemma walked over to the side of the stream, sitting down and watching the current taking the water along with it. Only the slight trickle could be heard. Lewis pulled his stained blue shirt off placing it into the running water. A gentle breeze blew through the trees which offered some shade to make it easier for them as the sun continued to burn down. Lewis wrung his shirt out and splashed the cool water over his face.

"So, what's the plan from here?" Lucas asked Lewis.

"We go onto Melbourne," Lewis repeated. "Then to the Davenport ferry, and then off to Tasmania—hopefully for a long time."

Juliana came over. "Do you think the navy will be there?"

"We can only hope," Lewis reminded her.

Lewis looked down onto the stream, watching the current taking it along. He started to lower his head. Tiredness was starting to kick in again. Lucas sat down next to him, his bag strap over his shoulder.

"Hey," a voice said, startling them.

Lewis swiped his handgun, seeing an elderly couple running towards them.

"Get away," the female snapped. "That's our property!"

Gemma looked to see that the man was armed. He was holding a twin-barrel shotgun.

"Okay, okay," Gemma said. "Sorry, we thought it was abandoned."

Lewis looked at Arron and Lucas as they had their firearms pointed at the couple.

"Lower your guns," Lewis ordered. "Now. Both of you."

The middle-aged man stood there, facing the group. Juliana held onto her small camcorder, filming the scene.

"Is that the train you came on?" the man asked.

"Yes," Lewis said.

The couple started to panic.

"We were going to have to move anyway," the man said. "Come on."

The female walked over and started packing the camping gear up.

"That noise could have drawn them things here," the man said.

"Look, I'm sorry." Lewis pleaded with the couple. "We thought it was abandoned."

"Leave our stuff," he demanded. "Go, or I'll shoot, I will."

Lucas faced the group. "Come on guys," Lucas said. "Let's get out of here."

"Go on," the man demanded, "and don't come back."

Lewis watched as Gemma, Juliana, Claire, and Lucas walked on. He kept his back turned, walking backwards and looking at the couple as they snuck back into the tent, preparing to move. "Come on," the man said at last. Let's get out of here. It's not safe here now."

• • •

Lewis walked through the dense shrubs looking into the clearing ahead. He looked ahead and saw a small outback town, but no one could be seen there.

Lucas stood behind him, looking at the small town. "Shall we?" he asked.

The sun was high in the sky, and it was getting hotter by the minute as the day wore on. "Yes, we shall," Lewis replied. "Try and find some water or a vehicle."

"How far is Melbourne?" Gemma asked.

"Your dad's warehouse is about a thirty-minute drive from here," Lewis said. "We are nearly there. We can do this, people."

Lewis walked out of the dense bushes onto the sandy ground. He looked up at the road sign. It read 'Bonga Wonga.' Lewis watched as it gently swayed back and forth with the gentle breeze. The town ahead was deserted. The shops were empty of stock. Lucas looked over at a jeep that was parked on the sidewalk. Lucas walked up to it. He pulled the door open, looking inside it.

"Anything?" Lewis asked him.

Lucas continued looking at the jeep's wires. "I could probably hot wire it," Lucas said. "However, there is no gas in the tank."

Lewis looked up along the deserted street. He squinted his eyes and saw a small petrol station. It was only a short distance away. "We may be in luck," he said.

Lucas reached in and lowered the handbrake as Lewis started pushing the jeep along the street towards the petrol station.

Lewis looked up at the station pumps as he and Lucas arrived there. Lewis walked over to the leaded petrol pump. He pulled the silver nozzle out. "Here it goes," he said. Lewis squeezed the small metal trigger in. A dribble of petrol leaked out the end of the nozzle.

"Fuck it." Lewis slammed the nozzle back into the socket.

"Well," Arron asked, "what do we do?"

"We walk on," Lewis replied. "We keep going until the end or find another vehicle nearby."

The group stayed quiet for a few seconds.

"Okay," Lewis said. "Arron, Lucas—split and go. Find some supplies, mostly water, and meet back here in ten minutes."

"Got it," Arron said. Arron and Lucas split up and moved into the small outback town.

"How long will it take to walk to my dad's warehouse?" Gemma asked.

"About an hour," Lewis replied. "That leaves us with just an hour to get to the Davenport ferry."

Lewis looked into the middle of the street, seeing Lucas and Arron had returned. "What have we got?"

"I found this," Arron said. "Just two small bottles of water."

"We'll have to make it last," Lewis comforted them. "What did you find, Lucas?"

Lucas showed Lewis the colt handgun. "Found a few rounds as well," he added. "May come in handy."

Lewis looked up the street. He stared at the road sign pointing towards Melbourne.

"Right," Lewis said, "let's hit the street."

"How long we got until the navy are at Davenport?" Arron asked.

Lewis looked down at his watch. "Two hours. I was just telling Gemma it is an hour's walk to her dad's warehouse from here." Lewis took one last look over his shoulder before slowly walking forward into the street.

"Do you know the way to Davenport?" Lucas asked Lewis.

"Yes," Lewis replied. "It's literally a straight line. Her dad's got a powerful car. If the streets and roads are clear. . ."

The group started to increase their walking speed. Lewis looked back at the town.

"Where did they all go?" Gemma asked after some time.

"Who?"

"The people from that town."

"Must have fled," Lucas said. "They obviously thought they were safer there than here and might have fled, but I am afraid they were wrong."

Gemma didn't reply as she walked by Lewis's side.

Lewis looked at Juliana as she walked along, the small camcorder still on her arm ready to snap another story. "So," Lewis said to her, "what are you planning to do if we get to Tasmania?"

"What?" she asked. "Do what with what?"

"Who are you going to sell the story to?"

Juliana continued walking along the road, keeping an eye over her shoulder as the outback town slowly started to get smaller and smaller as they walked away. "Oh," she replied. "I don't know. May try and broadcast it to the world from Tasmania; may even get a raise!"

Lewis looked at Juliana. He kept eye contact with her as he continued to walk at her pace.

"Just joking," she replied.

Lewis didn't reply as they continued walking along the street. He picked up his pace, catching up with Lucas, who was still carrying the huge black bag on his back.

"You okay, man?" he asked.

"I guess so," he replied.

"What are you going to do if we get to Tasmania?" Lewis asked. "How are you going to get back to America?"

Lucas panted in the heat. "Guess I could catch a ride with the Air Force, or the US government may fly its own people back home when all this is over."

"I guess so," Lewis replied. "Look what the New Zealand PM did."

Lucas stopped. "Did what?" he asked.

"He sent a jet over to get some of his people out of the county," Lewis said.

"Okay, there may be something waiting for me—or a rubber dingy back to California."

Gemma slowed down as she wanted to be with Lewis. "Do you have family?" she asked Lucas.

"Do I?" Lucas replied. "No—well, my mom's in Nebraska."

"Does she know you are out here?" Lewis asked.

"She does, yeah."

"She must be worried. Has she called you?" The concern was clear in Lewis's question.

"Oh, I have spoken to her, yes. Told her I was okay."

Lewis didn't reply as the group continued to walk along the road, Lewis constantly looking down at his watch. The time was slowly passing by. It was less than two hours now until they had to be at the ferry port.

Lucas peeked into the plains out to his right. Something captured his attention there. "Hey, wait." he ordered.

Lucas looked out across the fields and saw a figure, just standing there, looking down at the ground.

"Lewis," Lucas murmured.

Lewis turned his head, looking at Lucas as he pointed over at the figure. Lewis looked at the figure standing in the middle of the plains. It was a female with clothes battered and torn to pieces. She was just staring at the ground, just like the zombies they saw back when they were refuelling the train, unaware of her surroundings.

"Shit," he gasped. "Come on, move quicker. Don't make any sudden noises or movements that could grab its attention."

Lewis continued observing the figure as she went on staring down at the ground. She slowly lifted her head, opened her eyes, and looked at the group as they trekked up the road leading to the hill.

"Don't see us, don't see us," Lewis mumbled. "Please

216

don't see us." Lewis looked at the glowing yellow eyes and he knew she had seen him.

"Fuck, move it," he ordered. Holding onto his handgun, Lewis looked at the screaming woman as she sprinted towards him, snarling and spurting blood out of her mouth. Lewis looked at the entire field covered with zombies running towards the group.

"Shit. Found out where the people from that town went!" Lewis gasped. "We got more company. Come on, let's roll."

"What do we do?" Gemma panicked.

Lewis started taking single shots at the zombies, trying to hit them in the head to take them down, one after the other. He slipped the last magazine into the weapon when he heard a sudden rumble. He swung his head to the left. He couldn't believe his eyes. Jumping over the hill was one of the military jeeps with a machine gun mounted on the top.

"Get back!" Lucas yelled.

Lewis pulled Arron and Gemma back away from the jeep's path as it landed in the middle of the street. The jeep slammed into the street, skidding to a stop, the wheels burning. The solider on the back ripped the machine gun lever back. "DIIIIIIIIIIIIIIIIIIIIIIIIIIIIIIII-IEEEEEEEEEEEEEEEEEEEEEEEE!" he yelled.

Gemma ducked down as the golden bullets poured out of the machine gun. The soldier screamed as he killed off the zombies, one after the other. Lewis looked up and saw one of the Australian Army trucks appear over the hill. The brakes skidded the vehicle to a stop.

"Get in," the soldier yelled. "Come on. We ain't got all day."

The soldiers in the jeep continued shooting at the zombies as they ran in from the field. Lewis helped Gemma onto the truck.

"Come on," the soldier yelled. "Get in quickly. There are more coming."

Lewis climbed onto the truck as the driver hit the accelerator down to full.

"GOOOOOOOOOOOOOOOOOOOOOOOOOOOOOOOOOO," the soldier screamed.

The zombies ran out of the field onto the road chasing after the military truck. Soon the zombies started disappearing behind.

"God, that was close!" Lewis exclaimed. "Thanks for stopping by."

Lewis looked at the troop leader. "Hello sir," the sergeant said. "Can I take your name, please?"

"Jackson," Lewis said, "Lewis Jackson, New South Wales Police Division"

"Sergeant O'Neil, sir," he replied. "Where were you going?"

"Melbourne," Lewis replied.

"Melbourne?"

"Yes," Lewis replied. "Her mum and dad are hiding out in his warehouse. Then we are off to the Davenport ferry to get to Tasmania. The Australian Navy are doing one last stop at the ferry port. Then it's off to Tasmania"

The soldier didn't know how to express what he was about to say. "I'm sorry," he at last said, "Melbourne was overrun ages ago by them things. No one is left alive down there."

Gemma stormed over. "What's that about Melbourne?"

"Melbourne is gone," Lewis told her gently.

"I know that," Gemma frittered, "but my dad's warehouse is just out on the city limits. They could be alive in my dad's warehouse."

"We are going to bypass the city, but if your dad's warehouse is on the city limits, we could drop by and see if any survivors are there," O'Neil stated. "If he owns a warehouse there may be more survivors."

Gemma sat down as the truck sped along the outback road.

"What's it like out there?" Lewis enquired.

"Horrific." O'Neil's reply was brief. "There is hardly anyone left alive."

"God!" Lewis exclaimed.

"Yes," O'Neil replied. "All of the densely-populated cities are finished with. We were going to check that last place and then break for Davenport and assist the Tasmanian authorities, as that is the only place free from infection. We should be in time for the last navy pickup, as you said."

"What's Tasmania like?" Lewis wanted to know.

"We don't know," O'Neil replied. "All I know is that security is tight there. The US has arrived to aid us, and New Zealand has sent some troops over. Actually, all Commonwealth countries are sending supplies to Tasmania."

Lewis looked into the soldiers' eyes, seeing accumulated fear in them.

"Let's just get to the warehouse, find her parents, and then get to that ferry," Lewis suggested.

"We have to stop at one small town a few miles ahead. We had dropped some troops off there." O'Neil turned his attention to Arron as he sat down on the side seat of the truck. "And who are you?" O'Neil demanded.

"Arron," Arron said, "Arron Philips."

O'Neil took another look at the orange robes Arron was wearing. "What were you in for?" O'Neil demanded to know.

Arron looked into Lewis's eyes as they hit a bump in the road. The bump made O'Neil jump. He swung his head looking out the front at the main jeep as they continued to speed through the streets towards the next town. O'Neil turned his head back looking at Arron.

"I said," O'Neil repeated, "what were you in for?"

"Burglary," Lewis intervened.

O'Neil looked down at Arron.

"Keep your head down," he ordered, "and do as my men say. You got it?"

Arron didn't reply to O'Neil.

Lewis looked out the rear of the truck as they closed in on the next outback town. Lewis looked out the front of the truck and saw the escorting jeep as it came to a stop. He looked at the few troops on the street, waiting to be picked up to be taken to Melbourne.

"Anybody?" O'Neil asked.

"Nothing sir," a soldier replied. "The place is completely deserted. How about the other places?"

"Nothing," he replied, "but we found some survivors."

"Really?" Jason Philips asked. "How many?"

Jason Philips climbed onto the back of the truck. Jason couldn't believe his eyes. He stared into the truck to see his brother, Arron, just sitting there looking at the ground of the truck not noticing his younger brother standing there.

"Arron," Jason said, "is that you?"

Arron slowly lifted his head. He looked at his younger brother standing there, holding onto his rifle as the sun continued to beam down onto them.

"We have to go," O'Neil reminded them.

Jason climbed into the back of the truck. Arron leapt into his arms.

"Oh my God, I thought you were. . ."

Before Jason could finish speaking Arron intervened. "What about Mum and Dad?" Arron asked.

Before Jason could reply, the back flap of the truck was raised. The engines powered up again as the truck picked up speed.

"Mam?" O'Neil asked. Gemma stood up as Lewis walked over as well. "Where is your dad's warehouse? You said it was outside the city limits,"

"It is." Lewis looked at Gemma as she pointed at the wrong place on the map. "It's here," she said

Lewis looked to see she had pointed down at the wrong place. He walked up next to her placing his arm around her trying to comfort her. "There," Lewis corrected her and pointed at a different location. "If we continue on this street

220

we can be there in about fifteen minutes. Then, it's about thirty minutes to the Davenport ferry."

"It's a plan," O'Neil said. "Let's get there, ASAP, and get out of here."

O'Neil turned his head, looking at Jason and Arron as they were still hugging each other. "One big happy family reunion!" he commented. O'Neil went on, looking out the back of the truck as they continued along the streets.

Lewis walked towards Gemma and sat down next to her. "Are you okay?"

"Yes," she said. "Well, a bit of a headache coming along."

Lewis looked down at her. The silence is broken from the front of the truck.

"Contact," a voice yelled.

Lewis jumped, swiping his handgun from the pouch. He looked out the front of the military truck. He looked at the hordes of zombies running towards the main jeep. The soldier on the mounted turret ripped the metal lever back to full, squeezing the trigger.

"Down," O'Neil ordered.

Lewis looked through the handgun sight.

"Go, go, go!" O'Neil yelled into the radio. "Hit the gas!"

Lewis and O'Neil looked out the front window as the brigade of military vehicles picked up speed.

"There are far too many of them," the soldier screamed.

Lewis and O'Neil watched as the Humvee in front of them spun out of control.

"Shit," O'Neil yelped. "Drive!"

"What about—?"

"Just goooooooooooo!" O'Neil ordered.

O'Neil watched as the Humvee slammed into the ditch. The zombies were dragging the soldiers out. Lewis looked up and watched as the chasing jeep stopped, trying to aid the comrades. But it was too late. Lewis watched as the zombies ripped the soldiers to pieces, dragging them out of their vehicles.

"Why didn't you stop?" Jason demanded to know.

"We would have been sitting ducks," O'Neil replied. "Just be grateful that I, once again, saved your arse."

Arron clinched his fist.

"Hey, don't speak to my bro like that," Arron got up.

Lewis looked, seeing the two starting to square up. "Guys," Lewis said.

"Do that again," Arron challenged.

"Or what?" O'Neil asked. "You'll do what?"

Lewis looked at Arron as he squared up to O'Neil.

"Sir!" the soldier yelled from the front of the truck.

O'Neil ran to the front of the truck. He looked out and saw that vehicles lay sprawled all over the place in the street ahead.

"They have come from the highway that leads into Melbourne city centre," Lewis said.

"Sit down, now," O'Neil ordered. "And hold on. All of you; this is going to get rough."

Lewis went and sat down next to Gemma. "It'll be okay," he said to her. "Trust me. I know the training they go through."

The truck swerved in and out of all the damaged and smashed vehicles. The zombies were still in pursuit of the truck and the following jeep. More seemed to be arriving to chase the truck and the escorting jeep. The weaving slowed the truck down.

Juliana let go of the leather strap on the side of the truck. She watched in horror as her bag fell onto the ground, her small camcorder along with it. "No!" she shrieked.

"What?" Lewis gasped. "Leave it, Juliana!"

Juliana ignored Lewis's order. She dove to the ground, grabbing the camcorder. The truck suddenly swerved to the right. Juliana rolled onto her side, slamming into the back of the truck and falling over the flap.

"Juliana!" Lewis yelled. Lewis ran to the back of the truck, still feeling it swerving in and out of the vehicles in the middle of the street. Lewis looked over the side of the truck, seeing Juliana holding onto the metal pole at the back of the truck.

"Help me!" she pleaded.

Lewis leaned over and grabbed onto the small camcorder which was the only link to her hand.

"I can't hold on!" she yelled.

"No," Lewis encouraged her. "You can. Come on. I can help."

"I can't!" Juliana said again. "Use the footage. Make sure it is put to good use. Please, promise me."

Lewis watched as Juliana's hand slipped from the camcorder. "No!" he screamed. Lewis watched as Juliana rolled off into the street. The zombies jumped onto her.

"No !" Juliana screamed at the top of her voice.

Lewis moved away from the back of the truck as O'Neil continued observing the road ahead. The jeep was close behind, still escorting the truck. O'Neil looked ahead to see that the road ahead was blocked. A tourist coach blocked both sides of the street, and there was no way around. "Shit," he gasped. He looked out the front of the truck and saw a break in the barriers. "There," he pointed.

"Do it," O'Neil urged the driver.

"Yes, sir," the soldier yelled.

Lewis looked at Gemma, Claire, and Lucas as they held firmly to the side of the truck. Lewis watched as the driver swung the truck to the right. The two back wheels came off the ground as they entered the field. Lewis held onto the metal pole as the truck bounced along the rugged terrain. O'Neil looked out the front of the truck as they entered a slope and then the truck picked up speed. Lewis looked out the rear of the truck at the chasing jeep which continued to follow them closely.

"Rock!" O'Neil yelled.

Lewis held onto Gemma as the truck swerved to the left. He looked back at the other jeep. They didn't turn in time, and the front left wheel clipped the side of the rock, overturning the vehicle. Lewis watched as it slammed into the ground, erupting in flames. The fire seemed to draw the chasing zombies towards it. O'Neil shook his head, and Jason Philips stood up, looking out the back at the burning jeep as they continued downhill.

The truck suddenly drove through a small ditch in the ground. Jason fell back. The front of his leg twisted around and snapped. He accidentally pulled the trigger on his rifle. Jason screamed in pain as he fell against the side of the truck. O'Neil saw that the bullet had pierced Jason's throat. He watched as blood ran down out of the wound, Jason's body slowly collapsing to the floor as he felt intense pain rushing through his leg. O'Neil slammed into the ground as Arron ran over.

"Hey, man," Arron yelled. "Stay with me."

"I can't," Jason replied.

"Yes, you can," Arron yelled. "I've lost Mum and Dad. I'm not losing you!"

Jason continued to hold his broken leg. Lewis looked up and saw a huge lake starting to appear. But there was a drop.

"Holy shit!" the driver yelled. "Hang on!"

Lewis looked out the front of the truck as they sped off the small cliff; the nose of the vehicle pointed down to the hill as the lake slowly came closer and closer. Lewis looked at the camcorder. He knew that if they hit the water, the story Juliana had laboriously filmed would be destroyed.

"Hold on," he yelled. Lewis looked out the back of the truck. He grabbed the camcorder and launched it out onto the small sandy beach that surrounded the lake. The front of the truck slammed into the lake. Jason felt some more intense pain.

"Gemma, get out," Lewis yelled, "Lucas, you too."

"Come on, bro," Arron wept. Arron reached down, putting his hands around Jason. "Come on."

"Arron, go," Jason pleaded.

"No," Arron yelled. "I'm not losing you!"

"Lewis," Arron yelled. "Help me."

Lewis tracked through the sinking truck. He looked into the front of the truck, seeing that the driver was dead. O'Neil lay down on the ground next to him. Lewis went to help Arron pick up Jason.

"No, Lewis, I'll only slow you down!" Jason pleaded. "Please go."

"Arron, come on," Lewis urged him.

Lewis pulled Arron away, but Arron still fought to save his brother. The water from the lake flooded the truck as the back started to point into the air. When it slipped off the rock it was on, it would sink. Arron and Lewis jumped off the back of the truck. The water was hot. The truck started to sink.

Arron heard a gunshot. He knew his brother was dead.

Lewis swam to the surface as the warm water covered his body. He slowly turned around in the water, looked over at the small beach, and saw Gemma, Claire, and Lucas there waiting for him.

"Arron!" he yelled.

Arron came up to the surface. He looked over his shoulder, seeing that the truck had gone. "Jason!" he screamed.

"He's gone," Lewis said. "I'm sorry."

"Shit! Fuck!" He yelled. "NO!" Arron punched the warm water of the lake.

"Come on," Lewis said. "Let's get out of here."

Lewis and Arron swam towards the small beach. Arron slowly walked out of the water onto the beach. It didn't take them long to dry, as the sun was beaming down on them. Lewis swam towards the other beach. He slowly crawled out and got up, feeling the hot sun beam down on his head.

"Where you going?" Asked Gemma

Lewis didn't answer. He climbed up the small hill. He felt his hands dry off quickly in the intense heat that burned down on the beach. He looked up and saw the camcorder, just lying there on the dusty ground. He reached down, picked it up, and pushed the small power button in. The screen came on. "Yes."

Lewis turned around and slid back down the hill. He trekked along the beach towards Gemma and the rest of the group.

She started to walk over to him. "Does it work?" she asked.

Lewis nodded. It was the only thing he could do. He turned his head and looked over at Arron, as he sat there overlooking the lake. Lewis slowly walked over to him. "Hey," he said. "I'm sorry about your bro, but we need to keep moving."

Arron didn't say anything. He turned his head, looking back at Gemma.

"My head!" she said. Gemma leaned against the rock, putting her hand on her forehead.

Lewis looked at her and asked, "You okay?"

"No," she said. "My head is getting worse,"

Lucas started reaching for his bag. "Here," Lucas said. "I may have aspirin in my bag. If it isn't completely soaked, you may get something." Lucas reached into the bag on his shoulder and searched for the tablets.

"Woah!" he gasped." Lucas watched as his bag fell off his shoulder. He watched as the small silver case fell out, opening after hitting the rock. Lewis looked at the small syringes and other gadgets that were inside the case. Two small explosives were also there in the case.

Lewis looked over his shoulder into the distance at the fields, verifying whether any zombies had managed to catch up with them after the chase. The coast was clear.

Lewis spun around, looking down at Lucas, who was sitting back against the truck. Lewis looked at the silver case open on the ground, with the blood sample, a storage place for the handgun, and the small, advanced laptop with wires hanging out the side, ready to be used. There was a lot more to Lucas than met the eye, Lewis was certain of that.

Lewis looked at Lucas and guessed he had a guilty look on his face. He swiped the handgun from his pouch, pointing it down at him. "Who are you?" he demanded.

Lucas started to breathe heavily. "I'm just a tourist," Lucas replied calmly.

Lewis felt his blood start to boil; he knew Lucas was lying to him. His eyes were shifting. "Don't give me that," Lewis snapped. "Who are you?"

Lucas didn't reply.

"Keep your hands up," Lewis ordered.

The sun was beaming down on them. Arron walked over. He looked at Lewis, who was still looking down at Lucas sitting on the ground, the silver case open next to him.

"What's going on?" Arron asked Lewis. Arron was still angry after the death of his brother.

"Our friend here," Lewis replied, "is not who he says he is."

"Who is he?"

"You tell me," Lewis replied.

Arron walked over and picked Lucas up, throwing him against a small rock. Lewis swung his head around, looking for any of the zombies that could be near. Arron and Lewis slowly walked away from the truck. Both were trying to keep a cool head as Gemma and Claire stood next to each other, looking at Lucas and sitting by the truck, thinking back to the times when he had saved him and gotten them this far.

"Okay, I'll talk," Lucas panted.

Lewis and Arron stopped, turned back, and walked over to Lucas as he panted in the intense heat of the outback.

"I'm not the average American tourist," Lucas said.

"Who are you then?" Arron enquired.

Lucas let his breath out and said, "I'm CIA."

Lewis widened his eyes in shock as he holstered his weapon. "What?"

"I'm CIA" he said again. "My boss is the United States government, not a mall in Honolulu." Lucas slid back onto the ground after trying to get up. "Let me explain," he said.

"Please do," Lewis said.

WASHINGTON, DC

Professor Allan Hain, the Harvard University graduate, pulled into his parking bay at the Pentagon in Washington DC, USA. It was a clear day as the sun was shining.

"Hello, professor," a voice called his attention.

Professor Hain looked over to see Doctor Christian Uplinger, also a Harvard Graduate and ex-service to the US Army Intelligence Corps.

"All ready for the test?" Uplinger said.

"Ready as I ever will be," Allan Hain replied.

Allan Hain and Christian Uplinger walked up the concrete steps that lead into the Pentagon. The security guard nodded as he looked at their identification cards, unaware of the experiment that was about to take place in the United States of America. The doctors stood quietly as they put their bags onto the conveyor belt. They walked through the glass doors into the centre. The air conditioner was still running, and the floors were clean. A slight scent of the cleaning fluid was in the air.

Professor Hain and Doctor Christian Uplinger walked into the briefing room. They both felt very anxious about the test they were about to take part in. They entered a huge, doughnut-shaped control room. Loops of seats and computers overlooked a huge screen in the middle of the room. Uplinger entered the confined walkway which led past some of the computers and seats. The room was full of top US government officials.

They both took a seat next to one another, looking down at the huge widescreen in front of them. It showed a live stream from a space station above Earth. It was currently over Europe. They could see the United Kingdom and France.

Uplinger's attention to Earth from space was pulled away as General Edelson walked out of a small door next to the huge screen. Not a crease could be found on his green uniform from which medals dangled, showing off the services he had done for the country. He stood up straight, walking over to a stand. He picked up a small microphone, allowing him to speak to the entire conference arena. He took a deep breath, looking at the people awaiting his instructions.

"Okay, gentlemen," General Edelson said. Professor Hain and Uplinger looked at the General. "As you are aware," General Edelson started, "you are here working for the United States Government, and you are still under the Official Secrets Act." Hain and Uplinger stood there, looking at the General. "If this test is successful, Project Phobos will be the first-of-its-kind space station. You will be helping to make the world a safer place to live in."

The two men looked at each other. The room stayed silent.

"Shall we proceed?" Edelson said. The two professors walked out of the briefing room and into the command centre which was a very short walk away. They looked at all the staff who were observing Phobos as it was positioned above the Earth's atmosphere. Professor Hain sat down next to Uplinger.

"Okay, now begins phase one," General Edelson said. Edelson watched over as the team from the space agency typed into the computer. It was currently positioned over the United States.

"Find me a prison" Edelson ordered.

"Sir," the operator replied. A few seconds passed. "Sir," the operator said. "Ironport Regional Prison, Texas"

"Bring it up."

The screen zoomed into the prison grounds. Edelson stood with his hands locked behind his back.

"Well, well, well," he said softly. "What have we got, here?"

"Looks like a knife fight," the operator replied.

"Let's do one a favour and finish him off early." The operator awaited the instructions. "How old is he?" Edelson asked

"Twenty, maybe"

Edelson frowned looking at the two boys who were waiting to fight. "Give him a heart attack"

"Sir. . ." The operator hesitated

"That's an order," Edelson stated

"Altering protocols."

Phobos started to open, pointing down towards the prison. The power surged up in the canon blasting down. Edelson looked up at the screen, seeing one of the boys start to stagger around the prison grounds. He hadn't moved his hands. His eyes were just locked onto the screen.

"Do you think it worked?" asked Uplinger.

"Only one way to find out," he said. "What are they saying?"

The operator typed into the computer. "'I think he is having a heart attack' is heard from the speakers."

"Successful test," Edelson said.

Everybody in the room started to clap. Phobos continued to orbit the planet. It was positioned above Australia and Asia. The operator looked down onto the computer, seeing that a red light had come on. Many warnings started to appear on the screen in front of her. They were all hard to take in.

"Sir. . ." she hesitated.

Professor Hain walked over to her. He looked down onto the screen. "What is it?" he asked.

The operator continued looking down onto the screen in front of her. "Phobos is preparing to fire," she said.

"What?" Hain gasped. "Well, shut him down."

The operator continued typing into the computer,

listening to the orders from the professor. "I'm trying," she replied. "He doesn't seem to be responding."

Allan Hain looked down onto the screen as Phobos was still positioned over Asia and starting to open, preparing to fire.

"Shut him down!" Hain ordered.

"It won't," she replied. "It won't respond to any orders."

Allan Hain watched as the operator typed away into the computer, looking up at the screen and seeing that the new space satellite had finished opening. The alarm was raised again. Phobos suddenly started to power up.

"Why won't it shut down?" Uplinger asked.

"I don't know," the operator replied. "He still isn't responding to any orders." Phobos finished spinning, and the power generator in the rear fired. "It has fired," the operator said. "I repeat, Phobos has fired."

"What?" Allan Hain gasped. "How could this have happened?"

"I don't know," Uplinger replied. "What did you do to make it fire?"

"Nothing sir," the operator replied.

Christian Uplinger looked up at the huge display board in front of him. He looked at it as Phobos positioned itself above Australia.

The operator typed into the computer, trying to bring Phobos back online. Nothing seemed to be working. The huge space station slowly started plummeting towards the Earth as it fell out of the orbit.

"Sir," the operator said, "Phobos is falling towards Earth."

The metal exterior started to warm up as it entered the planet's atmosphere.

"Bring it back," General Edelson yelled.

"It won't respond," the operator said again. "And it's too late. It's in our atmosphere, and there is nothing I can do. We have lost Phobos!"

Phobos erupted into flames. The plasma trails ripped over

the metalwork of the space satellite as it plunged down towards Australia. The operator looked down onto her computer.

"Sir," She said "Phobos is gone."

Professor Uplinger and Allan Hain sat back into their seats, looking up at the screens in front of them on the command centre at the graphic image of Phobos bleeping red, showing that the station was gone.

"Where did it land?" General Edelson asked.

There was a short pause. "It hasn't landed yet, sir," the operator replied.

General Edelson walked away with his chest pounding frantically. He picked up the telephone on the side. He pushed three buttons in on the telephone and waited for a response from the operator. "Get me the president," he demanded. "Now." There was a short pause as he continued holding the phone to his ear. "Yes, of course, it's important," Edelson snapped.

* * *

Lewis looked down as Lucas looked up at him.

"Phobos was designed to implant a medical condition into an individual human being," Lucas said. "With no trace, it was going to be used to get rid of some of the world's leaders, prisoners in the USA, anybody who we don't want in the way. They were also going to try and sell the service to some of the world's richest countries! Lewis clenched his fist, looking down at Lucas. "After Phobos failed, the computer told the space agency what it had implanted into people here in Australia. They had no name for it and were unaware of what it would do to people," Lucas explained. "So, I was sent here to try and get to Ayers Rock, not far from where Phobos crashed. I was to destroy it and erase all American data on it, and to get a blood sample from an infected individual to bring back to the US before. . ."

"Before what?" Arron asked.

"Before a global pandemic happened."

"What? So, the US could create a cure and profit from all of this?" Lewis asked. "Is that what you are saying?"

"Well. . ." Lucas said. Lewis looked down at Lucas. "Yes," Lucas agreed. "And to cover up all evidence of its existence."

"When were you planning on telling us this?"

"The plan was this," Lucas said. "Once I had erased all of the information of Phobos, I was to destroy it with the explosives and to get a blood sample from an infected individual if there was one. They were going to get an extraction for me as they didn't know who or what Phobos had planted into about twenty-thousand people across this country."

Lewis looked at Arron

"What do we do?" Arron asked.

Lewis looked at Gemma as she held onto the small digital camcorder. "We tape the story," he said. "And we will put it to good use. We will show the world what the Americans have done to us; once again the Americans trying to police the world!"

Lucas didn't reply. Lewis reached over, pulling the camcorder from Gemma. He saw that there was enough battery to tape a short video.

"Up," Lewis demanded. "Now." Lucas sat up. "You're going to repeat what you just said to me," Lewis demanded. "And we are going to film it. You are going to say to the people, when this goes out, what your corrupt country has done."

Lucas let his breath out as he slowly started to sit up again. Lewis aimed the camcorder at Lucas. He slowly pushed the record button and whispered, "Go." Lewis aimed the camcorder at Lucas as he leaned against the back of the rock. "Speak," he ordered.

Lucas took a deep breath. He was about to breach the oath

he swore to protect the country. If he got out of Australia, he would be in prison when he returned.

"My name is Lucas," he said into the camera. "I am an agent working for the CIA in the United States."

Lewis looked through the small TV screen as he filmed Lucas. Arron, Gemma, and Claire were standing behind the camcorder, watching as Lewis filmed the story that was going to bring the current government of the United States down if evidence was found to be correct.

Lucas went on. "I was assigned the destruction and data erasure of a space station called Phobos. Phobos is a space station that was designed and created by the United States government and space administration, which has the power to pinpoint an individual person, mainly created for world leaders, such as Kim Jong-Il and other leaders who pose a serious threat to the human race. It has the ability to implant a medical condition, disease, or anything, that could leave no evidence behind of anything but a natural death."

Lewis watched as the battery symbol on the screen started to flash and the small side screen of the camcorder slowly turned black. The battery was finished.

"Okay," Lewis said. "Let's get to that warehouse. It's not that far from here. If I remember correctly, the road is over there. That means your dad's warehouse is that way."

"Well, let's go," Gemma said.

Lewis looked back at Lucas. "Give me your gun," he demanded.

"What?" Lucas gasped.

"Give me your gun now," Lewis demanded again.

Lucas handed Lewis his handgun, which Lewis slipped into his pouch. "If I wanted to kill you, I would have done it by now," Lucas said.

"Five minutes ago, we didn't know that it was the Americans that caused this," Lewis replied. Lewis walked forward again. "Now come on," he snapped. "Let's keep going."

* * *

Tony Brown walked into his room, seeing his wife lying on the clean bedding, his daughter by her side.

"Hey," she said, slowly opening her eyes. "What are you doing?"

Tony sat down on the side of the bed.

"I've been drawing up a speech to say to the people of the world that will be waiting for me to appear tomorrow."

"What are you going to say?" Amelia asked sitting up, trying not to wake her daughter.

Brown took a breath. "I'm going to tell them the truth."

"The truth about what?" she enquired.

"That Australia has been completely overrun by the Z virus," Tony replied.

"What?" Amelia gasped.

"I'm going to say that, no matter what happens from here onwards, I am going to rebuild Australia to what the nation once used to be." Brown looked down at his daughter as she continued to sleep on the bed. "I'm going say that Australia will return to normal. Australia will return to having people from the international community spending their holidays here in Australia. We will have an economy again. People will want to move to Australia to live here. People will want to invest in Australia again. It will happen, and I promise you that."

Amelia smiled as their daughter slowly started to move.

"Anyway, you get back to sleep," Tony ordered. "You need rest."

Amelia smiled as Tony got up. He looked down towards the ground. A few seconds passed, and then he lifted his head and walked away, heading back to finish the speech he would give to the world the next day.

CHAPTER EIGHTEEN

Lewis looked ahead. He looked up and saw Gemma's dad's warehouse coming into view as he looked down from the small hill that overlooked the industrial estate near it. Not a worker or person in the buildings or in the estate was in sight. Lewis stopped and looked at Lucas and Arron. He could still see the anger in the latter's eyes after the horrific death of his brother.

"Gemma," Lewis said. "Stay by my side." Gemma complied readily. Lewis and the group walked up to the huge metal gates of the warehouse. There was Gemma's dad's car.

"It's quite powerful," she said "We could be at that ferry port in under thirty minutes, provided the roads are clear."

"Well, let's go," Arron said.

Lewis walked alongside Arron, trying not to look at Lucas in any way whatsoever. The road was clear ahead. The industrial estate on the opposite side of the warehouse was deserted. The entrance gates to the warehouse were locked and sealed by a chain.

"Oh? What?" Lewis said looking at the bulky chain.

"No, that's a good thing," Gemma said. "Shoot it off."

Lewis looked at the huge padlock on the chain that was holding it closed.

Lucas stepped up. "Here," Lucas said.

Lewis pointed his handgun at Lucas. Arron observed the roads around the warehouse. Lucas reached into his bag, pulling out a small lock pick.

"The CIA trained us to do this," he explained.

"And what else?" Lewis asked. "What else do they train you to do?"

Lucas didn't reply to Lewis's comment as he poked the pin into the hole of the padlock. Lewis placed his hand onto his sidearm as Lucas undid the padlock to the warehouse gates. The huge padlock was unlocked and slammed into the metal gate. The echo of the crash reverberated in the whole warehouse.

"Hey, be careful," Lewis warned.

"What?" Lucas asked.

Lewis stopped to take a breath. "It has a horrible creak," he explained. "Open it a bit so that we can get in, and then we'll open it fully when we drive out of here."

Lucas slowly slid the gate open. "Let's get them," Lucas said. "And then to the Davenport ferry."

Lewis heard a sudden scream coming from behind the group. "Shit," he gasped and turned in an instant. Lewis and Lucas spun around, looking into the industrial estate and seeing the long line of the infected, snarling towards them.

"Shit," Lewis said again. "Inside."

Lewis watched as Gemma, Claire and Lucas ran into the yard of the warehouse. "Aaron, help me," Aaron ran across to Lewis as he struggled to slide the gates closed. "It's stuck," Lewis said in dismay.

"What?" Arron gasped. "Oh, fuck. No, no, no!"

"It's stuck," Lewis said again. "The fucking thing is jammed."

Arron swiped his handgun and looked through the sight at the zombies as they were getting closer to them.

"Lewis, go," Arron yelled. "I'll distract them and get them away from here."

"What?" Lewis gasped. "That's suicide."

"Just go," Arron yelled. Arron pushed Lewis through the gates. "Hey!" Arron yelled.

Lewis listened as he got ready to run in.

"About that time. . ." Arron said. "I'm sorry."

"Leave it," Lewis cut him off.

The snarling zombies slowly crept towards the warehouse gate. Arron put his hand through the gate. Lewis grabbed onto Arron's hand, shaking it. "Thank you," Arron said. "Thank you."

Lewis looked up at the sprinting zombies.

"Make sure that the story gets put to good use," Arron requested of Lewis. He spun around as Lewis ran towards the warehouse entrance.

Arron took a deep breath. "For you, Jason," he mumbled. Arron ran into the fields with the zombies chasing after him. Arron continued into the field. He could see the snarling zombies still chasing him as he looked over his shoulder. He looked forward again. He didn't have time to react as he stumbled over a log on the ground. He slammed into the dry ground, feeling a huge rush of pain in the lower half of his foot.

"Aggggh, fuck!" he screamed. Arron crawled backwards, trying to get back up. The pain was too unbearable.

He looked at the angry eyes of the group of zombies as they dove onto him. Their teeth started piercing his neck without any mercy, just as in a revenge killing. He felt his inner body start to warm as the rest of his body was torn to pieces. Rivers of blood ran from the wounds into the dry outback field. Arron's eyes slowly closed as the gleaming yellow appeared. He stood up, turning his head, looking at the warehouse walls, blood still running out of his neck onto the dry ground.

· · ·

Lewis entered the warehouse. He looked at the group as they stood there waiting for his next orders.

"Where's Arron?" Lucas asked.

Lewis shook his head slowly. "Come on," he snapped. "Let's do this." Lewis pulled his handgun out and wiped his forehead. He entered the huge warehouse, looking into the empty office. Gemma looked inside the room only to see the picture of herself and her parents on the fishing trip with Lewis a few months before this nightmare began. She picked it up, looking around the office for the car keys.

"They are not here," she said.

"What? Not here?" Lucas asked.

"My dad's keys." She showed that the keys were not there.

"Come on," Lucas said. "Let's not get too far from Lewis."

Lewis walked through the door. He looked onto the balcony that overlooked the warehouse. He stared at all of the metal columns holding the electrical and electronic supplies ready to be distributed to the cities within Australia: computers, washing machines and several other household amenities.

"Mum," Gemma called. Gemma's voice echoed as it travelled around the warehouse.

"Gemma," Lewis scolded her, "please!"

"Sorry," she replied.

Lewis climbed down the metal stairs, looking around the warehouse. No one was to be seen.

"Mum, where are you?" Gemma mumbled. "Make them be alive, please, God!"

As Lewis and Lucas searched through the warehouse, they saw two figures sitting down next to each other, gently rocking back and forth. Gemma's eyes opened wide with shock.

"Mum," she gasped.

"Gemma, wait," Lewis warned her. Lewis grabbed Gemma as she charged towards the two figures who were her mum and dad. She could tell by the dress sense of her dad. He continued to rock back and forth.

"Hey," Lewis called. "Can you hear me?" Lewis put his hand on his firearm.

"Mum," Gemma yelped again. "Mum, please. It's me, Gemma." Gemma walked up to her mum and dad and kneeled. "It's okay," she said. "We are here, and we are going to get you to safety."

Lewis walked up to Gemma's parents. He watched as her mum slowly lifted her head. Her eyes slowly started to open. Lewis looked at them as they started gleaming yellow.

"Mum," Gemma screamed.

"Gemma, move!" Lewis shrieked. Lewis pushed Gemma out the way as her mother jumped up. Lewis stepped back and looked at her as she stood there, looking at him. Blood was running out of her mouth.

"No, no!" Gemma pleaded.

Lewis put his fingers onto the trigger of the handgun. Gemma's mum's mouth slowly opened up. He looked at her once white teeth slowly starting to die away. He squeezed the trigger, launching the bullet from the canister. Gemma watched as the bullet went straight through her mum's head. Her body slowly fell to the ground. Her eyes started to fade away as the lower half of her body went down onto the concrete ground. Lewis watched as her dad's head shot up as well, his eyes also gleaming yellow. Lewis didn't hesitate before he squeezed the trigger, slamming the bullet into his head as well.

"No, please!" Gemma yelled. "Please!"

Lewis put his hands on her shoulder as her dad slowly fell to the ground.

"No, please!" Gemma wept.

Lewis holstered the handgun. He looked at Gemma as she collapsed onto the ground by her mum. "Gemma," Lewis whispered. "Gemma, come on, we have got to go. Come, it's just under an hour until that pickup by the navy."

"No, no, no," Gemma cried. "Please, why?"

"Gemma, there's nothing we could do," Lewis tried to reason with her.

Lucas looked away as Claire started to weep.

"Gemma," Lewis called her again.

Gemma continued to cry. Lewis reached into her dad's pocket, looking down at the two corpses. He rummaged around the pocket, feeling] tissues and coins. He dug deeper into the pocket and felt a slight jingle in his palm. He pulled out the keychain, looking for the keys to the car.

"Gemma, we have got to go," Lewis said to her again. "It's just under an hour until the last pick up from the Davenport ferry takes place."

Gemma stood up, taking one last look down at her deceased parents. Lewis also stood up, looking at the remaining members of the group. "Okay," he said. "Let's get out of here."

Lewis started walking towards the stairs to see if the coast was clear to leave the warehouse by the main entrance. He heard a sudden crash. He looked up at the glass door he had entered the warehouse through, seeing that the zombies had broken into the warehouse.

"Oh, fuck, no!" he yelled. "Not now."

"What do we do now?" Claire asked.

Lewis had to think. All of the front exits had been sealed off by Gemma's dad. He looked over his shoulder for the walkway leading through to the refectory. His days in the service flashed back to him.

"Lucas," Lewis snapped. "Them explosives—how long do they take to set up?"

"Couple of seconds only," Lucas said. "Just have to flick the switches up, and the timer is done."

Lewis looked up at the glass panel as it started to crack.

"Go," he ordered. "Get it."

Lucas dropped his bag, pulling out the explosive charges. He ran towards the back wall. He slammed the silver explosive into the wall, flicking the switches up. The twenty-second timer came up. The zombies continued to scream through the glass. Lucas pushed the activation button down. "Get your head down!" He ordered.

"Gemma, move!" Lewis ordered.

Lewis and Lucas ran into the warehouse as the timer hit zero. Lewis ducked down by the metal racks that were holding the washing machines and other household appliances in place. The explosive detonated. Gemma yelled as the pulse travelled through the warehouse. The top of the warehouse rattled. Lucas saw Lewis was right underneath one of the racks. The metal bolts and hinges slowly started to break away; they couldn't hold the weight anymore.

"Lewis, move!" Lucas screamed. Lucas ran over, diving to Lewis and pushing him out of the way of the tumbling racks. Lewis looked back after he landed onto the cold ground to see the lower half of Lucas's body had been crushed by the huge boxes and containers.

Lucas screamed in excruciating pain.

Lewis staggered up off the ground and moved over to Lucas. He noticed that the door leading towards the reception was starting to break. They didn't have much more time.

"Lucas," Lewis whispered. "You just saved my life."

"I know," Lucas replied. "Don't brag about it."

Lewis struggled to move the heavy appliances out of the way. "Come on," Lewis gasped. "Lucas, can you move?"

"No," he said. "No, I can't." Lucas panted for breath, looking at the small river of blood running out from under the boxes. "Lewis," Lucas said, still panting. "Just go, please. You have the evidence. Use it to tell the world that the US government has gone too far."

"No," Lewis replied. "We need you to say to the world what your government has done to the people of Australia."

"Lewis," Lucas said again. "You go ahead. You have the story on the camcorder. Take my bag; the access code for the laptop is three, one, six, nine, two."

Lewis reached into his pouch, catching a glimpse of the door. He watched as the glass started to break. He wrote the code down on the paper. Luckily, it had dried well.

"If you do the wrong code," Lucas explained, "the hard drive will fry, and you will have nothing to show the world." Lewis showed Lucas the code on his notebook. "That's it," Lucas replied. "On the laptop, you'll find all the information on Phobos. Prove to the world what the US Government has done to your country."

Lewis looked up and saw that the door was breaking away. "Lewis, the gates are jammed," Lucas said. "Use the last explosive to blow the wall. Go. I'll hold them off."

Lewis picked up Lucas's bag.

"Oh, one thing," Lucas remembered. Lewis looked down at Lucas. "Can I have my gun back?" he asked.

Lewis pulled the shiny handgun out of the pouch and chucked it over to Lucas, who reached up to grab it.

"Now go," Lucas demanded.

Lewis ran towards the blown hole in the warehouse. He reached in, pulling out the explosive as Gemma and Claire waited for him by the blown back wall. "You two okay?" he asked.

Lewis looked at the door that had been blown off the hinges from the explosion. "Claire, is the coast clear?" he asked.

Claire looked out the side of the warehouse. She looked towards Gemma's dad's car, which was parked and ready to roll—their chance to escape. "It's clear," Claire replied. "We can do it. Let's go."

Lewis reached into the bag and pulled out the explosive. "See this?" he said. Claire and Gemma looked down at the explosive. "Go and stick it to the wall," he said. "Flick the three switches up and hit the red button."

"What?" Claire gasped.

"Claire, just do it."

Lewis looked through the damaged door as the zombies

broke through the door leading into the warehouse. Lucas looked up at the zombies as well. "Come on!" he yelled.

Claire grabbed the explosive. Looking at Lewis, she ran out through the broken wall.

"Gemma," Lewis said. "Get the keys out of my pocket and start your dad's car."

"Got it." Gemma reached into Lewis's pocket and pulled out the keys. She ran out, looking at Claire as she flicked the switches up on the explosives. The twenty-second countdown timer appeared on the screen.

"Run!" Gemma screamed. Gemma and Claire ran away from the warehouse wall. Lewis looked through the gap in the broken door as the zombies tumbled down the metal stairs towards Lucas as he lay on the ground of the warehouse in pain.

Lucas held onto his handgun, looking through the sight. He squeezed the trigger, shooting at the zombies, one after the other. It didn't seem to be slowing them down at all. He watched as the top of the weapon pinged back. He had no rounds left at all. He looked up towards the gleaming yellow eyes coming towards him.

Lewis closed his eyes as the zombies dived onto him. He watched as the zombies feasted on Lucas. Lewis kept quiet, hoping that the zombies hadn't seen him.

The timer hit zero as Gemma and Claire arrived back at the warehouse, ready to escape to the Davenport ferry. The explosion ripped through the wall and Gemma and Claire screamed as they ducked down. Lewis looked through the gap in the broken door.

"Come on," Gemma shouted.

Lewis looked up and saw one of the zombies running towards him. He didn't have time to react. He held the door closed as the rest of the zombies followed like a pack of wolves. The zombies slammed into the door. Lewis struggled to hold it closed as Lucas's bag seemed to be weighing him down.

"Lewis," Gemma screamed. Gemma watched as Claire got into the car, looking out for zombies and watching as the smoke from the blown-away wall slowly started to disappear.

"I can't hold them," Lewis said. "Gemma, go."

"What?" Gemma yelped. "No, I'm not leaving you!"

Lewis continued to hold the door closed. Gemma watched as one of the zombies pushed its head through the broken wall. It squeezed through slowly, blood running out of its mouth.

"Look out!" Gemma yelled.

Lewis looked down, seeing the male zombie coming through the wall. Its mouth was wide open. Gemma watched as it slammed its teeth into Lewis's arm.

"Agggh!" he screamed.

"No!" Gemma screamed.

Claire got out of the car, running towards Gemma, who was still looking at Lewis's arm. He looked down at the blood as it rushed out. His body was starting to heat up.

"Gemma," Lewis panted. "Just go. Please."

"No, please," Gemma pleaded. "Please, not you!"

"Gemma," Lewis said again. "Go, for God's sake. I can feel it trying to take over."

Gemma watched as Lewis's eyes closed.

"Damn," he moaned. "Gemma, go. I'll hold them off."

Gemma went to kiss Lewis.

"No," he shouted. "No, I could infect you. Go, go straight down this street. It's a straight line to the ferry port from here. Trust me."

Claire looked at Gemma as she stood there crying.

"Take the bag. It has got everything in it. The code for the laptop is in the notebook. Use it, Gemma, and show the world what the Americans did to your mum and dad," Lewis demanded. Lewis's inner body heat started to increase as he started to lose grip of the door.

"Tell my unborn," he coughed, "I love. . . love. . ."

Gemma looked as Lewis started to collapse.

"Come on!" Claire shrieked.

Gemma picked up the bag as Lewis fell to the floor. The zombies burst through the door. Gemma stepped into the car and threw the bag over the back seat. She pushed the accelerator down and sped through the car park of the warehouse to the blown-away wall. The ground was dry, and the dust billowed up from behind the wheel as Gemma held on to the steering wheel. She pulled onto the road. She looked into the mirror as the warehouse slowly started to disappear.

Claire watched as Gemma wiped long, heavy tears away from her face. She didn't know what to say. The sun shone down as the industrial estate disappeared from sight. "How far is the ferry?" Claire asked.

"About twenty minutes," Gemma said amidst her tears.

The drive to the ferry port was easy; there were no cars in the way, nothing. All the streets had been cleared. Gemma looked out of the window, seeing the road leading down to the docks. No one was seen and there were no blood-thirsty zombies waiting to kill them. It was completely empty. Gemma pulled onto the road leading down to the docks, her eyes peeled for likely hindrances. The sea was calm, and the sky was clear. Gemma pulled the handbrake up, looking out across the ocean.

"Well," She quietly said. "Where are they?"

Claire looked down at her watch. They had a few minutes more. Claire and Gemma sat down on the benches. No one was about. The tourist shops were shut and sealed, still filled with souvenirs for tourists.

Claire slowly lifted her head and saw something bubbling in the water. "Gemma," she whispered.

Gemma lifted her head. She had dozed off for a few seconds. They watched as the water continued to bubble. Slowly appearing from under the sea water, was one of the Australian Navy's submarines. Gemma and Claire watched as the surface of the long machine rose to the surface. It was a sight they are never going to forget. Clair watched Gemma break down into tears. Soon, the top of the submarine opened up. Climbing out of the submarine were some of the Australian submariners, who were armed.

"Move out," a voice asked them.

Gemma picked up the huge, black bag as she walked over to the edge of the dock. The silver bridge came across allowing them to board.

"This way," the submariner said. "We got survivors."

"How many?" The captain asked.

"Two."

Claire and Gemma took one last look at Australia as the air-tight door was sealed.

"Prepare to dive," was what they heard next.

The submarine submerged under the water. Gemma sat down as a medic arrived.

"You okay, ma'am?" he asked.

Gemma gently nodded.

"We'll get you something to eat and drink and get you to the safe zone in Hobart," the submariner said. "We'll be at a navy vessel in about three hours. From there, we'll arrange for transport to get you to Hobart."

Gemma didn't reply. The submariner walked off as the submarine left the Australian coast behind it. The burning buildings and the famous landscape of the nation disappeared from sight. Gemma lay down on the bed, thinking about Lewis, her first true love who had lost his life to save her life from the Z virus.

* * *

Tony Brown stood up straight. He tightened his tie, looking into the media room of the ship. "Let's do this," he reminded himself.

Brown walked into the room. He looked at the cameras set

up by the Australian Navy, ready to broadcast his speech to the people of Tasmania and the world that had tuned in to watch this iconic piece of history. Brown took a deep breath, looked at the spotlight as it beamed down onto him from above, and spoke.

"To the people of Australia and the world, a devastating act of terror has been waged on the people of Australia. It hasn't just affected the Australian people, but families from all over the world who have lost loved ones in this horrific event that is never going to be forgotten." The camera crew continued to film the prime minister. "I am determined to find out who and what caused the outbreak of this virus. Whether it was an act of God or an act of science or terrorism, I will rebuild Australia back to its original state. The economy will thrive again, and people from all over the world will still want to spend their holidays in Australia. It is my ultimate goal to achieve this. I would also like to thank the people of Tasmania who have provided refuge and nice hospitality to the citizens and people we flew into Tasmania. I would also like to thank the chain of hotels and restaurants that have spent their own time and money to provide for them. Thank you all, and God bless you."

Tony Brown walked away from the cameras as Thomas Legg walked in.

"Impressive speech, sir," Legg said.

"It had to be done," Brown replied.

"Oh, Thomas," Brown continued. "Thank you."

"Not a problem, sir," he replied.

Brown smiled as he headed back to his cabin. "Right," he said. "Now to find out who did this."

* * *

Gemma looked out of the helicopter window as they touched down in Hobart city. Claire and Gemma stepped down from the helicopter. Gemma walked around the city centre, looking at all the white tents that had been set up. Hobart was now a refugee camp. Hotels were filled with families.

Gemma looked for one of the soldiers. "Hi," she said. "Who is in charge of your operations?"

"Carl Farrington. He is in that tent over there."

Gemma and Claire walked over to the tent where Carl Farrington was. They turned the corner and walked into the building.

"Carl Farrington?" Gemma said.

"Yes, ma'am. How I can help you?" Carl Farrington replied.

Gemma put the bag down on the ground. Then she undid the zipper and handed the laptop and files over to Carl Farrington. The room stayed quiet as he looked down at the laptop when it was opened up. Carl Farrington's eyes opened with fear as he looked down onto the screen of the computer, learning about Phobos and what the United States government had tried to cover up.